One

I stared pensively through the window in its rust-streaked and swollen iron frame, my gaze directed up into the sullen haze that was the London sky on this hot and humid August day. Eventually I moved over to the open window, to be greeted by the familiar sights and sounds of city life being played out four floors below. God, it was hot! Looking down I could make out the taught sinuous figure of a boy struggling manfully to push his heavily-laden barrow across the cobbled square, steel bound wheels grating, leaving white trails into Shepherd's Market.

On the far side, a liveried chauffeur stood smartly against the door of a gleaming black Mercedes, the bright sunlight accentuating the dark mystery of its blackened windows. Its owner, I mused, was probably visiting Trumper's for his afternoon shave. The ubiquitous London taxis scurried about in all directions, their characteristic diesel rattle clearly audible above the general cacophony. In the distance a Police siren wailed, its urgent scream making a fitting contribution to the cosmopolitan din. Suddenly I was conscious of the stench and fumes drifting up from the teeming streets below, and found myself desperately yearning for the wild, windswept moors of my native Yorkshire.

I turned away, my damp shirt sticking momentarily to the wall where I had been leaning, and looked slowly around the room, taking it all in. My gaze took in the single lamp hanging from the faded white ceiling, it's green and white shade standard issue in all Government buildings of the time, the grey filing cabinets with their brass combination-locks, the big inlaid leather-topped desk, the button-leather chairs and the fraying carpet. Father in full uniform glared down at me from the mantelpiece above the huge Adam fireplace. The now-faded and yellowing photograph that had always served to remind me that I was expected to follow a well-established tradition of service to one's country, the steely eyes never seemed to leave me.

The decision I was about to take had not come easily. I sat down with a sigh, glancing once more at the window. I reached slowly for the top drawer, took out a single sheet of headed paper and a fountain pen and began to write.

It took me less than two minutes to throw away a life's work, a secure future, maybe even a pension! everything. I sealed the envelope, picked up the phone and dialled.

'Jean, is the Old Man free?' I asked.

'Yes, but not for long,' came the reply.

Carlos ll

James Hayward-Searle

A

A KIT MARTIN   SPYTHRILLER

ISBN: 9781520698250 (paperback)

Other novels by the author:

Deep secret

No replacement

And so to return

The meeting

Part 1

London – August

'Fine,' I said cheerfully, 'I'll be right there.'

Martin, Lieutenant Colonel (Hon), Kit Martin! Rt. I muttered to myself replacing the phone, what the hell have you done, impetuous as ever, but what was I supposed to do? the cold war now long gone, Perestroika in full swing, ministry cut backs, and a new openness within the service being called for, my expertise, my training, experience of what use now?

I rose and strode once more to the window, no, hell! my mind was made up, I turned swiftly on my shoe, it grating on polished wood as it turned off the fraying Indian carpet, I moved across the room, grasped the brass door knob firmly and twisted hard left, pulling the door towards me, my decision made! I closed my door and flicking in the code, I walked out into the corridor breathing a little heavier than normal, and so I should I thought.

The smell of polish drifted everywhere, pervading the dark, high-ceilinged corridors with their well-worn carpets. I took the lift to the fifth and highest floor, where the Old Man's lair was tucked away. The polished brass trellis gates slid open, and a long maroon carpet stretched down the corridor away from me. Shiny brass knobs decorated every door, and the lenses of surveillance cameras winked in the gloomy corners. A myriad of dust particles danced in the shaft of sunlight that came through the armoured skylight, captured in a brilliant moment of time.

I decided to make a direct approach, rather than

through the secretary's office, and knocked purpose-fully on the huge old door of the Old Man's personal domain, the gruff voice boomed, 'Enter!' and I did so, the heavy door brushing on the thick pile carpet as I pushed it open. He rose from his desk, smiling; a huge man of immense presence, his tweed suit and craggy face more befitting a grouse moor or the front cover of Country Life. I grasped his outstretched hand and shook it firmly, and he waved me to the inevitable chesterfield against the wall.

I stood for a moment, reaching into my pocket for the envelope. Passing it over to him I remained standing. He took it from me, his smile disappearing as he did so, and returned to his chair without once taking his eyes off me. This time he pointed firmly at the sofa to indicate that I should be seated.

He opened the letter, and proceeded to read it in silence; a heavy silence, broken only by the slow, pendulous ticking of the old Grandfather clock. As he read, a wistful smile gradually spread across the weathered face, face hiding a million thoughts.

'I suppose I was expecting it,' he said resignedly. 'Your father would turn over in his grave.'

Casting my eyes down, I nodded curtly.

'I know,' I said. But I didn't want any discussion.

He looked at me quizzically, one eyebrow lifting slightly.

'I suppose I can't change your mind?'

'My   mind   is   made   up,'   I   replied   firmly, uncomfortably aware that this move, which was to affect the whole course of my life, had been taken on a mere whim, and I didn't have a clue what I was going to do next.

It was not a time for chatter. The Old Man rose from his chair, looking me in the eye. I stood up and offered my hand, and for a moment I thought he wasn't going to take it. In the end he shook it firmly, I said.

'It's not the end, Sir.'

'It never is the end for us, Kit' he said slowly. 'However, you've made your decision.'

'Yes Sir, I'm sorry!' I said as resolutely as I could, and with that I turned and walked, probably for the last time, across that carpet of secrets. As I opened the door I could feel for the last time, his gaze on my back. I could feel the hairs on the nape of my neck and without turning around, I slowly closed the door behind me. I forced my tensed body to relax and releasing my breath I walked thoughtfully down to the fourth floor and toward Stuart's office.

Two

S tuart, my oldest friend and immediate senior, not that that made too much difference, we had been at school together, shot at Bisley together, and in the British team, later we went on to University where Stuart had excelled while I had hobbled through, studying Psychology and languages but we had never lost touch, indeed it was Stuart who had come to see me one bleak winters day at Catterick.

I had watched his powerful figure, thinly disguised in a London suit, walk determinedly across the parade ground, and I noted, unusual as he was not escorted, he had thrust the door open before I could get to it, we had shaken hands vigorously, caught up on family happenings, talked quickly about old friends. But I could tell he was only skimming the surface, this was not a social call!

He had sat down and looked thoughtfully at me for a moment, before drawing in breath and asking me

'Kit, how would you like to have some 'sun and sea' on the Government?'

'Why not?' I had instantly but curiously replied,

and within days or so it seemed I was heading South and on my way to London, seconded to 'The Service' and in those heady, often an eighteen hour stint. I remembered it fondly. We were ever on alert, and 'active,' not as today!

Stuart had been the best man at my wedding, and he was the first to know of the rumblings that all was not too rosy now in that direction.

'Our job' he had said, 'puts too much pressure on wives, we are loners 'Kit,' they never know when they will see us, they are home makers, they like to arrange things, we let them down, and we cannot always tell why, our secretiveness destroys them.' He had said.

I remembered this as if it were yesterday, and now here I was walking towards his office. Would he feel let down? Surely not, he of all people knew I just lived for the action. I raised my knuckle and knocked purposefully.

My knock was responded to immediately by the familiar voice calling.

'Come in!' and I did so, smiling.

'Good afternoon, and how are you today?' I asked jovially.

Stuart waved me to a chair with a grin.

'What have you got to be so bloody cheerful about?' he asked.

I sat down and brandished a small cigar.

'May I?' I asked.

'Must be important,' he said, still grinning.

'I suppose you could say that,' I said, then after a moment, 'Stuart, I've resigned.'

'Holy shit!' he exclaimed, 'You've done what?'

'I've resigned,' I repeated.

He got up and crossed to the cafetiere on the side table and poured two cups of black coffee, without a word. He handed one to me.

'But why, for Christ's sake?'

'Long story,' I said. 'Too long to tell you now.'

He was just about to protest when the phone rang. He threw me a look which said

'Don't go away!' and picked up the receiver.

I wandered over to the window and looked down into the street once again. The Mercedes had gone, the build-up of evening traffic had started. I made a mental note to visit Trumper's the following day for a last shave before I went North and home.

The phone clattered down.

'Well, that's certainly put the cat among the pigeons!' sighed Stuart, 'The Old Man is beside himself.'

I made no reply.

'So, what next, Maverick?' asked Stuart.

'We'll talk,' I said quietly.

'You're damn right we will! Listen, I've got to go now, and I can't see you for dinner tonight, but how about tomorrow?'

'That'll be fine,' I said.

'Good, I look forward to it!' he replied, rushing

out of the room. 'Shut the door after you!' he called over his shoulder, then re-appeared in the doorway. 'On second thoughts, you'd better leave. After all, you could be a spy now,' he laughed.

Stuart dashed off upstairs, and I walked quietly back to my own office. I put my head round the dividing door and spoke to my secretary.

'Anything for me?'

'Plenty,' she said, 'but it's all straightforward paperwork and I've done it. At least now we'll be able to read it!' she smiled. Her breasts heaved invitingly, firmly encased in untouchable diplomatic bags, so to speak.

'Your eyes give you away,' she said tartly, sitting up straight, making it worse as the thin cloth tightened across her chest.

I laughed.

'It's not my eyes I was thinking about,' I chuckled, 'I'll be in a bit later in the morning.'

'Okay,' she said smiling. I closed the door, hesitating. Should I tell her now? No, I thought, tomorrow would be better.

I looked around my own office. No so far, no regrets. The place depressed me, and it would a relief to leave it all behind me. I poured a small scotch and soda, sat down and did the unthinkable, by putting my feet on the desk.

I soon lapsed into deep thought, staring out of the window at aircraft crawling slowly across the late afternoon sky towards Heathrow. Where had they come from? I wondered. I would take a long holiday, lots of sea and sun, somewhere that I had always promised myself. The thought cheered me up.

The silence was shattered by the phone. It was Stuart.

'Have I got news for you!' he said.

'Go on,' I growled.

'You may well sound curt,' he said.

'They want Liam as your replacement.'

'Smart Arse!' I shouted, incredulous at the thinking.

'In one, you've got it,' he gasped.

'Well, I suppose there wasn't much choice,' I said warily. 'What's your view?'

'I think it stinks, but as you say, there aren't too many people available at your level, and he is 101% computer literate, and has more electronic qualifi-cations than all of us put together. Anyway, I have to give my view within twenty-four hours.'

'Should keep you busy,' I said, amused.

'Thank you Kit, you've been a great help!' A fur-ther groan whilst, slamming the phone down.

I needed fresh air. I got up, stuffed my mobile and pager into my pocket, and walked down floor by floor, across the hall and through security.

'Goodnight, Harold,' I said to the commissionaire.

'Goodnight sir, be sure to go straight home now!' he smiled.

'Absolutely,' I replied, and strode out into the cool evening air of Curzon Street.

I was never really sure how we ended up in Curzon Street, our section had moved here temporally some time ago. But as with most bureaucratic establishments temporary could always be a lot longer than anyone envisaged.

I personally had no complaints. Yes, the building itself and fittings are quite antiquated but it had a sense of style about it. I suppose we will move into the new block eventually. But for me Curzon Street suited me admirably. Situated in the West End, close to the Park, the bars and nightlife of Shepherds market, Trumper's the gentleman's Barbers just below, elite restaurants just a stone throw away, Bond St, Berkley sq, Jermyn St, and Piccadilly. Famous stores and hotels, gentleman's clubs and card schools.

No, I was happy here. !

Three

The walk through the park to Knightsbridge and Ennismore Mews was uneventful, and gave me an opportunity to gather my thoughts and reflect on things. Before I knew, I was putting my key in the lock of Number 12. I flicked off the alarm and went up to the second-floor lounge. It was good to be here. But for how long?

I poured a drink and relaxed in my favourite chair. I looked around the familiar room. If only these walls could speak, I reflected. This room had held some of the country's leading figures over the years, some well-known, some not, but all men of considerable power and stature. The shatter-proof windows and armoured door had been installed for good and serious reasons.

The peaceful silence didn't last long. A fast-moving car came hammering down the cobbled street outside, horn blaring, and screeched to a halt at my door. I was familiar with the style, and I was pretty certain who it might be. I ran down to the front door, and checked the peephole just in case. I was right. I opened the door to see Tina Del's exquisite, silk-clad legs slither out of her silver Mercedes sports.

She manoeuvred her incredibly beautiful body to its full height, and stood by her car, smiling broadly, her perfect teeth flashing in the early evening light.

'Hi!' she said, not moving.

I moved towards her and kissed her, and she wouldn't let go. I could feel her hard nipples straining the silken fabric of her Harvey Nichols blouse.

'Hell, I don't know why, but I've missed you!' she whispered urgently, squeezing me hard. I felt the muscles of her back flexing sinuously. She was fit, a superb athletic body, honed by hours of relentless gym! She pulled away.

'Well, speak to me,' she laughed.

'Drink?' I asked.

'Typical!' she retorted, pushing past me and into the house. I slammed the door and followed her upstairs, her stunning perfume filling the air. She pulled a bottle out of the rack, turned and handed it to me, an inviting smile playing about on her lips. I cut the foil and drew the cork with the satisfying sound that only a wine-cork can produce, and filled her proffered glass. She looked into my eyes, a look laden with sultry promise.

'Tina, your beauty stuns me to silence,' I whispered.

'Bullshit!' she said heartily, looking even more beautiful as she smiled. We went through into the lounge, and Tina moved to the window, standing with her back to me. I put my hand gently on her shoulder, and she turned to face me. She looked at my expression.

'What is it Kit?'

Without preamble I answered.

'I've resigned.'

'Resigned from what?' she asked simply placing her hands on her hips.

'Ah yes, point taken, I wonder.'

Her face took on a look of genuine concern.

'You won't be leaving London?'

'Not altogether,' I tried to reassure. But probably not convincingly.

'You're really serious, aren't you,' she said quietly.

'Yes, I am.'

'Then will you take me for dinner?'

'I might,' I said teasingly.

'Sometimes you're an absolute bastard,' she laughed, 'And I suppose you want to fuck me as well.'

'Before or after dinner?' I said.

'Bastard!' she screamed, and laughed as the half-full wine-glass came hurtling towards me.

I ducked, and the glass thumped down onto the settee, throwing its contents over the Laura Ashley fabric. I was glad couldn't stand it. I placed my own glass on the table and made a grab for her. She squealed with delight as I pulled her to the floor, and we rolled about laughing. Tina's knee caught me in the groin.

'Oh, sorry,' she exclaimed, 'You okay?'.

'No problem,' I rolled in fictious agony.

'I'd better be careful,' she whispered mischievously, 'I might be needing those!' She thrust her hand down the back of my trousers, and I lay still. Slowly she manoeuvred round to find my rampant erection.

'Missed me?' she whispered, as one by one I undid the buttons of her blouse with my teeth. She began to squirm as I released her magnificent breasts from the restraining bra, two plump doves with pink inviting beaks reaching up to me. I captured one in my lips, gently rolling its tumescent hardness between my teeth, and carefully sliding a hand down to her dampening mound. I brushed her throbbing clitoris and she moaned ecstatically, her nails digging into my scrotum. With her free hand she deftly undid my belt and pushed down my trousers and pants, then rolled away and quickly shed her remaining clothes, and lay back for me to take her, a vision of stupefying sexual beauty.

Then it happened. At that crucial moment, that most rewarding moment in a man's life, the answerphone whirred and clicked into life, and I realised my mistake. I had switched off only the bell, leaving the dreaded machine still active. Damn!

I tried to ignore it, but a second later Camilla's voice filled the room.

'I know you're there …… … come on, pick up the phone … … I suppose after your last call you've gone into hiding with some tart.' Tina froze beneath me. 'Well, if you really have quit, I suggest you get yourself home a.s.a.p. .... you have responsibilities here, and masses of work to do. Just don't get under my feet ...... or catch anything! Give me a ring when you've finished.'

The phone clattered down, a click, and the most awful silence. Damn the woman! Even at that distance she could call a halt to my little games. Tina pushed me away violently.

'You really are a shit!' she said, raising herself on one elbow.

'Probably,' I said, getting to my feet.

'Sometimes words fail me, they really do,' she said, shaking her head, her eyes brim-full of tears.

I went off to take a shower, and by the time the water was warm to my touch I heard the door slam.

She was gone.

Four

The following day I rose early, keen to sign off and get on with my new life. I left the Mews and hailed a cab. No walk today, I just wanted to get on, to get the whole business finished in case I changed my mind. Or in case it was changed for me.

We turned into Curzon Street.

'Anywhere here,' I called through to the cabby. I climbed out and paid my fare. Trumper's was on my left. I hesitated, looking in the window, a treasure trove of gentleman's paraphernalia, huge natural sponges, back-scratchers, shaving brushes, creams, old-fashioned violet and lime colognes, in fact every aid to perfect grooming. I went in, and was instantly greeted.

'Good morning, sir,' said the white-coated attendant.

'Good morning,' I said putting put a hand to my chin. 'Any chance of …'

He cut me short.

'But of course, sir, this way please.'

He led me to a mahogany-partitioned cubicle concealing a classical marble sink with Victorian brass fittings. I sank into the big leather chair and closed my eyes. Soon my face was being swathed in hot towels, my thoughts drifted and I relaxed.

Somewhere in the background I could hear Major Tom Laxton's crisp military voice.

If the Russians had planted a barber in here, what a coup d'état I thought, they would have heard half of the MI6 rumblings. The sound of a blade being sharpened on a leather strop brought me back to reality.

I kept irregular hours at my office, and my late arrival brought no comment. The dividing door to my secretary's office was ajar, and I smelled coffee.

'Please!' I called.

'Do they all come running?' Susan laughed as she came in with a cup.

'Sometimes,' smiled.

'M'm,' she said, raising her eyebrows, 'By the way, Stuart asked for you to ring him as soon as you arrive, and all the mail and daily notices are on your desk.'

I watched her leave, and she turned before closing the door and caught me watching her.

'I should put something in your coffee!' she joked.

I picked up the phone and dialled Stuart's number. 'Morning,' I said.

'Kit! Pleased you could make it, not too early for you is it,' he said sarcastically,

'Pop up can you.'

'On my way,' I said, downing the rest of my coffee as Stuart waved me to a chair.

'Well, looks like it's your old pal Liam,' he shrugged.

'The Old Man's not too happy, but he feels we should move with the times and give it a shot. So, I've asked Liam to be here at eleven. I'll have a chat with him, then we'll go to see the Old Man at eleven thirty, and we'll be with you in your office at twelve. Okay?'

'That's fine by me,' I said. I was not looking forward to it.

'Don't you feel a twinge of guilt about all this?' he asked with dry humour.

I smiled, but didn't answer.

'Twelve o'clock,' I said, 'Good luck.'

At twelve prompt there was a rap on the door, then the handle turned and the door was thrust open before I could speak. How bloody rude can some people be, I thought, even the Old Man waits for a reply to his knock.

The unmistakable tanned Liam entered, with Stuart at his heel. Stuart's face said it all. Liam looked slowly around the room, his eyes resting momentarily on anything personal. He looked directly at me with a sort of challenging insolence. We had never really got along, and there was certainly no love lost between us. I felt a particular distaste at his dandified appearance, always immaculate in an unsuitable sort of way. His ready-made mohair suit and ornate shirts, and the shoes produced from the skin of some unfortunate reptile. These things, together

21

with his fondness for designer aftershave, I found incongruous with the Service, and I just couldn't take to the man.

Stuart glanced at me over Liam's shoulder, his expression mirroring my own feelings. However, I thrust out my hand firmly, and Liam took it half-heartedly.

'Like an antique shop in here,' he said scathingly.

'Does that include those present?' I enquired smoothly.

'That will be for me to find out,' he replied, parrying my blow. 'But you must admit the place is crying out for modernisation. I mean, you're not even on line here, no computer. It's unbelievable!'

'That's all in another room,' I said quietly.

'Oh great,' he said, 'for all the world to see.'

'When I'm out on assignment, Sue has to deal with all incoming traffic,' I said firmly. Undeterred, he blathered on. He wasn't going to be put down, I thought; then I suddenly lost interest.

The meeting dragged on, my mind wandering half the time. Liam boasted about his expertise in the world of technology, and his ability to speak several Eastern languages. I virtually ignored him, looking out of the window and up at the aircraft heading to and from Heathrow, wishing I was on one of them, bound for anywhere away from this detestable creature.

Stuart's voice brought me back to reality.

'Well Kit that's about it for now,' he said, 'We have other people to see.'

I tried half-heartedly to recall what had been said, as I turned back to face the room. Stuart had noticed my lack of attention.

'I'll send you a memo.'

'No need,' I said winking, 'You've been taped! I'll have a printout.'

Liam flashed me a venomous glance.

'We're not that much in the past, you see,' I said, opening the door.

'We will see,' he replied.

Liam, much to Stuart's surprise, actually had the good manners on this occasion to open the door and allow Stuart to go out first. I smiled as pleasantly as I could, and stood in the doorway.

'Good to meet you again Liam, I wish you well in your new post.' They walked off down the corridor, and I closed the door behind them. To hell with it, I thought.

I poured a small scotch and sat down, and the phone rang. It was Stuart.

'Pompous little prick, isn't he?' he quipped.

'Certainly is,' I said, 'I suppose, but he's not daft, and I can well see why he's been selected. I wish you well with him!'

'Yes, well thank you very much!' said Stuart sarcastically. 'Listen, I'm seeing you for dinner tonight, aren't I?'

'That's right, but where are we going? I asked curiously.

'Oh, just a small place you won't like. That way it won't cost me much!' He laughed and slammed the phone down.

I sat for a while, quietly reflecting on my situation. The last fifteen years had been a hectic time, an interesting and action-packed time, often a dangerous time. But in recent months' things had begun to change. The raison d'être of the Service had started to disappear. Its role in the scheme of things was not nearly so important or exciting as it had been; assignments were now much more mundane. I was convinced it was the right time to move on. I was so very tired of the whole business.

Five

I t was 8.15 pm when I left the office, and I needed to
be ready so as to be collected by Stuart's driver by
9.30. He was always very punctual. I grabbed a cab,
and told the driver to get me to Ennismore Mews as
quickly as possible.

I turned to put my briefcase on the seat beside
me, and glancing out of the rear window as we
pulled out of the traffic, by chance I noticed a dark
blue Daimler Sovereign, similar to my own car, ease
itself into the line of traffic two or three cars behind
us. At the time I didn't attach any great significance
to this. After all, I thought, there must be hundreds
of cars like this in London. I dismissed it from my
mind, and sat back to think over the events of the
day. We turned into Ennismore Mews, and as I paid
off the driver, I noticed the Daimler slide quietly by
at the end of the road.

I let myself into Number 12 and automatically fell
into the routine of long habit, running a bath, pouring a scotch, and checking the answering machine.
Tina had rang, apologising for last night. Tina had
rang again, asking why I hadn't rang her back. Tina

had rang yet again, and this time she wasn't at all apologetic. There were two other calls of no importance, and a surprisingly and embarrassingly a long call from Camilla in Yorkshire. I think she had finally taken on board the fact that I had actually resigned, and would be coming home permanently. No doubt she found the prospect somewhat daunting! I decided to ring them both later; this was not the time to get involved in long discussions.

I re-set the answerphone, reached for my glass and glanced out of the window. My attention was immediately held by a movement in the shadows across the darkened street. I could just make out the figure of a man standing quite still, looking directly up at my window.

I pretended not to notice him, and stood there sipping my scotch in full view, careful not to look in his direction. After a couple of minutes, I casually turned away and moved slowly out of sight. I went out of the lounge, closing the door behind me, then bolted up the dark stairs and into the unlit bedroom. I moved carefully towards the half-open curtains, and peered out into the street. There was no sign of him. He had been bloody quick, I thought. He could have simply been waiting for someone in the house opposite to answer the door and let him in, I mused. Yes, that was it. Simple! Except that there were no lights on in any of the houses, no parked cars, no sign of life. Disturbing.

I sat on the edge of the bed for 15 minutes, watching the street carefully. Nothing happened, and our man did not return.

Time to move if I wasn't to be late. I quickly showered, dressed, and checked my watch. It was 9.29. I grabbed a coat and opened the door, and to my amusement Charles was on the doorstep, about to ring the bell.

'Good Evening, sir,' he said cheerfully, and returned to the car, holding open the door for me.

'Good evening, Charles,' I returned. I set the alarm and double-locked the door, and climbed into the waiting Daimler. As we turned right at the end of the mews, I glanced to the left, and there, just perceptible in the shadows was the man I had seen earlier. The set of the shoulders, the shapeless raincoat and 'pork-pie' hat all were unmistakable. It was him all right. There could be many reasons for a man to hang about in that area, and I found myself giving him the benefit of the doubt, but I made a very definite mental note of the incident.

We drove swiftly up to Prince's Gate and into the Park. Stuart was not a man of idle chatter, and Charles, his chauffeur for many years, was by habit a man of few words, who rarely spoke unless spoken to. I took the opportunity to settle back in the cool comfort of the big car's rear compartment, and enjoy the sumptuous feel of the sheepskin rugs, the inimitable smell of Connolly leather, the street lights reflecting on the polished walnut door capping's.

I felt a surge of pride at the knowledge that the drawing-room environment in which I was travelling was the work of British designers and British craftsmen, handed down through generations of traditional coach-builders and unique to British luxury cars.

I collected my thoughts as we glided round Berkeley Square, down Bruton Street and past Holland & Holland, the gun makers; another splendid example of British traditional skills still surviving. Left into Bruton Place, and the car drew smoothly to a halt. I waited for Charles to open the door, knowing how offended he would be if I so much as touched the handle.

A few strides took me inside the Kaspia Restaurant, one of Stuart's favourite eating houses. Specialising in caviar, vodka and all manner of things Russian, it had been heavily frequented by Russian Embassy staff and diplomats in former days, and was still quite busy in the late evening when the theatres emptied, sight of a celebrity was almost guaranteed, but at this time of night it was quiet and peaceful, an ideal venue for a relaxing meal. Stuart, I knew, would be sitting at the far end of the restaurant, where his favourite table was situated behind a frosted glass partition. This structure was quite opaque, but it featured a 1-inch border of clear glass, its edges bevelled to give a prism effect, and I knew that Stuart would be looking through this and watching the door, and was probably already aware of my arrival.

I was greeted by the head-waiter, who said obsequiously,

'Good evening, sir, you'll be dining with Mr Stuart?'

'That's right,' I said, 'Has he arrived?'

'He has indeed, sir. This way, please.'

I was led through the restaurant to the expected table, the quiet strains of a balalaika played in the background and Stuart rose to greet me.

'Ah' good evening Kit, a pleasant journey I trust?'

Stuart's formality never ceased to amaze me. Here we were, close friends and colleagues for many years, and he still afforded me a politeness more suited to a virtual stranger. It was a personal trait of his which I found both endearing and infuriating.

'Drink?' he asked the obvious, lifting the bottle. He knew exactly what I would have. The Kaspia was famous for its quite unbeatable house Champagne, its crisp dryness and slight almond bouquet quite unrivalled.

'Cheers,' I quietly raised a cold misting glass, and watching the bubbles rise slowly.

As I sipped, I ran my eye along the clear border of the opaque glass partition. Stuart caught my eye.

'Good, isn't it?' he said with a smile.

'Excellent,' I answered, 'From where I'm sitting,

I can see the door and the window. Turn my head slightly and I can see the bar and the far corner. How did you come to find it?'

'I didn't, he replied, 'You remember the big Russian who used to come in here from the Embassy?'

'You mean Volanovitch,' I said.

'That's the one. He always used to request this table, and after he was re-called, I made a point of booking it myself. Just curiosity really. Then of course I saw its usefulness.'

'I see, I even thought you might have had it bugged at some stage.'

'Never entered my head,' he smiled.

We gave our instructions to the head waiter, both ordering caviar, and as Stuart was footing the bill, I followed his lead and ordered Sevruga, the cheapest of the four varieties available.

Stuart looked across the table at me.

'Well Kit, do you think is this the last supper?'

'Hardly,' I replied, 'You're at a dinner party in Yorkshire in two weeks' time. I think we'll be having suppers for a very long time.'

'Sounds good to me,' he smiled, 'By the way, what do you think of the new man, Liam, your successor?'

'Well, it wouldn't be difficult to find a nicer man, but he's bright, intelligent, full of modern ideas and computer technology, so maybe he's the right guy for the job. But can you handle him?'

'Only time will tell,' he replied thoughtfully. 'He

certainly isn't the traditional type, but there is something there that the department can use.'

I nodded, and waited as Stuart stared into his glass, watching the bubbles rising in the exquisite amber liquid. This was a sure sign that he was preparing to say something.

'Listen, Kit' he said at last, 'do you remember that business of the freighter CarlosII?

'Yes, what about it?' I asked, surprised. This had been some time ago, and was well forgotten.

'Is it dead and buried?' asked Stuart.

'Completely,' I said, 'I have a small file in my office containing the details of the vessel, but nothing more. Everything else is on the main computer and can't be accessed unless you and I are both present. I suppose from now on it'll be yourself and the Old Man. Anyway, why do you ask?'

'Well it's just that the Old Man spoke to me about it this afternoon. Called me into his office and asked me if it was properly dead and buried. At first, I wondered if he'd had an enquiry from elsewhere, but thinking about it, I suppose he just wants to make sure there are no loose ends anywhere after you've left the Service. Perhaps if you could let me have the file in the morning, I'll go through it with you and then I'll take it up to him and he can satisfy himself.'

'You'll have it first thing in the morning,' I said.

At that point a waiter arrived with two silver trays each displaying a small cut-glass bowl of Sevruga caviar lying on a bed of ice, and side plates with egg-yolk, egg-white, chives, and warm thin bread toasted on one side only. The waiter, clearly Russian, smiled ingratiatingly.

'Vodka, gentlemen?' he asked.

I looked at Stuart, who nodded agreement.

'Most certainly,' I said, 'Two of the Zubrowka, with the Bison grass?'

'An excellent choice sir,' replied the waiter, and moved silently away. The meal continued quietly, each of us deep in our own thoughts, enjoying the excellent fare. Two halves of Scottish lobster arrived, bedded on salad as we had requested, we gently ate our way through to coffee, savouring every morsel.

Stuart sprinkled the brown Russian sugar into his black coffee and stirred it gently.

'You won't change your mind?' he asked, looking down into the swirling liquid.

I laughed.

'That would be a little difficult now, as my replacement has already been appointed.'

'That is a matter of conjecture, as I said earlier, the Old Man called me, this afternoon, he wonders if he has done you a miss service? He wants to offer you a higher rank, along with a salary increase and so on.'

'I'm grateful for the offer, I really am, and I could certainly use the money, but I've made my decision and must stick by it. As for rank, it's never interested me too much as you know, and I only ever used it at Embassy dinners or State occasions and that sort of thing. No Stuart, I'm sorry, I just can't accept the way the Service within its self has changed of late. Being desk-bound is not for me. This is where I depart, gracefully, I trust.'

'What about the protection assignments you've been given lately, didn't you enjoy those?' Stuart asked.

'To a degree, yes it got me out of the office, and there was a good deal of satisfaction when a job was safely completed. But there was a certain lack of communication which I found worrying sometimes. There seemed to be no direct contact with the people one was working with, orders often having passed through several departments foreign or otherwise before reaching me, sort of remote control.'

'You were damn good. Do you still train?' asked Stuart.

'A little,' I said. 'Hyde Park Barracks every two weeks for 150 rounds, but it's more from habit than anything else. I don't think I could hit Westminster Abbey if I was inside it nowadays.'

There was a short silence, then he spoke softly.

'I don't think I've ever seen you miss anything. You have a magnificent gift, don't lose it.'

We finished our meal and Stuart paid the bill, which would, of course, come out of his own pocket. It was accepted by all in the Service that no costs of this sort should ever be claimed against expenses, it was far better to deal with them personally. This was principally a point of honour but also avoided recriminations.

We stepped into the night air, to find Charles waiting by the Daimler, rear door open, ready for us. We moved off up Bruton Place, and left into Berkeley Square. Stuart interrupted my thoughts.

'I think I'll stop off at the office, just for a few minutes. Charles can whisk you back to Ennismore and collect me on his way back.'

'Whatever you say,' I agreed.

As we rounded the corner into Curzon Street, Stuart exclaimed,

'Well, well, someone burning a bit of midnight oil, by the look of things!'

I followed his gaze, and saw two lit windows on the fourth floor – my floor! Odd, I thought. I felt sure I'd been the last to leave. Cleaners perhaps?

As we drew up outside the entrance, the doorman stepped forward and opened the door, and Stuart slid nimbly onto the pavement.

'Good Evening, Colonel,' said the doorman, himself ex-military.

'Good Evening, Harold,' Stuart returned the greeting, 'I won't be more than five minutes, Charles will be back for me.' Turning to me he said,

'A good evening, Kit see you in the morning.'

The big car slipped away, taking me home to a much-needed bed. It had been a hectic two days.

'Charles,' I said, 'I'm sorry to drag you back to Ennismore, especially at this time of night.'

'No problem, sir.'

'Well, it must have been very boring for you sitting outside the restaurant all that time.'

'Not at all, sir. I have always something to do, making sure the car is clean and warm, and that everything is ready at all times for any situation that may arise. Never apologise, sir.' He went on, 'Two years ago I had to retire – my age, you know.'

'I didn't know,' I said softly.

'Yes sir, it was a very sad day for me. I had tears in my eyes as I made my way home on the Tube, the earliest I'd made that journey in thirty years. I was bewildered, sir and when I got home to the memsa-hib, she felt the same way. The prospect of spending the rest of my days sitting in a flat in Battersea appalled me, and I sat around not knowing what to do. The next morning, I got up at 0500 as usual, and without further ado, put on my uniform, and made my way to the Tube station. I sat in the car in the garage and waited until the Colonel arrived.

'Charles!' he boomed, 'What the hell are you doing here, you've retired.'

'I can't, sir,' I muttered. He looked at me for a long time without a word, and then.

'Well then, you'd better get that bloody car cleaned and ready to go, instead of moping around!'

I've been with him ever since. It's a long time now

sir. I was only twenty when I drove his father just after the war. Real gent he was, sir. Very strict, but a real gent. Time for everyone he had. Yes, sir a real gent…… but never apologise sir, 'cos this is my life.'

The car slid to a standstill outside number 12.

'Goodnight Charles,' I said quietly. 'Sorry.'

He nodded almost imperceptibly, and got back into his seat, taking the big car silently off into the night.

I put my key into the lock, automatically scanning the street in both directions. There was nothing. No movement, no sign of life, nothing. I flicked off the alarm and went upstairs. I checked the answerphone, only Camilla had rung. I rang her back, but the number was engaged, so I poured myself a nightcap and slumped into a chair.

A few seconds later my reverie was interrupted by a violent banging on the front door. Someone obviously knew I was in and demanded an answer. I ran downstairs and switched on the outside light, and looked out through the spy hole in the door.

I'd had this door specially made so that it appeared outwardly to be a perfectly normal solid oak-panelled door, but sandwiched between the two substantial veneers was a sheet of quarter-inch armour plate. My idea had been that it might protect me from an external bomb or a push-bell assassin, but as I peered out, I realised it was worse than either.

Tina was standing outside, arms akimbo, nostrils flaring, and clearly very angry.

I braced myself, fixed a smile and swung open the door.

'Hi,' I said brightly.

'Where the hell have you been?' she yelled.

I took her arm, pulled her into the house and closed the door before she woke the whole of Knightsbridge. As I did so I caught a whiff of her unique perfume, strangely enhanced now she was mad.

'Where have you been and who have you got here?' she demanded, walking straight upstairs.

'There's only me, the whisky and the cat, and I think the cat's left me,' I said. She was not amused.

'Don't you ever listen to your answerphone?' she asked scathingly.

'Yes, I do I'm sorry, but as you know I've been at bit busy. Resigning has left me with a lot to sort out.' The idea that I was going to leave London for good seemed to soften her, and she sat down.

'What can I get you?' I asked her soothingly.

'A small brandy and soda please,' she replied quietly.

The phone rang, and I continued to pour Tina's drink and let the answering machine take care of it. Camilla's voice filled the room, asking virtually the same question Tina had done. The phone clicked off, and Tina said,

'What's it like to be chased by two women, and not answer the phone to either of them?'

I apologised again.

'I am very pre-occupied.'

'In that case,' said Tina positively, 'let me try to occupy you. Let's go to bed!'

She came out of the bathroom looking absolutely stunning in her total nakedness, long dark hair flowing down to her perfectly formed breasts, flat stomach and designer pubic stubble and long, sleek legs. As she strode purposefully towards the bed, I wondered what man could deserve this. One of life's finest experiences in anyone's eyes.

The night passed on, not a tumultuous, thrashing affair by any stretch of the imagination, but more one of gentle affection, wondering if we'd ever see each other again. I was awakened by the phone, to find sunlight streaming through the window. By the time I'd finished on the phone, Tina was standing there, showered, dressed and ready for the city.

'This time, you will ring me, won't you?'

'Yes,' I promised, 'I will.'

Six

As usual, Harold the doorman when I arrived at Curzon Street ostentatiously glanced at his watch and shook his head. I grinned at him and started up the stairs. I punched my code into the office door, and it opened with its customary click. I walked across and pressed the button to release the dividing door. Susan was at her desk.

'Good morning,' I said brightly, 'Anything for me?'

'Morning,' she replied briskly, 'just a request for a file you promised Stuart.'

'Ah yes. Straight away.' I turned towards the 'A-B-C' filing cabinet, and stopped. Something was wrong. The cabinet was a little out of line with the others, and at a slight angle. I probably knocked it yesterday, I thought. I moved towards the lock, and it also was not as I had left it. My habit was always to leave the combination on a row of zeros, but two digits had been altered because 12 was showing. I'd had people in the office yesterday, and it was possible someone had brushed against it. I took out the file on Carlos II, and everything seemed in order, in fact there was more in there than I remembered, but then, it had been a difficult case to which nobody wanted to put their name.

I buzzed Stuart.

'Can I come up?'

'Yes, crack on,' he said.

Moments later I knocked on his door.

'Come in, good morning,' showing a broad smile.

'No recriminations from last night?'

'How could there be?' I asked, 'It's still one of the best places. Here's the file you asked for. You'll probably need me to brief you on it.'

'I'm sure I will, but I'll go through it first.'

As I was leaving, I turned,

'Tell me, Stuart, you didn't by any chance go into my office last night?'

'No,' and with a frown why do you ask?'

'Well, it's just that you're the only one who can remember my code number,' I shrugged.

'You're not supposed to know that!' he joked.

'I remember you telling me how you do it,' I said, 'Coburn's 1929, one bottle, two glasses and two people, which makes the number 1929:122.

'Correct,' he laughed I thought somewhat falsely, then his expression suddenly changed to one of concern.

'But no Kit, I didn't go into your office, why do you think someone did?'

'Not sure,' I mused.

'Then I have a question for you. Did you leave your office light on last night?'

'Not to my knowledge,' I don't like waste.

'Well, when I came back last night,' Stuart paused then, 'The light was on in both your and your secretary's offices, the corridor light was on too. I suppose the corridor light, we could perhaps put down to the cleaner? maybe you were in a rush to leave, were you?'

'That's certainly true, I suppose,' I nodded thoughtfully.

'We'll play it by ear, see what happens,' Stuart decided. 'Meanwhile Kit give me a couple of hours with this, then we'll work through lunch on it and you can put me right on things before I take it up to the old man this afternoon.'

I returned to my office, deep in thought. Questions were arising now to which I had no answers. Passing the open doors of the lift I picked up the unmistakable, near-toxic smell of a pungent, fashionable after-shave, which could only belong to one man. I wondered what he was doing creeping around on this floor already. I sank into my chair, and went over in my mind the points that were disturbing me.

The filing cabinet? I suppose I could have knocked against it myself, but it was quite heavy, and would need a fair bit of force to move it. Surely, I would remember such a collision?

The lock? Could it have been altered by a passing trouser-leg? Possible, but somehow unlikely. The lights? Did I really leave them on?

41

Yet again it was possible and I couldn't be certain, but the element of coincidence was uncommonly strong here, perhaps too strong. Unable to reach any definite conclusions, I decided to take a walk to clear my head. I needed to see Turnbull's, my shirt-maker in Jermyn Street, so I decided to kill two birds with one stone, and set off in that direction.

When I returned Susan was at lunch, and I found a note on my desk to say that Stuart wanted to see me immediately. As I approached his office, I could see that his door was open.

'Come in,' he said, looking up as I reached the threshold.

'It's unusual for you to work with your door open,' I commented.

'Yes well, it's suddenly become rather hot in here,' he seemed to grumble. 'I didn't appreciate the gravity of the Carlos II affair. I think it's raised the temperature by about five degrees!'

'Well, it was quite a big one, bigger than we thought it was going be, but it passed off quietly enough,' I raised my eyebrows in exclamation, 'I don't think there are too many pointers left about. There are only a handful of people world-wide who'll remember it, and they won't have all the pieces to complete the picture.'

'Ah' but you do,' Stuart said pointedly. 'In fact, you're probably the only one in the world with all the pieces, and now you've got to brief me.'

'That's true,' I nodded 'just the file, the computer, and myself.'

'Yes, but your computer is on your shoulders and always will be. Very wise. Anyway, let's make a start on Carlos II.'

What put you on to it in the first place?'

Part 2

Operation Carlos II

Seven

'Russian Embassy please,' I said quickly to the cab-driver, and the gruff cockney voice came back, muted by the glass partition.

'Righto Guv' and we moved off into the hell of the evening traffic.

I began to reflect, as we slowly picked our way through the busy streets of London.

A week before in the morning mail an invitation had arrived from the Russian Embassy, for Cocktails at 6 p.m. 'A Farewell' it read, I wondered now for whom and on what this gathering might involve. Lots of goodbyes? Some sad perhaps, some tinged with relief maybe.

Gorbachov's Perestroika was now well established, welcomed universally as the start of a new and exciting period in world history. The Cold War was at an end, and the need for a Russian presence in London, as in many of the world's capital cities, was greatly reduced. The central purpose of the gathering to which I had been invited, I thought, was the announcement that a large number of Russian diplomats were being recalled to Moscow forthwith, which meant that several people with whom I had forged relationships in recent years would disappear out of my life.

The glass partition slid back, bringing me out of my reverie.

'There we are Guv, that'll be just four quid.'

I gave him a five-pound note, told him to keep the change, and strode across the pavement into the Embassy building.

The duty receptionist was sitting at her desk just inside the door.

'Good Evening, sir,' she said pleasantly.

'Good Evening,' I repeated, handing her my invitation, my eyes taking in the room and what occupant's I could see.

She examined it carefully.

'Do you have any …'

She stopped as I offered my identity wallet.

'Thank you, Colonel.' Again, she scrutinised my papers, finally handing them back with a radiant smile.

'That's fine, sir, please go in.'

She handed me a clip-on identity badge, which I put into my pocket out of site, and I made my way up the wide, thickly-carpeted staircase to the first floor.

The heavy, gold-inlaid double doors were opened for me by two plain-clothes security men, whose typically Russian features assumed an automatic pale plastic smile as I approached.

I nodded in reply to his murmured greeting, whilst showing my card from my pocket, and descended the six steps to join the gathering ensemble. Immediately, waiters appeared from either side, bearing trays with champagne glasses and canapés of caviar and smoked sturgeon. I accepted one of each, and started to mingle.

Several familiar faces were in evidence, and it seemed strange that some of them I would probably never see again. For perhaps half an hour I moved about the room, chatting to acquaintances, a nod here, a word there, all very relaxed and civilised.

Then I came across Yanovich, I had seen him earlier but did not want to make an approach and it seemed neither did he. Yet he was standing against the wall on the other side of the room, his shining pate reflecting the light from the ornate chandelier, a fixed smile on his moon-like countenance. He was looking directly at me, and when he realised, I had seen him, just perceptibly to me, he flicked his round head a fraction, in the universal 'follow-me' gesture, and ambled unhurriedly away towards the open French windows, beyond which lay the balcony at the back of the building. Fresh air and a five-storey fall … I wondered how many.

I waited a couple of minutes, then slowly made my way over to the windows, nodding and smiling at people as I did so, and eventually I was standing beside my old friend in the corner of the balcony.

'It's good to see you here Kit, how are you?' The sound of the traffic in the street below almost drowned out his low-pitched voice. 'It is better this way,' he said gesturing to the cars and taxis below.

'It's like the Cold War all over again,' I said smiling.

'No,' he replied, 'that has finished – for the time being anyway.'

'Sceptical?' I enquired.

He turned to look at me, his flat, pale face devoid of emotion.

'There is so much change, so quick,' he said, 'the people don't understand.'

Looking at him, standing there in his suit of Huddersfield cloth, champagne in hand, I thought, I'm sure they don't.

He continued to look straight at me, so that I wouldn't miss any of his words.

'Kit my friend, I have something to say to you.'

'Go on,' I encouraged, intrigued.

'I may be recalled, quite soon, even tomorrow, but before I go there is something, I must do for you.'

'For me?' My interest quickened.

'Once you did something for me, and you made me a happy man. I have not forgotten.'

'How is she?' I asked, 'Zara,' realising who and what he meant.

'She is fine, excellent, thanks to you. But now I must repay your kindness.'

'But, and I was about to protest, however he raised a podgy hand to stop me.

'Please! Such a favour should not go unrewarded, it will not.'

A couple of years ago he had told me that he desperately wanted to get hold of a work permit for his daughter, so that she might go to America and study law. I had been instrumental in getting the papers sorted out for her, and she was now happily living and working in New York, a solicitor.

He paused for a moment then continued, 'Murmansk? You know Murmansk?'

'Indeed, I do'.

'Well, as we speak, there is a freighter being loaded with wheat for export. Did you ever hear of Russia exporting wheat?' he demanded raising his furry eye brows.

'It does sound a little strange,' I agreed cautiously.

He lowered his voice even further. 'Want to know why?' he asked, leaning closer.

'It would help,' I replied.

'Then I will tell you,' he said somewhat dramatically, 'Beneath all that wheat will be Scud missile parts, or even the complete Scuds'

'Right,' I said briskly, 'Where is she bound for? When does she sail? What is her name?' I fired the questions at him.

'Kit, I am repaying a debt, not working for you,' he said, managing a furtive smile.

He continued, 'She is loading now, so she will be leaving quite soon, maybe even tomorrow, her name is Carlos II.' He stood looking at me making sure that I had digested all his curt facts, then hurriedly, he said, 'That is all I can tell you.'

He moved quietly away without another word, never turning. It was the last time I would see him. I stood for a moment looking at the traffic below, then trying to assess the implications of what he had told me, I moved casually back into the room. No one was looking, no one had noticed.

I mingled with the diplomatic throng for a while, noting that the Norwegian Consul's wife was astonishingly attractive, she smiled back interestingly, but my heart was not in it. I was still trying to make sense of Yanovich's story.

Eventually I finished the appropriate round of thanks and goodbyes and slipped away, Yanovich's information still eating into me. I decided that I would act on it first thing in the morning, I'd have to be careful, he was a notorious misinformer, and yet he did owe me one.

Eight

The following morning, I arrived early at the office, keen to verify Yanovich's story and to decide on what action to take, if any. I cleared my mail, giving my secretary Susan the bulk of it to deal with, and then set about my task with alacrity.

My first move was to contact Lloyds for any information on a vessel registered as Carlos II. I knew from previous experience that their report would take a little time to compile, so I pressed on with other avenues open to me. I called through the dividing door to Susan, in the next office, 'Sue, can you send a fax to the British Consulate in Murmansk.'

'Can do,' she said, appearing in the door way with a note pad and pen.

'To read as follows: 'URGENT. Please confirm Spanish registered ship Carlos II is loading, or has loaded, possibly grain. Sailed or sailing time, destination if known, and any other relevant details Yours, Kit, London, and mark it for the attention of the Consul.'

'Right away,' Susan said, quickly feeling the urgency.

If Yanovich's information was correct, this vessel needed to be found, and found fast, and I intended to find it. But there was the nagging knowledge that he had given me information in the past which some-times turned out to be worthless. Still, this latest tip had an air of intrigue about it, and more to the point I had a feeling about it.

I heard Susan send the fax, and I called her through again.

'Sue, fax Group Captain Roger Mulhouse up at RAF Kinloss, and ask if there are any sightings in the last twenty hours or so of a Spanish bulk carrier that could have come out of Murmansk, ask him to let me have any details, and further details from now on.'

'Consider it done,' she said, mischievously wig-gling her way round the door. Within seconds I heard the fax being typed.

I poured myself a coffee, and went down to the Operations Floor. I found an empty room and closed the door, and set about studying the maps and charts of north west Europe from the Barents Sea down to the Canaries, spending some time on the areas con-cerned, trying to get the overall picture of the area, and what I was dealing with.

Clearly, she had to be heading south, there was no point in hauling grain across the Atlantic, they had plenty! It had to be South. But if that was the case there were several routes open to her, maybe north of Iceland and through the Denmark Strait, between the Faroes and the Hebrides or even down through the North Sea and at this stage I could only rely on the Nimrods of Coastal Command at Kinloss to locate her.

I returned to my office and asked Sue to get me all the information on Scud missiles, dimensions, weight and types, etc. Within about fifteen minutes she came through with a Scud print out, and good, all the dimensions were here. Now I needed to know whether they could be transported in sections or as a whole, and I needed some idea how they could be stored under a cargo of grain, if indeed they were!

Now I had set all the wheels in motion there was nothing more I could do until more information came in. I decided to go to Curzon Street for a shave at Trumper's, a hot wet shave always helps the mind, and then an early lunch.

When I returned there were a couple of faxes waiting for me, the results of the first two lines of inquiry. The Group Captain's fax stated that for the moment flights were grounded due to a bad weather front. I would ring him later.

The second fax was from Lloyds, giving me chapter and verse on the Carlos II. She was a bulk carrier of some 22,000 tons, built in Yokohama in 1970; she was now Spanish registered to a company in Barcelona, but was currently on charter to a Maltese company of no known origin or trading record. Her hull was painted maroon with the white superstructure at the after end, and with a red and yellow band round her single short funnel on the top deck behind the bridge. I could see from the accompanying plans, which were not too complicated, that there were many large holds, and numerous derricks. There was no mention of any major refit but she had been docked in Cadiz for bottom cleaning and a repaint a year ago, so it was safe to assume that she would look reasonably well kept.

I did a memo to Roger at Kinloss with her description to help him locate her, and faxed it off myself straight away.

Within moments the fax burst into life again.

Nine

The fax read:

Carlos II, Spanish merchant vessel, departure delayed due to late arrival engine spares, now sailed at approx. 0530 hrs. Cleared port limits 0645 hrs, manifest shows cargo grain, crew 26, destination Valletta.

Shit! The bird had flown! Why was I always bloody late? Maybe I was losing interest. But I knew I wasn't; this was intriguing. I thought, there was something about it, the tip off had proved correct; that in itself was unusual. I'd had plenty of misinformation over the years from Russian contacts, but my gut feeling was there was far more to this than met the eye.

Now was the time to stir up Roger Mulhouse at Kinloss, the Coastal Command Long Range Maritime Patrol search and early warning base, direct. I dialled them up, after a moment the Staff Sergeant came back to me, 'The Group Captain was out on the field,' he said, but he would relay the message immediately, and he'd ring me back.

I poured a coffee and thoughtfully stirred the black liquor, but within moments it seemed the phone burst into life. I leaned over quickly and grabbed it with anticipation.

'Kit, its Roger. Got your fax, how can I help? We're all still on the ground here so no change.'

'Not even the Nimrods! Something must be airborne,' I said surprised.

'The only thing that's 'up' is my blood pressure,' he said joking.

I had a mental vision of his overweight frame squeezing behind his desk, with the round florid face blasting into the phone.

'But apart from that, Nimrod 486 will be airborne at 11.00 hrs'. He sounded as if there would be no doubt about it.

'Well, don't worry too much,' I said 'but the vessel in question has now definitely left Murmansk, 05.50 hrs today, yeah, so I faxed you a bit prematurely. Sorry. However, it's on its way South, I presume you can keep an eye out for it? I just need it verifying.'

'No problem, how official is it?'

'Well, I have no authority yet, but I have a feeling I may go for it soon. It depends where she's heading to. I'll speak to you later in the day anyway, and by the way aircraft are supposed to be in the air not on the tarmac.'

'Tell that to the ministry,' came back the terse reply.

I laughed and the phone went dead.

Stuart was away. Do I speak to the Old Man? No, not yet, I thought, give it a little more time to develop. I went down to the operations floor, found the empty room I'd been using and looked at the charts again. If I had something to hide which course would I take? There were short cuts, maybe? But the best course looked to be straight out to sea and straight down through the Atlantic, wherever it was bound. Then, off Portugal to turn east, if it was bound for the Mediterranean or, straight on if going to Africa. But the company is registered in Malta, as stated, m'm, I'd have to wait and see.

The following day I was at Curzon Street before most of the day staff had arrived. When Harold, the commissionaire saw me, he glanced at his watch, and shaking his head simultaneously, gave me a friendly scowl. I raised a clenched fist in salute and rushed past, and as ever, gave the lift a miss and strode forcefully up the stairs. The overnight cleaners were just completing, wheeling away floor polishers and giving a final shine to door knobs as they passed, as usual everything smelt of polish.

As I punched my code into my office door, I could not help the feeling of excitement at being onto something at last. I walked through into Sue's office, only to have all excitement drained, no messages and no faxes. I picked up the internal phone, and called the communications room.

'Anything come in overnight, Jill,' I said hopefully.

'No, not a thing, oh and what's got you up so early,' she said caustically.

'Depravity,' I said laughing and banged the phone down.

The next twenty-four hours were hell, I had kept everything to myself as yet, and all the pressure was on me not to blow it. Carlos II had still not showed up, admittedly the search was not official, but I would have thought we should have got something by now, it simply couldn't vanish. I felt like a Father waiting for his first born, pacing up and down, snatching the phone every time it rang, had I made a mistake?

It was lunch time the following day when finally, the call came.

'Roger,' I bellowed, 'tell me'.

'Your luck, as always,' he said, 'She has turned up, it's her all right, at about 58.10 North, 9.28 West, seventy odd miles west of the Shetlands.'

'Are you sure?'

'Squadron Leader Baxter is. Well, about as sure as he can be without alerting them, do you want him to pop down and ask?' he said facetiously.

'No, but I have to be sure,' I said seriously.

There was a pause at the other end, then Roger said,

'What about a Fisheries Protection Vessel, there may be one in the area that can have a closer look it can seem to be a casual inspection?'

'Makes good sense,' I said, 'can you do that?'

'Cost you, but yeah, give me ten minutes. Oh, and by the way Baxter sends his regards, says it's as bumpy as hell out there today, and hopes it's worth it to you?'

'Send him mine, tell him to keep his eyes skinned. And Roger, I'll stand by here till you call? OK.'

'Fine.' The phone went dead.

I walked to the window as I had done a thousand times before and looked down into Curzon Street. Let's hope, I thought. Sooner than I expected, the phone rang again.

'You're in luck, Kit, there is a Fisheries boat about forty miles south of Carlos, they may possibly already have her on radar, but Carlos will not pick her up for a while yet. So, they will steer for an interception, close enough to make a positive ID, but it will be done with the utmost nonchalance, i.e. they will not alter course after this, and will steam straight past and away, OK?'

'Brilliant!' I said, 'An enormous help, you'll get back to me?'

'Will do,' Roger put the phone down with typical abruptness.

I quietly went down to the operation rooms again, and looked at a chart. A parallel ruler and the given bearings, soon gave me an idea as to where she and the Fishery vessel were. With a convergence speed of, say 35 knots, I would expect contact in under the hour.

I closed the door, this time locking it and taking the key with me. On the way back up to my office, in my haste I nearly bowled over one of our new recruits.

'Busy today,' he jibed.

'Busy enough,' I said, I didn't like him, couldn't remember his name, just his fancy suits and a pervading odour of aftershave. I thought, too full of himself, too familiar, then again, I was a loner, and preferred it that way, safer.

The wait! I knew I shouldn't be tense but I hated these times, then after what seemed an age the phone rang again.

'Its your day, Kit,' Roger said, 'Carlos II right across the stern, and flying the Spanish flag, all looks normal, according to Fisheries. What next?'

'M'm, how far south do your Nimrods go?' I asked.

'Far as you want, if you get authorisation,' he said, 'We could move an aircraft down to St. Mawgan in Cornwall.'

'Get back to you, and thanks,' I said slowly putting the phone down.

Stuart still being away, I decided to go and see the Old Man.

I dialled his extension, instantly getting his secretary,

'Any chance of an audience?' I asked.

'Ooh, well now, there's a question, it'll cost,' she said with a giggle. This had connotations of James Bond, I thought, but somehow without Miss Moneypenny's panache. If only it was really like that.

'This has cost me plenty today already,' I sighed.

'So, it should,' she retorted, 'hang on.' Within seconds she came back to the phone,

'Come straight up, and don't be stuffy.' She laughed again.

Within moments I was up the stairs and opening the heavy door into the Old Man's outer office, thick pile carpet under foot, the slight aroma of pipe tobacco and gentle perfume hung in the air.

'Is he in a good mood?' I asked.

'He always is when you're on your way,' she flannelled, 'Go on, go straight in.'

I knocked, and the heavy voice came back,

'Come in, Kit.'

I opened the door and strode in, purposefully,

'Good afternoon, Sir.'

'Hello, trouble,' he smiled, standing, and gesturing towards a chair, 'to what do I owe this dubious pleasure?'

This room was like going back in time. It always had an effect on me, rather like going to see the Head at school, Sir Edward standing there in his sombre tweeds, holding his pipe, eyes soft yet searching, puissance emanating from his very presence.

I sat down in the chair offered. He was a man who appreciated facts only, so it did not take me long to bring him completely up to date. When I had finished, there was a short silence as he looked at me thoughtfully. Then, and I was waiting for it,

'Kept it to yourself as usual,' he boomed. I didn't answer, we always played this tiresome little charade, and I was used to it. I waited.

'M'm well, we have a perfectly normal bulk carrier going south, we have a tip off from a known misinformer, and he has gone back home. You have already alerted Coastal, what do you want me to do? We have no proof of anything out of the ordinary, it's a non-starter, Kit.'

'Maybe, Sir, but can't we follow it for a bit longer, we do have surveillance down to Biscay and beyond,' I said hopefully.

'So, she goes into the Mediterranean. We have no reason to apprehend her?'

'But we may have more information soon.'

'How,' he said grumpily.

'I am working on it, Sir,' I said unconvincingly.

'Sure, you are, but it doesn't look promising to me, can't go boarding vessels without a reason.'

'But …' I never finished.

He raised a hand,

'If it fits in with near normal routine for Coastal, ask them to keep an eye on it, don't know what you'll do though.' And as an afterthought, 'Nothing without my nod, I trust, and keep me up to date.' raising one of his furry eye brows, questioning.

'Thank you, Sir.' I rose to go, he smiled,

'Good luck.'

Well, that was straight forward I thought, what now? Back in my office I faxed out a memo to Kinloss.

F.A.O. Group Capt. R. Mulhouse.

Continue with surveillance of bulk carrier Carlos II, any deviation from known   course and destination please report.
       *** Authorisation sheet on its way.*
                   Regards A. 6 London.

Now the waiting again. Was she going to the Med. as stated on her manifest? If she was, would the destination be Malta? I thought not, so where? Somehow, I had to verify what, if anything was on board, how was I to do it? So many questions, I needed some fresh air and thought. As by now it was about six p.m., I decided to leave, and take my thoughts for an evening drink, deciding to walk back to Knightsbridge, and stop off at Bentleys of Beauchamp Place for a 'freshener'.

On arrival it was full of the 'early doors' solicitors and barristers who seemed to frequent the spot, but for me tonight, it was just too busy, so after a couple of scotch and sodas, I decided to go straight back to

Ennismore Mews, tomorrow was going to be busy anyway.

That night I could hardly sleep, thinking of Carlos II making her way down through the Atlantic, more than likely in rough weather, spray and foam howling over her decks, one man in near darkness, peering out of a dimly lit bridge, keeping watch as the others slept, the deep slow beat of engines, and the creaking of steel plates as she made her way through the sea, with a cargo of hell. Southwards?

The next day things were quiet. We had a report in at about 12.00 hrs, and another later in the day. Carlos II was making steady headway in poor weather, she was steaming in an almost direct line for Gibraltar but if anything, she was further out to sea than one would have expected, and maybe not making as much headway as expected, either. She seemed to have slowed down a little, but the weather might have caused that, maybe?

Down in my now private ops room, I plotted her suspected course on, and my estimate of her going through the Straits of Gibraltar would be in about thirty-six hours.

Somehow, I or someone had to get on board, for some spurious reason, and in an official capacity so as not to cause any alarm. Even then I would have no reason as yet to authorize a search. I needed to know if the Scuds were under the wheat before any definitive plan of action could be put in to play. Even then, what legality if any would I have?

A plan had been slowly forming in my mind that perhaps a sea rescue could be staged somewhere along her route; myself and a small crew in a broken-down drifting vessel, sending up flares or putting out an SOS to get her attention? She might answer, would she offer to pick us up? If so, we could get on board. But one main problem of course was that other vessels might also come to our aid, and defeat the object. This and other ideas occupied my mind for the remainder of the day, till by evening I had formulated the plan of a 'Rescue'. It would be an exercise mounted out of HMS Rooke, the Naval Base at Gibraltar, and timing was all important. We only had a token force nowadays in Gib., nearly all administrative, but by morning, a small unidentifiable vessel could be made ready, with a crew of a couple of ratings, for the adventure.

Then; 'best laid plans,' as they say. The phone burst into life.

'Kit!' Roger Mulhouse from Kinloss bawled.

'Yes, just going to ring you,' I said, 'Problem?'

'Yeah! Carlos II is stationary off Cape St. Vincent; the bottom end of Portugal to you.'

'How long for,' I asked.

'Don't know, only just picked her up in a routine sweep, and didn't want them to hang about.'

'When are you due round again?'

'Shan't be, old boy, bit out of our area now, and you don't want us buzzing around all the time.'

He was quite right, I thought.

'Er, OK, I'll get back to you, and thanks for the call,' and the phone went dead. Simultaneously the fax chattered, verifying the position and everything he had said. Blast, what now?

Within moments I was speaking to the Commanding Officer of HMS Rooke, the Naval Base at Gib; and told him I was on my way as soon as might be, but in any event, I would be on the Rock early afternoon tomorrow. I was about to close, when he said, nearly as an afterthought,

'What's the problem, anything we can do?'

So, I relayed very briefly what had happened in the last few hours, though not of course our suspicions of the cargo. After a pause, he said,

'We have no aircraft here, but we do have a Hercules aircraft due in from Ascension early tomorrow, maybe I could have a word?'

'It would be an enormous help,' I replied. 'I will fax you the aerial photos of the vessel and its last known position as of now, as soon as you have anything let me have it and my secretary can contact me. I'll be with you tomorrow.'

'Scheduled flight?' the C.O. said. 'Yes, of course.'

'Till tomorrow then,' and he hung up.

The following morning, I called the office before leaving. Gibraltar had made contact, leaving a long message for me, but on having the main content read to me I nearly fell through the floor. It was----

'No vessel sighted, further search tomorrow.'

By the time I arrived at Heathrow, I was nearly fraught, I didn't like public phones but there was no choice. Sue was at her desk now and there was still no further news; absolutely nothing had come up, not a sign, not a trace. My head was on the block.

I signed for my diplomatic bag, and boarded the British Airways 737 for a direct flight to Gib. The flight was uneventful, save for the pleasure of half a bottle of duty-free champagne, and a delightfully leggy air hostess, who nearly made thoughts of Carlos II vanish. She had mentioned that she was staying overnight in Gib. I wonder, I thought.

Ten

Landing at Gibraltar is quite spectacular. One cannot mistake the Rock standing proud at the gateway to the Mediterranean, often topped with a little white ring of cloud, not unlike Sugarloaf Mountain in Rio. To the south lies Africa looking blue and pink in the distance, with the drying green of Spain to the north, with Gib's runway stretching out into the sea, white surf breaking at its edges. Circling out over the sea, the inexperienced traveller could be forgiven for thinking that we were about to land in the sea, as no sign of the runway is visible till the last minute as it flashes by under the wing. We came in on a westerly approach putting La Linea and Spain on the right, and the Rock on the left. With a jolt and a roar, we touched down on the tarmac, juddering as the engines reversed, and as we slowed the smell of burnt aviation fuel permeated through the air. We taxied gently to the terminal, and one could see way over to the right the old Royal Air Force buildings still visible. Within moments of the doors being opened the heat and the smell of Spain invaded the now inadequate air-conditioning, warm damp air, with a strong smell of sea and humanity. As I waited for the other passengers to disembark, I felt for my Serengeti sunglasses, then moving into the aisle the brilliant sunshine met me as I stood at the cabin door momentarily before descending the steps, on to Gibraltarian soil.

Over on the far side of the runway I could see a dark blue Land Rover making its way toward the aircraft. It soon slowed and stopped behind the transit bus. A Royal Marine jumped out as I approached and saluted inquiringly,

'Colonel, good morning, it is you isn't it, Sir,' he said a little unsure of himself.

'Yes, good morning,' I replied smiling.

He held the door open for me, and I climbed up and in, slamming the door with a resounding metallic bang.

'Where to, Sir? I'll come back for your bags.'

'I'm booked in at the Rock Hotel,' I replied.

'Been here before, Sir?' he asked as we made our way past the huge Avro Vulcan in desert camouflage that was parked menacingly as a 'Gate Guard,' a reminder of the not too distant past.

'Oh, once or twice,' I said, as we were waved through the gates, and turned towards the Rock. The old cannon embrasures hewn out of the cliffs during the days when the Spaniards besieged the garrison glared down at us ominously, reminding me that there was some 27 miles of tunnels inside the Rock, 'more roads on the inside than the out,' as the saying

goes. Against the skyline the Rock bristled with an-
tennae, and radar aerials; my mind jumped, I wonder if they have found Carlos II?

I snapped out of my thoughts,

'Er yes, straight to the Hotel please, and can you
bring up the diplo bag as well as my own gear as soon
as possible?'

'Sir.' He saluted.

'The Base Commander, its Commander Bairstow,
is it not.'

'That's right, Sir, he's a real gent, but can be a bit
strict some days. But if you want to know where to
wine and dine, he's your man, Sir.'

We passed through the old fortified gates, with
castellated walls and battlements to the right, and
into the Old Town, London cabs, old British cars,
horse and traps and naval three tonners all hurtling
along clinging to this mad anthill of Gibraltar.

'We won't get through the centre, Sir,' he said, 'full
of street traders, people everywhere, we'll take the
old Dock Road, and go around that way.'

I noticed fishing boats, a jumble of small craft
and a marina as well as the quay where the Tangier
ferry berthed. Ahead I could see the gates of the naval
Dockyard, when we swung left and started to climb.
Just as we started to claw our way up the Rock, the
driver swung left under some palm trees and into the
court yard of the Rock Hotel. A well-tanned gentleman of Asian origin wearing a long red jacket and a

blue cummerbund round his waist rushed forward as we halted and opened the door.

'Welcome to Gibraltar,' he said with a distinct accent, holding the door open, 'Any luggage?' he asked, peering in the back.

'No, it will be here shortly,' I said not wishing to get entangled. I quickly turned to the driver. 'Thanks for the lift, tell the Commander I'm here, er and ask him if he would like lunch up here,' I said, pointing toward the terrace, that was overflowing with brilliant purple bougainvillaea, where tables were just being laid, the white table cloths moving in the breeze.

'Will do, sir,' he replied, and looking at his watch, 'Any specific time sir?'

'About half an hour after you have delivered the bags, I need a shower,' I called going up the steps after the colourful doorman.

The receptionist greeted me with a smile,

'Good morning, Sir.'

'Morning,' I said, taking in the panoramic views of the bay with all the tankers and ships lying at anchor, and in the background the steep hills behind Algeciras shimmering in the heat. 'I'm booked in under Balearic Yachts, I hope,' I said, smiling back.

'You are indeed, sir, a double overlooking the bay,' she said, her flashing brilliant white teeth contrasting with her long jet-black hair, 'Will you be taking lunch?'

'For two,' I said, signing the register, 'and two bags will be here shortly, please send them straight up.'

'No problem,' she smiled back somewhat sensuously, eyes sparkling, m'm Spanish, I wondered?

The concierge coughed, I turned and followed him down the long bright airy corridor to my room, and gave him a tip on entering. Closing the door behind me, I turned, the view again was staggering, the huge windows opening onto the balcony allowing the sun to beam in, and it was hot.

I poured a scotch and soda from the tray, and added ice from the fridge. Then I picked up the phone, dialled the naval base and asked for Commander Bairstow. He answered impatiently,

'Base Commander.'

'Commander, I'm your visitor from London, do, you have any news for me.'

'Not a thing as yet, but I'll take you up on your offer for lunch. May have some news by then.' He said, 'Good flight?' almost as an afterthought.

'Fine, OK, see you in about three quarters of an hour.'

I rang off and then dialled London, taking the phone out on to the balcony.

'You sound cheerful,' Sue said.

'I am, the view is fantastic from here,' I took a small sip, ice tinkling on the cut glass.

'You're drinking,' she laughed, 'all right for some.' I didn't answer.

'There's still no sign of this dammed ship, have you got anything there?'

'Nothing's come in, the office is very quiet.'

I could see the returning Land Rover winding its way up the hill. 'Fine. I'll ring in later, er, maybe after hours, OK.'

All very frustrating, however, I started to run a bath; then there was a knock on the door, my bags had arrived.

A little time later, feeling fresher, and wearing just light trousers and short sleeved white shirt, I made my way through the marbled corridors to the open colonial style bar on the veranda, a slow punkah fan on the ceiling circulating the warm damp air, and stirring the perfume of a million garden flowers ablaze with colour in the sunlight. I ordered a Perrier.

The Commander arrived on the dot at 14.00. He strode straight into the open bar, and looked around then walked straight over,

'Long time no see,' he laughed. 'You look fit, how is your room?'

'Fine,' I said, not wasting any time, 'but is there any news?' He was somewhat taken aback by my sudden urgency.

'No, I'm sorry to say there isn't! Are you buying?' he said, gesticulating a little impatiently toward the smartly attired barman.

'I'm sorry, David,' I said. 'I just need to get cracking

on this one, and the bloody thing has vanished.' I turned to the bar and ordered him the predictable large gin and tonic.

'Happy?' I asked.

'Delirious,' he said drily. 'Shall we sit down? I presume you have booked a table.'

Somehow, I didn't think I was scoring any points so far at this meeting. As we moved towards the balcony, we were intercepted by an immaculate head waiter, dressed in white jacket and trousers.

'Gentlemen, your table, this way please,' he said with a slight bow, wafting a large red menu with tassels dangling, in the direction intended. We took our places looking out toward the old town below, its battlements with shadows growing longer in the afternoon sun.

'Any idea where Carlos II has disappeared to, David?'

'The Hercules has had a sweep along the coast,' he replied thoughtfully. 'It can't be too far away, but we really don't have the search facilities here now. We are trying, I'll out line it to you,' and he took a drink from his glass, making himself comfortable, but just as he said those words, the wine waiter and the concierge arrived simultaneously.

'Who's first?' I laughed. The concierge moved forward.

'Sorry to interrupt but we have an urgent call for Commander Bairstow?'

'I'll call back,' he said stiffly.

'They said it was urgent, Sir.'

'Oh, very well,' he said and rose irritably. Must be very serious to have your lunch interrupted in Gibraltar I thought and smiled inwardly.

I ordered a bottle of Marques de Caceres rosé and perused the delightful menu.

Within moments the Commander was back, beaming all over his red face, nearly laughing.

'Have I got news for you,' he exclaimed.

'Come on then, tell me!' I said frustrated by his obvious delight in his secret.

'Well, Kit, you're looking at it!' He laughed again, sweeping his arm broadly in the direction of Algeciras and the bay, 'It's there somewhere, Carlos II is there, broken down, just called up Algeciras Port Radio.'

'Unbelievable,' I said standing up to look out at the bay, a bay full of vessels riding at anchor. 'How on earth …?'

The Commander put his hand up, enjoying every moment,

'Aren't you lucky? About fifteen minutes ago Carlos II made a ship to shore call for spare parts and an engineer. She's had engine problems all the way down, apparently started in Murmansk, is that right?'

'Yes, we believe they were held up,' I said.

'As a result, she's had to heave-to here, in the bay. Our boys in the signals office picked it up, can you believe it!' he exclaimed, jubilantly pouring himself a large glass of rosé from the frosted bucket.

'Right,' I said. 'We need a plan, I have to get on board before she sails, I need to locate her amongst all that lot, I really need to get going,' I said, getting up.

'Relax, relax!' the Commander said, whilst pouring me a glass, 'you're in Spain now; well, nearly, it's Friday and she isn't going anywhere'. He laughed. 'Not at least till Monday or Tuesday at the earliest, no engineers will be working over the weekend.'

I wasn't convinced,

'We should make the effort,' I said, urgency in my voice.

'I'll make you a deal,' the Commander said, obviously settling in for a good lunch, 'you order lunch while I go and organise an inconspicuous launch, and when we've eaten, we can go for a little trip and have a look round the bay, and in the meantime my boys will monitor the air waves, if anything changes we will be notified immediately. OK?'

I didn't really agree, but I as I had little choice I reluctantly conceded. The Commander went to phone, and I ordered a mélange of fresh Mediterranean shellfish for two, with a dozen oysters, and waited for his return. He came back looking more florid than ever,

'Everything sorted,' he said' we'll pick a boat up from the Dockyard at 17.00.'

'No, we won't,' I said quickly, and he looked up at me, startled. 'We'll go from the Marina, I don't want any suspicion about us, we could be noticed motoring straight out of the yard.'

'Is it that serious?' he said looking surprised and off guard.

'It may be, and I like to be low profile just in case,' adding 'Sir' as an afterthought.

A most magnificent display of sea food arrived and we sat quietly until our waiter left.

'I shall come with you,' the Commander said.

'Certainly, no problem. You can show me the area,' I said, 'but dress in civvies, and if you can get some trolling lines? Might as well look as if we are fishing.'

'Absolutely,' he slurped, as the first of his oysters went down, I wondered what state the Commander would be in by five p.m.

The resounding blast of a siren echoed round the bay, and the steady clang, clang of chain cable thumping against the lip of a hawse pipe from an anchor being raised, made us look out to sea.

'What's your plan?' the Commander said, relaxing now.

'Difficult to say without further knowledge of f possible check what is in the hold, and if they are hiding anything, within the cargo itself.'

'Like what,' he said.

'Well, we're not too sure,' I said evasively, believing as always that the fewer people in the know; the safer ultimately, I would be, and the operation.

'Maybe drugs,' I said, hoping that would suffice for now. what we are dealing with, but somehow, I have to get on board the vessel.

'M'm, most likely,' he nodded, 'especially down here, the Spanish coast is alive with the stuff, especially Marbella and Fuengirola.' He leaned forward, taking a crab claw.

'They really do this very well here,' he said 'I'm glad you asked me to lunch'.

'I can tell,' I said with a wry smile, turning the cold misted glass in my hand and admiring the pale rosé.

Eleven

F ive o'clock soon came and I had decided to meet the Commander at Shepard's Marina, rather than get too involved for the moment. From the room, I'd scanned the bay through binoculars, but frankly there were just too many vessels to make a decision and to make matters worse, several had the red and yellow Spanish colours on their funnels. I changed into scruffy sea fishing clothes, ordered a taxi, and walked down to the foyer. By the time I got there an old Morris Oxford taxi had arrived.

'Shepard's Marina,' I said climbing in.

'Round the Rock, Sir? See the Rock,' he asked. 'Feed the Apes, Sir?' he said, smiling to show a mouth full of rotten teeth.

'Later maybe, just the Marina for now,' I said, and with a jolt and a rotating growl from first gear, off we went. Shepard's was on the left as we went back toward the airstrip, a large sprawling marina full of yachts, and many broken dreams. Sailor's intent on crossing the Atlantic who never made it, others arriving down from Northern Europe full of hope for a life in the sun. 'Gateway to the Mediterranean.' Gibraltar is often called.

I paid off the driver and walked through a massive chandlery shop and out on to the pontoons of the marina, yacht halyards rattling against masts in the afternoon breeze.

'Bang on time, that's what I like to see,' said a voice from behind. Half turning, I was joined by the Commander, dressed, surprisingly, in old denim. I had underestimated him, he looked the part.

'Just over here,' he said, pointing to a small plain wooden boat flying a small Spanish flag from the gaff of its stumpy mast, with a couple of rods hanging over the stern. 'Will that do you?'

'Excellent,' I said. 'Yours?'

'No, borrowed from a Spanish friend of mine in La Linea, just over there,' and he pointed to some low-lying white pueblo houses in the distance. 'Other side of the border, a restaurant owner, you get a very good meal there too,' he said happily.

'I can imagine,' I said jumping aboard. 'Right, let's get on with it,' I said and moved towards the forward warp. The Commander fired her up, and the old fashioned double knock of a twin cylinder Lister diesel rattled below the sun bleached boards, with the odd fish scale glistening from the caulking.

The Commander, his more practical naval days not forgotten, cast off astern, swung the wheel over and backed off the pontoon, then briskly applied opposite lock and pushed the gear lever into forward. We headed off towards the centre of the bay where scores of assorted vessels lay at anchor, the cool sea breeze welcome in the sticky afternoon heat.

'Anywhere special first?' the Commander hollered, pleased to be at the helm.

'Just start on the right and pass by the big vessels over there, and we'll chalk 'em off.'

I pointed toward several ships at anchor that I had observed from the hotel room.

'We're only interested in bulk carriers flying the Spanish flag, and with the yellow, red and yellow coloured bands on the funnel,' I said, producing a copy of the photo taken a few days ago off the Shetlands, and passing it over. The Commander glanced shrewdly at it and passed it back, swinging the boat to the left. As I started reeling out the trolling lines, the Commander threw me a bottle of San Miguel beer. 'Look the part,' he said, passing me the opener, so, 'when in Rome' I thought whilst opened my beer with a satisfying hiss. We passed by a huge rust streaked ship, plimsoll marks high out of the water and registered in Panama. As we rounded her prominent bulbous bow, from the bulwarks high above us a Filipino deck hand offered a half-hearted wave.

After a good hour we still had not located her, indeed if we had not known that somewhere amongst this confusion of anchored vessels Carlos II was lying, I would have been very down hearted. Even the Commander was quiet as his eyes searched the scene.

'We'll try over the Spanish side,' he said, pointing a sun-tanned arm in that direction. 'She may be lying close to Algeciras port over on the far side.'

'Don't point.' I said

'You're right, sorry.'

Within fifteen minutes we were approaching several container ships, a couple of tankers low in the water waiting to unload, then at last we had a likely target. Without pointing, I nodded in the direction of a large bulk carrier flying what looked like the Spanish flag, and with a banded funnel, but the Commander had already seen it. I moved aft to sit at the stern where I would have a better view without making it look too obvious. I checked the lines, sat down, and pulled out another San Miguel, while the Commander reduced speed. As we approached, she seemed much bigger than I had imagined, then as we passed between two other ships she came fully into view.

There at last were the words 'Carlos II,' in huge white letters on her bow and she looked a good deal rustier than she had appeared in the photo. As we came closer, we could hear the hum of generators from deep inside her hull, a thin wisp of smoke slowly rising from her funnel. We motored slowly down her full length, nonchalantly looking at her, taking in every small detail. Just forward of the accommodation a companion ladder sloped down to the waterline. Right aft under the funnel, presumably where the engine room was, water was pumping from various outlets, and we could hear the sound of heavy metallic banging echoing from inside the hull. Mooring lines from the deck held two tenders lying alongside; another seemed to be approaching from the mainland Spanish port of Algeciras. Looking up, we could see a couple of crew men leaning on the rail, having a smoke. When they looked casually our way, we raised a hand and they waved languidly back.

The Commander feigned a complete lack of interest and motored on past the stern toward the shore. When a good distance away, well out of earshot, he nudged our boat out of gear and walked to the stern, took up a fishing rod, and sat next to me.

'What now, Kit? I've done my job, over to you,' he said smiling, lighting a cigarette.

'Didn't know you smoked,' I said.

'I'm trying to give them up,' he replied, 'but I can't resist the duty-free price. Besides, it helps me to think.' He laughed.

'Somehow, David, I have to get on board that vessel.' After a pause, I said,' I think it will be too risky to try get on at night, I haven't had the ship's internal plans yet, with luck they should be faxed down from Lloyds by the time we get back.' Looking back at the sheer height of Carlos II's deck from the water, it must be forty feet, not easy to get up there I thought.

'Do you speak Spanish?' the Commander said thoughtfully.

'I can get by, what have you in mind?' I said inquiringly,

'You might board as an engineer. We know the firm in Algeciras that owns the tender that was just arriving.'

'A bit difficult to search the holds when I'm supposed to be in the engine rooms,' I objected. But if you could get me on as a customs officer, that might give me a chance?'

'Possible,' the Commander said. 'She's in Spanish waters here so we would need the help of the *Aduana*, but if we go under the auspices of a drug enquiry, they might go along with it. We'll get back and see what I can arrange.'

Without further thought, he looked at the setting sun, rose and slipped the gear into forward, and the Lister resumed its characteristic knock. We quietly motored back towards Gib giving Carlos II a wide berth, the sea like glass around us.

The setting sun lit up the Rock, sharply outlined against the deep blue behind it. As the sun set the stone face of the Rock turned deep crimson, and the sky behind it darkened to indigo, with a pink blue smoky haze over North Africa to the right, and lights just beginning to twinkle in the shade of the 'Rock' behind the hundred or more masts from the marina pointing skyward.

As we approached the harbour entrance, small fishing boats were leaving for a night at sea, men on board sorting their nets, and large wired gas lamps hanging over the stern to attract fish in some distant bay.

We came through the entrance just as the lights on each mole started to flash green and red, and I turned to look back in the direction of Carlos II hoping that I would still be able to locate her through the glasses later, but from the maze of lights now appearing on the vessels at anchor, it would not be easy.

The Commander slowed to the pontoon, I took the after warp ashore, and he threw me the forward one.

'Right, Kit, make her fast,' he said, killing the engine, 'and I'll take you to the Officer's Pavilion for a swift gin,' he said, climbing ashore.

'The idea is terrific' I said as we walked down the pontoon, 'but duty calls. I've really got to make some progress now, and I'll have to get onto London right away.'

He looked quite crestfallen, and I felt for him, but there's a time and a place for everything.

'Well, later then? I'll go and see if I can speak to the *Guardia* or the *Aduana* now, and see if I can't get you onto this dammed ship of yours, but it is Spain and things don't happen at the same speed y'know.'

I needed the Commander's help desperately but I could also see that he was after a bit of a session, and at the moment I dare not let him into the secret of what might lie under the wheat in her holds, so the urgency was not apparent to him.

'I'll go back and get any messages that might have come in, then have a shower. If you could give me a call with your results, I'd appreciate it 'I said a little apologetically

I declined the offer of a lift back, preferring to walk through the palm lined streets toward the old town enjoying the warm balmy air of evening. Yes, his idea could work, I thought, an Officer of the *Aduana* would be a good cover. A taxi came clattering round the corner looking for a fare, so changing my mind I obliged him with

'Rock Hotel, please.' Within minutes I was collecting messages and various faxes from the reception desk.

'Several phone calls came in, Sir, they said that they'd ring back, are you staying in your room a while, Sir?'

I said I was, turned and walked away down the cool marble corridor, lined with old prints of the various sieges of Gibraltar. Once in the room I rang London, and found the message was, could I ring the Old Man on his private, number at home, and Sue also. The night staff said nothing else had come in that had not been faxed down to me.

I dialled the Old Man.

'How are things, Kit,' he asked in a deep quiet tone. I brought him up to date by relating the events of the afternoon. He listened intently, then after a pause, 'That's good, very good, may be a stroke of luck the breakdown, I have developed a feeling about this one' he said. 'So much so, I am going to fly down on the morning flight.'

'Don't you trust me, Sir?' I said.

'I certainly do Kit.,' he laughed, 'but why should you have all the fun and sun? I'm on my way. Anything you need?'

'Ask them to put a magnetometer in the diplo bag,' I said, 'could be useful, a hand held one, nothing conspicuous, and a locator beacon.'

'Right Kit, I'll be at the Rock Hotel around lunch time, arrangements have been made' and the conversation closed.

I called room service and ordered a bottle of their red Rioja, took all the messages and various faxes onto the balcony table, found an ashtray for a paperweight them and sat down. I looked out once more across the bay, to the position where I now knew Carlos II lay at anchor.

A knock at the door confirmed the arrival of the Marques de Riscal Rioja. I signed the chit and returned to the table, picked up my binoculars and focused in the general direction of Carlos. She was difficult to pick out among so many vessels and so many lights but I reckoned I had her marked down pretty well.

A fax had come in from Lloyds with the ship's detailed plan. As I had requested, they had changed the ship's name to 'unknown'. I wanted no give away's at reception or anywhere else. The other fax was a confirmation of the arrival time of the Old Man, and a good night signing off from Sue with nothing to report.

I had a much needed shower, and on trying my first sip of Rioja the phone rang, typical! I dragged it out on to the balcony and sat down, overlooking the bar and the couples preparing to dine.

'David,' I said, recognising his voice.

'Right, Kit, you're on! It's all arranged and not easy either, the *Aduana* is going to request a look at the ship's documents first thing Sunday morning. I know it's an odd day, but may be better for it, half the crew will be on shore leave, and the officers will be in bed or ashore at Mass, not bad, eh! You'll be dressed as a Customs official, we have to meet about an hour before, and you'll be going with two other officials, both Spanish chaps from the *Aduana* at Algeciras Port, I'll drive you there, and hang about till you have finished,' he said somewhat breathlessly.

'I think that's terrific news, but don't come in your land rover,' I said. 'What time away from here?'

'About seven, think you can make it?' was the reply. 'And oh! What is the size for your clothes? I don't want any slip ups.'

I gave him all the information, but I knew what was coming next.

'Fancy a look at the Old Town tonight?' he said hopefully.

I broke the news that the Old Man was flying out on the morning flight.

'You're a keen lot, I'll give you that,' he laughed, 'probably see you tomorrow then.'

I agreed that it would be more sensible, and it would give me time to work out a game plan. I said that I would be back at the Hotel by midday and would he join me for drinks at 13.00 hrs; he could meet the Old Man too if he had arrived. He accepted enthusiastically!

Twelve

S aturday morning; it was already hot and the sun was streaming down onto the flower covered balcony ablaze with colour, the weather forecast indicated that there could be a change, and I just hoped that we wouldn't get a 'Levanter' blowing up through the Straits otherwise boarding could be a wet and blowy job, even if possible. But I could already see the wind had changed, and through the glasses I could see Carlos II at anchor had swung toward us, but no sign of any further activity, no tenders along side, all looked quiet.

Peace was suddenly shattered as a pair of RAF Tornadoes left the runway, tails glowing as the afterburners punched in. I watched them curl away to the left, and vanish to join some far away exercise, I suppose they only came to fuel, I thought, now we don't have an active base here any longer, more is the pity.

I swam twenty-five lengths in the pool as a quick workout, breakfasted lightly, and decided on a brisk walk, to collect various items for tomorrow. Quick Tan to bathe in, some form of moustache, and hair dye. I tried to think of anything to try change identity slightly, and to look a little more Spanish. Saturday morning, and the Old Town was heaving, Asian traders in all directions, radios, cameras, and watches being sold, 'very cheapest, sir,' 'no tax, sir,' shouted by small Indian boys. It was hard work finding everything I needed, but find it all I did.

On getting back to the Hotel, I was told the Old Man's flight was early and he was on his way up. I had a quick shower and made a call to the Commander, but no answer. Checking on Carlos II I could see that nothing had changed, all looked quiet, for the moment anyway.

Feeling refreshed I went down to the veranda bar restaurant, where there were a few pre-lunch drinkers taking the sun, and then I spotted him in the far corner, looking like something from Agatha Christie novel completely dressed in whites. It was the Old Man. He rose as I approached.

'Good morning, Kit, how are you?' he said, shaking my hand firmly.

'Good flight, Sir?'

'Excellent, now take a seat, and bring me up to date.' The waiter hovered, so we ordered a couple of Campari and sodas, and I proceeded to tell the O.M. what had happened.

'M'm, so it's floating amongst that lot, is it?' he said grumpily. 'And in Spanish waters, and registered to them? It's not good, you know.'

'They have been most helpful, Sir, the Base

Commander here also, anything to do with drugs and they are all up in arms about it.'

'Yes, Kit that's all very well, but it's not bloody drugs is it? Has anyone got an inkling?'

'No, Sir,' I smiled.

'As usual, a one-man band; it will catch you out one day,' he muttered pleasantly.

'I would prefer to keep it all under wraps until I have had a proper inspection,' I said. 'Then if it is what we think it is we will need help. What will you do, sir, if they are on board?'

'Difficult in International waters, but if Spain were to play ball, we could impound her,' he said, thoughtfully downing his Campari, then as an after-thought, 'What did you buy me this for?'

'It's long and refreshing.'

'I'll be the judge of that,' he said scowling at the glass, 'let's go for an early lunch.'

At that juncture the Commander joined us, intro-ductions went around the table, and the Commander announced that everything was ready for tomorrow, but he had found out that the engineers were go-ing on board on Monday. We then outlined the plan in greater detail to the O.M. He sat in silence for a moment, then, 'it's all 'favours' on the Spanish side then?'

'Yes, but if it is successful and there's a good drugs haul it will look very good for them. And for us,' he added, 'both we and the Spaniards would like to nobble the smugglers from Morocco and there are constant problems with dealers up the road, Costa del Sol, y'know.'

The old man cast me a glance.

'Very well, go on with your plan, but I don't want an incident, Kit,' he said, looking at me firmly. 'The 'diplo' bag will be in your room. I wish you luck.'

Thirteen

It was 06.45 hrs on Sunday, and no Levanter blowing yet, the bay was calm, and from the balcony I could see that Carlos II was still at anchor. I checked my equipment for the second time, no need for any guns, but I still put a Beretta .380 Auto in my holster on the right lower leg, and strapped a knife to my left leg I would wear the official Spanish side arm anyway. The magnetometer and a magnetic stick on locator beacon were in a cheap but official looking brief case. OK, Carlos, I thought, pretty soon I'll know your secret.

The Commander arrived promptly, red faced but unflustered.

'Christ! I didn't recognise you,' he laughed, 'With that instant tan and all that grey hair you look about twenty years older. Yes, m'm, well done.'

We moved off swiftly.

'Your car?' I asked casually.

'No, took your advice, we won't be recognised, I borrowed this old Spanish registered SEAT. Happy?'

'Tell you in about three hours,' I said.

After that we drove in silence down to the border

at La Linea, cleared it, and drove through the quiet Pueblo style village of La Linea. For the faithful a single bell tolled in the small white horseshoe tower of a small white church, a rope pulled from the side of the building, a priest in black with his shovel hat, small white house's bright to the eye, and little old ladies in black sweeping the doorways in the morning sun. Dodging dogs and the odd out-numbered cat, we were soon on the coast road, and within about seventeen minutes or so we were pulling into the commercial port of Algeciras; the *Aduana*, a square grey building standing on the left of the huge iron gates.

The Commander drove straight round the back and climbed out, as if he'd done this a million times before. An obviously well known friend came to meet him, looking for all the world like a South American President in a comic opera. There was much back slapping and noise, both of them quite oblivious to me standing there, then he looked up.

'Hola,' he laughed. 'I Manolo, a Coronel,' he beamed proudly, and it was my turn to be embraced, his breath making my eyes water.

'So,' he exclaimed. 'We go hunting, eh, drugs, eh, and in my harbour! Come I find you uniform.'

The office reeked of black tobacco, with strong overtones of garlic and rancid frying oil. A Sergeant rushed to stand up, knocking a half full cup of coffee over the typed lists of cargo on his desk. Manolo thrust a small grubby glass into my hand, full of a transparent oily liquid, the aqua dente.

'Success, eh,' he downed his glass in one, and David's went the same way, I thought what the hell, it burned my throat as it went down, it was good. I wouldn't feel a bullet.

The Sergeant came back with a grey uniform; and that smelt the worst yet, but within moments I'd pulled it on, straightened the belt and holster, made my black shoes look dirty, twisted my tie and I was ready to go.

'You're keen,' David said.

'When this is over,' I retorted, 'you and I can have that night out.'

'Let's get on with it, then,' he laughed, as Manolo gave himself another shot. The Sergeant was looking a bit nervous; he had obviously been on this type of trip before.

'El Barco,' Manolo roared, and as an afterthought 'I tell you on the way,' slapping me on the shoulder, but I never found out what. 'How long you want in sheeep,' he asked. 'How long you take, eh?' I estimated that I'd need about half an hour at the most, providing I could get the deck to myself, and that I had memorised the hold pattern correctly.

We walked down the quay which was covered in a heavy coating of dried black fuel oil and tar. At the bottom of sea-weedy stone steps a grey customs launch was banging merrily against the quay, its bow line held by a soldier dressed in grey. The Sergeant jumped in and held it steady for his Colonel, who nearly fell in and went to stand proudly in the stern, firmly clasping the ensign staff and flag in one hand, and his coffee soaked papers in the other. He gestured for me to jump in and join him, so holding the brief case I jumped in; the bowman jumped aboard and instantly the Sergeant hit the throttles. There was a roar and a jerk, but we stayed where we were. Unfortunately, we were still firmly tied by the stern rope to the jetty. After considerable abuse and gesticulation directed toward the Sergeant from Manolo and an apologetic shrug and raised eyebrows to me, we were away, and heading towards Carlos II at about 15 knots. They bay was no longer calm and getting covered in spray, Manolo soon took shelter with me under the cabin roof. We were soon at the stern of the vessel, she lay heavy in the water and towered above us, rust streaked and not ship shape, showing that she may have had a battering coming down through the Bay of Biscay.

With an air of full authority, the Sergeant tied the launch to the gantry steps and gave Colonel Manolo and myself a hand up onto the companion ladder. Manolo turned looked at me.

'Half hour, eh,' he said with a wink, and impressively he just strode straight up the steps as if he owned it, got to the top and shouted, 'Hola' and banged the steel rails with his gun butt. A dark tousled head, with an unshaven face, the ubiquitous Gauloise hanging from the corner of his mouth, and wearing a grimy vest, suddenly appeared out of what appeared to be the galley, by the sound and smell of the crackle and spit of cooking oil and garlic coming from somewhere within. God! If that's the ships cook, I thought.

'Si hombre! ah, es un Coronel,' he said in sobering amazement, gesticulating at the sky above, his black eyes darting from one to the other of us.

The Colonel took his time, letting the surprise visit sink in as more crew appeared from the accommodation door aft of us as we stood at the top of the ladder. 'Donde el Capitán' he said authoritatively, as the waterproof door on the boat deck above us opened with a metallic clang. An old man with a white moustache wearing a faded navy blue uniform looked down at us.

'Si soy el Capitán, Coronel,' and indeed he had four tarnished green gold stripes on each arm. The Colonel looked at him unimpressed, announcing that he represented the Aduana (Customs), and would like to see the ships manifesto and crew list.

'Es normal,' the Captain shrugged, and you could see he was trying to argue that it wasn't necessary, our total cargo is all wheat, why the manifesto, he questioned? Then

'Anything for an easy life,' he gestured to us to come up to the bridge deck. The Colonel glanced at me. I had to get myself into a position where I could look inside the cargo holds, and I knew I wouldn't have long; the bridge deck was no good to me.

The Captain frowned at me, sensing my reluctance, his eyes glancing at my brief case. As the Colonel moved toward the outside ladder going up to the boat deck and bridge, he turned to me and said.

'Juan, walk the topsides. How many life rafts?' he said looking up at the Captain,

'Four,' he replied curtly.

'So Juan, you have four life rafts to check as a matter of course, also see if she is carrying totally wheat, please now,' he said tapping one heel on the steel deck.

The Captain at this point said that he must come with me, to show me the cargo and started to move toward the ladder. The Colonel, who was already half way up towards him, raised his hand and said no, he wanted him on the bridge to look at the ship's papers, as we 'had not much time'.

That was our break.

'Not much time,' the Captain repeated, this seemed to please him, he smiled for the first time and said, 'be my guest,' extending his arm in an arc toward the bow.

He then quickly spoke in another language – could it have been Maltese? – to one of the more seamanlike looking crew members dressed in what may have once been a blue uniform. The Colonel glanced down at me, he had not understood either.

Raising an arm in an elaborate salute I sauntered off nonchalantly towards the bow of the vessel, fully aware that the man in blue was also following me equally nonchalantly.

As I walked this huge deck my mind was running riot on how to shake him off. The four main cargo hatches were all covered by mechanically operated metal covers all held firmly down by numbers of wooden wedges along the sides. Beside them though, on each side of the ship, were the same number of small hatches about six foot by three and the lids of these were open at right angles to the deck. They looked to be open to let air circulate or perhaps to make security rounds easier.

As I bent down to look down the ladder inside the hatch, I saw the shadow of the man in blue suddenly close behind me. Leaving well alone and standing up, I turned and said.

'Rough trip,' in perfect Spanish.

'Si, mucha aqua, mucha aviento,' he snarled at me, with an aggressive manner.

I had realised from the plans that there was a 'tweendecks in each hold, a wide shelf running down each side of the hold about 15 feet down, so that lighter bales or boxes could be carried above the loose bulk cargo below it. I had to get down one of these trimming hatches to see anything, I had to shake off my guardian, and the time was ticking away every moment.

I shrugged at my guardian and walked over to the other side of the deck. Looking aft I saw another large lifeboat painted Day-Glo orange hanging from the boat deck davits on this side, and further aft two white plastic shells containing the life rafts. My brain worked like lightening. Pointing, I said.

'Test certificates for the rafts, and safety survey for the boats, if you please.' His mouth dropped, he was just about to say something, he looked again at me,

'Please, Chief Officer, it will be quicker,' I said, giving him a rank which seemed to please him momentarily.

'Wait here,' he said, and moved off in the direction of the ladder up to the bridge. Those papers will take time to find, I thought, walking back to the original side of the deck where the kingposts and derrick winches were between me and his return. At the nearest open hatch, I looked over the coaming and saw a vertical steel ladder leading down into the semi-darkness below.

Without hesitation I stepped over the coaming and climbed swiftly down.

It took time for my eyes to adjust, there was so much dust suspended in the air and the only light was from above, where daylight shone through the open hatch. Breathing was nearly impossible, and the heat was already making me sweat profusely. The 'tweendeck shelf stretched away into dim obscurity with a repeated pattern of frames supporting the deck above. I moved swiftly towards the inner edge and looking down, all I could see was wheat and more wheat, golden grey, a level surface about two or three feet below me. Looking back through the suspended dust I could just see the entrance and steps.

Kneeling, I flicked open the brief case and quickly took out the magnetometer, set it to 'Directional' and waited for the red light to turn to green 'ready'. My heart missed a beat, as from the deck above I could hear and recognise the steps of the man in blue. The magnetometer indicator turned to green; swiftly I began moving along the edge of the 'tweendeck with the instrument held out over the wheat in the lower hold. Within moments I was getting a reading, a positive indication of an object or objects lying about four to five feet below the surface of the wheat, with a total depth of about 10 ft more.

A clatter at the hatchway told me I had an unseen and unwelcome guest. Packing the magnetometer away, I grabbed the locator beacon, moved to the side of the ship and crouched at the side of a massive ventilation fan, and held my breath. I could hear the sound of metallic footsteps descending the rungs of the ladder. I held my breath and peered through the mist of dust but could only make out a vague shape. The sound changed as the feet shuffled on the steel deck, he'd arrived at the bottom; there was a spate of muffled coughing, and then the unmistakeable 'click, click' of a hammer being drawn back. Christ! He was armed. The footsteps started again, slowly coming this way, grain cracking under foot.

As he came into sight, I recognised him as the man I'd called Chief Officer. He stopped, looking directly at me, but obviously he could see nothing, he crouched a little peering down the 'tweendeck past me, so close now I could smell him, hear his breathing laboured with the heat and dust. As he stopped moving, I saw his arm raised to shoulder level, so it was as I thought, he had a gun in his right hand. Sliding my hand down to my .380 on my leg, I palmed it.

In the bowels of the vessel a generator burst into life, the roar echoing hollowly inside these metal walls. It seemed to draw him on and he walked slowly past and on into the darkness. I pressed the adhesive locator beacon onto the back of the ventilation fan, flicking it to transmit mode as I did so, and replacing the .380 in my leg holster, removed my shoes and stealthily made for the ladder, and welcome daylight.

I was now confident that the hold held some ghastly secret, but what was it? Was our tip correct? And why should a innocent merchant seaman be carrying arms?

At the top of the ladder I peered cautiously over the coaming of the hatch. I could see some of crew gathered some distance away by the galley door, but no one appeared to be in the immediate vicinity, so I climbed out slowly so as not to attract attention. I replaced my shoes and walked forward till I reached the forward end of the main hatch where I turned and crossed to the far side of the ship. I slowed to a saunter and headed back towards the ship's accommodation as though I was returning from the bows.

I heard a voice from behind me shout coarsely.

'Donde usted' (Where have you been?). I pretended not to hear and strolled on, deliberately slowing my breathing so as to appear calm. He shouted again, louder this time but less angrily, 'Donde usted'.

This time I turned around slowly,

'Hola,' I said, smiling, I was on the forecastle, and in return I asked him where he had been, hoping he was not noticing my dusty footprints on the deck. He eyed me suspiciously, but he bore no obvious signs of any gun, and grudgingly he proffered an untidy folder of documents. I led him aft to the poop deck and made a great show of comparing the serial numbers of the life rafts with the annual test certificates in the folder, glad that the dust wouldn't show on my greasy grey uniform.

I had just finished the fourth and last when the door to the boat deck flew open with a clang and the Captain and the Colonel appeared exchanging extravagant and noisy farewells. I saw the Colonel starting to move down to deck level, and by the time

I had got to the companion ladder, both of them were waiting for me and possibly the 'Officer' also.

'Every thing in order, Coronel,' I reported, with another elaborate salute.

The Colonel said indeed it was, revealing a canvas bag in his left hand with a smile. I did not inquire what it was, instead turning to bid farewell to my shadower, but he had gone, and looking forward I could see him slamming the lid of the nearest trimming hatch, and looking thoughtfully in our direction as he did so. The Captain, a man of few words, bade us farewell. Manolo, the Colonel, was trying to catch my eye but I didn't want to make definite eye contact, so I moved toward the upper platform and led the way down to the launch, and we descended in silence.

Once aboard, the Sergeant cast off and as we motored swiftly away, I turned once again to look at Carlos II. The Captain was lounging on the guard rail listening to his mate who was pointing forward, and speaking it appeared in a forceful manner. They both turned to watch us with a questioning interest.

Out of ear shot, the Colonel leant over saying.

'Drugs eh, information yes?'

'May be,' I said, 'but I didn't find anything definite as yet. It means we shall have to follow the ship some more,' I said evasively.

'Ah, you Briteesh are so in secrets,' he laughed, 'but I find drugs. Look,' he said, smiling and holding up the bag I had seen him with earlier. Delving deep he produced two large bottles of vodka, and a box of Cohiba Habana cigars.

'The Captain he no give me all papers, just theese, much bezza, yes?'

I panicked for a moment.

'Did he declare where he had come from? And, for that matter, where he was going?' I asked nervously.

'Si, Si, señor, Stolichnya from Russia,' he said, holding up a bottle. 'And cigars, what other country gives Cohiba for preesents, eh!'

'The bill of lading, was it Murmansk?'

'Si, Mrrmask,' he said, peeling the wrapper off the box of cigars.

'And destination,' I asked hopefully.

'Si, Si, tranquil señor, she sails to Malta, here in our beautiful Mediterranean. But engines no good, new part,' he said, committing sacrilege and biting the end off his Cohiba, before passing me the box. Meanwhile the Sergeant at the steering wheel watched, as a dog would watch a chocolate biscuit.

At the quay side stood the Commander, looking his usual flushed and jovial self. Lucky he was in civvies, I thought, knowing full well that Carlos II would have the glasses on us, and I resisted the temptation to look back. I would use the glasses from well inside the Customs Office.

The Commander called for a line to be thrown up,

and made the boat fast forward. Then he promptly walked off, stating over his shoulder.

'I'll be with you shortly.' I followed the Colonel to the office, away from the sea breeze the heat was fierce, the quay was even tackier under foot than before and I was dying to get out of this uniform. Once inside, I stood well back from the dirty windows, picked up the Colonel's binoculars and focused on Carlos II. They were still watching, the 'Mate' leaning on the rail and staring at the port through binoculars.

The rear door opened and in walked the Commander.

'Success?' he boomed, and then 'Are they still looking? Good job I left you, eh!'

'Good move,' I agreed.

The Colonel, not wishing to be left out, said.

'A leetle success perhaps, but your man, he tell me nothing, just maybes, like all Breetish. He only smoke, my cigars,' he laughed.

The Commander looked at me and I nodded in what could be described as the affirmative.

I changed out of that awful uniform quickly, wishing I could have a shower, and aware that I needed to have a meeting with the Old Man as soon as possible. We were just saying farewell when the Sergeant who was standing near the window spoke rapidly in Spanish to the Colonel, who promptly took the binoculars off the table and joined him at the window.

He stared intently in the direction of Carlos II, and after a moment he handed them to me.

'They have veesitors, engineers from Barcelona. I know those people.' Re-focusing the glasses, I could now see there was a tender alongside and three men manhandling machinery in the tender.

'When are they due to sail,' I said, showing no emotion.

'He not say, but soon I theenk, Tuesdays perhaps.'

I looked at David and said.

'We must go.' He nodded, and refusing all his offers of a glass of vodka, we thanked the Colonel warmly and having shaken his hand, left by the back door.

I still felt I could not relate my findings to David so our trip back to the rock was virtually in silence. We were soon through the check point, across the airstrip, past the Vulcan and wending our way back up to the Hotel. I thanked him for his help profusely but just as I was closing the door he said.

'It isn't all over yet.'

'How do you mean?' I replied.

'You said we would go for dinner, I know the very lady for you,' he laughed.

'You're married,' I said.

'Yes, mine is,' he winked.

'I'll ring you,' I said, slamming the car door, and as an afterthought 'When I've finished my report,' raised my hand and swiftly strode up the steps, passing an amazed porter on the way down to greet me.

I went straight to my room showered and changed, then noticing my binoculars had been moved, I put them up to look once again at Carlos, but damn the maid! They were also out of focus. The ship had swung on her anchor again and the gangway was now on the far side. I couldn't see the tender, but there was activity on deck, the after derricks had been topped. I'd keep a watch.

I took the locator receiver out of my suitcase, and placing it on the bed, turned it on. Brilliant! I had a bearing of sorts, but not very strong, it must be because of all the steel around the transmitter. I cast my mind back to its position stuck on to a ventilation fan in the middle of a huge ship, not the best of places. Now to find the O M.! I glanced quickly at my Ulysee Nardin, 13.00 hrs exactly. As I couldn't think there would be a Golf course in Gibraltar, the obvious spot had to be the balcony restaurant. My hunch was right.

'Thought you'd gone off me KIT, saw you arrive.'

'I'm sorry, but the way I looked and smelt, you would have done!'

'Quite, quite,' he said dismissing this trivia, 'So what have you got? I saw you go down below.'

'You couldn't! You can't see her properly from here,' I said, turning toward the bay for a better look. 'She is hidden behind those two tankers, and you said you couldn't see her from your room,' I said curiously.

'I used yours,' he said, smiling and dangling three skeleton keys in front of me, and taking a sip of white wine.

I sat back in amazement.

'Old habits die hard' I said shaking my head in mock annoyance, which didn't make the slightest difference to him.

'So, Kit, what did you find? Was your hunch right?'

I told him the sequence of events in great detail, and he raised one eyebrow a couple of times.

'M'm, he would have used his weapon you say. Don't like it. We're on to something Kit, but we need now to verify for definite.' And after a pause 'I'm sorry, but you're going to have to go back onboard again, we need to know precisely what is under the wheat.'

'It'll be a hell of a job,' I said. 'Digging into wheat is nigh impossible, it just runs back again. I may be lucky and find a hold where they're not too deep, but I won't have too long in there, even if I can get in. I'll need a rope to lower myself into the hold, you can vanish in grain, suffocate y'know,' I exclaimed, looking at him to get my point over. 'Once there I'll have to dig with bare hands, some hell of a job' I said again.

There was a silence. I looked up.

'And, I have to get there, can't go as a customs man again.'

A longer silence was now broken by the Old Man.

'Kit are you going grey?' he asked, staring at me bemused and upsetting my train of thought.

'Ah! I forgot, it's all part of this morning's little episode.'

He didn't seem to believe me.

'Have you been listening, Sir?' I said.

'I have indeed Kit, too far for a night swim I suppose?' he said smiling, and then thinking, 'but of course we haven't got the equipment.'

'Equipment would be no problem, Sir. I'm sure there'd be diving equipment and bottles available, but getting on and off Carlos? I'd need to take equipment with me, OK I could disguise it as flotsam maybe and push from below, or behind, but then I have to get on board and into the hold without being seen, not easy Sir. I suppose I could dump the diving bottles when I got there, go in unencumbered, check it out and swim back on the surface.'

Whilst he was mulling these thoughts over in his mind, I ordered a bottle of rosé for us and excused myself for a moment, wanting to go back up to the room to have yet another look at Carlos, and see if the engineers were still on board. As luck would have it, the wind had backed a point or two so that I could see the gangway again. I could see that the engineer's tender was still alongside, but no sign of any other activity.

'Kit,' the O.M. said on my return, 'I think you're

going to have to go for a midnight swim, are you in agreement?'

'Must admit, Sir, it looks a bit like it,' I said, wondering how the hell I would put it all together. I took a sip of the beautifully cool rosé that had now arrived.

'To your liking?' he said smiling, but a little cynically.

'The other alternative of course would be to try to board tomorrow as an engineer? Whatever we do, it will be better tomorrow. Give 'em a day to cool off, eh!'

'Pushing it a bit, Sir,' I said, 'they've seen me once already, and my disguise wasn't the best. If it's to be a night swim, tomorrow may well be too late, but you're probably right to let em' cool off a bit. In the meantime, I'll have a word with the Commander and get his help on putting the gear together, also talk about the possibility of going as an engineer.'

As soon as lunch was over, I took the opportunity to leave, I didn't want to wait another day. Anything could happen, but at least now we had her in the bay. During my meeting with the old man the weather had been changing, and the wind was getting up, although there was not a cloud in the sky. I made the decision that if at all possible, I would try to get on board tonight.

I called the Commander, saying I would be able to find out a lot more if I could get back on board and move about unobserved. He fully understood, also saying that going as an engineer would be possible. After a moment he spoke.

'What about recognition, for Christ's sake.' He then also mentioned that the glass was dropping. A Levanter was now due, 'a day late but that's Spain.' he laughed.

At six o'clock that Sunday evening, I took a taxi and left the Hotel, noticing that the wind was howling round the Rock. The Commander had asked me to meet him at the old Dockyard gates although I pointed out that any operation would still have to be mounted from the cover of the Marina. When I arrived at the gates, he was standing waiting, still in civvies, I was glad to see. I was even more impressed by what I saw lying on the work benches of a small office close to the classic Victorian administration buildings. He had all the diving equipment laid out in perfect order, with black self seal waterproof bags for it, everything else was black, even to the

10 litre aluminium air bottle which had just been sprayed, and the mouth piece touched in. The smell of cellulose thinners hung in the air. Waving his arm over the benches he smiled proudly.

'Perfect, eh! bloody perfect, just a shame you won't be able to use it, though.'

'Why not, don't tell me, not the weather, though I must admit I was beginning to wonder,' I said.

'Not only the weather but the currents generated by it,' he pointed out. 'It can end up like a small whirlpool the bay can, always a lot of currents in the straits.' He was right. By seven o'clock it was blowing an absolute bastard, wind screeching through the masts of boats in the harbour, halyards thrashing against masts, and in the fading light you could make out the large vessels sheltering in the bay, waves breaking against their bows as though they were under way, riding heavily at their anchors. Carlos II tonight, it was a non starter.

I was by now in a bit of a dilemma. Should I tell the O.M. of developments? The possibility that the Levanter would last for about three days, which made a dive not practical for one man plus equipment with the storm blowing, but he had said leave it a day anyway! The other point was that now the only other realistic option was to board with the engineers. The Commander had a contact within that Company; David seemed to have an enormous number of useful contacts. A Mediterranean way of life.

Back in the room at the Rock Hotel the wind howled, and the dining area had been moved inside. I sipped the remains of the Rioja, and pensively looked out at the bay and Carlos II. I didn't like what I saw. She seemed to have arc lights on her deck, noticeably more than the others at anchor.

That night, what with the wind and noise, I slept badly. At seven o'clock I got up, had a shower, put on a dressing gown and walked into the sunshine on the balcony.

Carlos II had gone.

Fourteen

Shocked, I lurched back into the room but before I could get to the phone it rang, and as I lifted the receiver, David's voice boomed in urgency.

'Kit, Christ! We've slipped up, she's sailed. Upped anchor and bloody gone, this morning in the early hours, about 04.00 apparently. We've picked a radio call up from her about eighteen minutes ago, but of no significance, she's gone through the straits and into the Med proper. Haven't got a course for yet her though, but we were able to get her position; a radio D/F fix, and she's making about fifteen knots and travelling southeast at the moment,' he said breathlessly.

'Thanks,' I said. 'It's no consolation but I'd just noticed she'd gone myself. What a cock up, call you back as soon as I can, got to speak to the O.M.' I banged the phone down and dialled, the phone was answered immediately if a little gruffly. I brought him rapidly up to date, while he listened quietly, I could hear his thoughtful breathing. When I had finished there was a slight pause, and then after ...

'See you in ten minutes, in the breakfast room,' the phone went dead.

Opening the briefcase, I took out the locator receiver, and flicked it on. The pin lights flickered, and I waited for a moment, hoping for it to pick up some signal information, but there was nothing. Five minutes later I had washed and there was still nothing. Typical, that was all I needed, but perhaps the Rock stood in a direct line between myself and the vessel at the moment, I would try later.

Now, swiftly changed, I strode to the breakfast room hastily buttoning my shirt as I went. Entering the room, I could see the O.M. seated at the far corner, m'm, he's moved quick, I thought. He gestured at a chair and passed the cafetiere across the table, waving the waiter away, looking glum.

'This is serious, Kit we've missed a perfect chance.'

'I appreciate that, Sir,' wishing to say that I'd wanted to have a go last night anyway, indeed I had got all ready for it, too! But that wouldn't get us anywhere.

'What ships do we have in the Med.?' I asked.

'Not many, if any,' he said, raising an eye brow. 'Commander Bairstow, have you spoken to him yet?' he asked.

'He rang me, Sir, confirming that Carlos II had flown.'

'Ring him, Kit it's time we brought him into the picture, ask him up for breakfast.'

Within ten minutes, David Bairstow was striding

purposefully into the breakfast room, resplendent in a immaculate white uniform. He shook hands and sat down, helping himself to a coffee.

'Still blowing like hell,' he said, looking out onto the bay, where white horses swirled in from Europa Point to the south.

There was a silence as we waited for the Old Man to speak. Clearing his throat, he spoke slowly and deliberately.

'Gentlemen, I may have made a huge mistake; the responsibility must for the moment lie with me. Looking on the black side, Carlos II has slipped away; it may prove to have been a grave mistake that we didn't find out all about her cargo when we had the chance. But we also needed to know where she was bound for, and why? So, I still believe we were correct, in that we kept it an under cover operation, and that we should not have declared our hand. The problem now is how do we salvage the operation?'

I interrupted.

'Sir, I would ... '

But the Old Man coughed again, raising a hand slightly, a signal for me to desist.

'Commander, how many ships do you think we have in the area?'

'Not sure, Sir,' he said, 'but I can easily check, I'll have the weekly status report on my desk when I get back' he said efficiently. Then he said what he had obviously been thinking since last night's abortive scheme. 'Is this all not a little over the top for a drug bust, or is there more to it?' he questioned a little pompously.

'There is, Commander,' the O.M. grumbled to himself, 'and now I'll confirm your suspicions.' He proceeded to bring David fully into the picture, emphasising that, 'Up until now only the two of us had been aware of the operation, Kit here, and myself.' then smiling he said, 'but now there are three; Commander, welcome aboard.'

'Good Lord!' said David, 'Isn't it worth a full scale onslaught?'

'Hardly,' said the O M. 'We could finish up with egg on our face, as we need to know whether or not this is the first shipment, whether there will be anymore, who is involved and, most importantly, where it is going. After all, the powers that have such weapons legitimately, as such, move them at will, we ourselves do not always transport arms in the conventional manner. No, it wouldn't do, certainly not.'

'I see, and how do I fit into the equation?' David said thoughtfully.

'For the moment just a little more help again would be appreciated. I'll need an office, phone and fax, anything suitable?'

'No problem, I can have an office brought on stream in less than an hour, up at the communication centre.'

'Then please do. Kit how are you fixed. Any more favours of our Commander here?'

'Er, well yes any chance of speaking to the marine engineering company that worked on her, I wouldn't mind knowing what her problem was, it could be useful.'

The meeting lasted for another half hour, then David left to start the ball rolling.

We had arranged to meet at 09.30, at the entrance to the communications centre in the Upper Galleries of the Rock, he'd send a car for us, which we could also use for the duration.

Knowing that every minute Carlos II was getting further and further away, time was of the essence. There was bad weather, yes, but it wouldn't make too much difference with a ship that size, even if she was plugging against a full Levanter, it wouldn't hold her up. The future looked bleak.

It was the first time I had been into the communications centre, that was hidden away at the top of the Rock, nearly in the clouds; and even though our minds were full of today's problem one could not help being taken aback by the centre. It was hidden by concrete buttresses overgrown with creepers. An unobtrusive small steel door was the entrance leading into a concrete reinforced tunnel, which led into yet another tunnel blasted out of the rock. It was cool but not damp; the air was clearly being circulated by a very efficient ventilation system. At the end of this tunnel was yet another blast proof door which led into the main room itself.

A large circular space held half a dozen desks in the centre, while the walls bristled with electronic equipment, lights flickered, radios crackled and eerie green radar displays rotated silently. There were also many corridors leading off the main room, some showing brightly lit side rooms, some going down and turning once again into tunnels entering the bowels of the Rock. From far below deep down under our feet generators hummed, the heartbeat of the brooding watchfulness that was the very soul of the place.

At the far side, through armoured glass windows I was now looking out from the other side of the Rock, the Mediterranean side. The massive steel bomb proof shutters that could be moved across the glass were rolled aside. To my right across the Straits lay the jagged hills of Africa, the sight was nothing short of fantastic. As I looked, I could see the wind lashed shipping struggling through the straits, decks awash, with howling spray flying as they butted into the sea. Farthest right in the distance I could see a huge hulk, a tanker stranded on a shallow shoal close to the shipping lanes opposite Tarifa, at the southern most point of Spain. Over Africa lay a purple and pink haze, to the left the Mediterranean stretched to the horizon, and somewhere out there Carlos II was getting farther and farther away from me.

'Some other time please,' said the Commander interrupting, and looking across at us.

'So, what vessels have we in the area?' said the O.M. looking at the Commander.

'Not a great deal, Sir, we have a frigate on her way up from the Falklands due in a day or two, maybe more with this weather, the only other activity is down at Malta.'

I shot the Old Man a glance.

'Apparently we have the carrier Ark Royal heading there.'

'A bit over the top,' I interjected smiling, and the Old Man glared at me.

The Commander continued,

'M'm, and the Britannia and the submarine Orca are also bound for Malta, all to do with the celebrations by the George Cross island I believe. Ending of the siege? Fortieth anniversary possibly, or something similar, and that's about it, not like we used to be. The frigate I suppose could be told to speed up, but she's only really coming in for fuel. C-in-C Home Fleet would have to give permission for her to divert, but what actually are you hoping to do, Sir?'

'We need to intercept her on the presumption of ...' his voice trailing away as there came a knock at the door. The Communications Lieutenant stood there again.

'They're talking again now sir, we are recording them, no rush, and I'll have a bearing in a minute.'

We moved back into the main room and over to one of the bays against the wall, where a radio operator sat in front of a pair of dark blue metal boxes with dials and meters, earphones clamped to his head. We were listening to their medium wave ship to shore, the Lieutenant told us, this time they were speaking to a harbour authority some four hundred and fifty miles away at Palma, on the island of Mallorca in the Balearics. Once again luck was with us, they were still having engine problems. Rough weather had prevented completing repairs at Algeciras, they said, they needed a more sheltered position with better amenities, now they wished to go alongside a proper berth on the commercial quay at Palma, after which the engineers could fly home.

'Well Kit, your prayers are answered,' said the O.M., now waving the Commander and myself to a large central table strewn with charts.

'Can we get some coffee,' he said aloud, to anyone who was listening, the Lieutenant, who had followed us, presuming the request was directed at him immediately said.

'Aye, aye, Sir' and disappeared down into the bowels of the Rock below the centre, the hum of generators or ventilation fans filling the room before the thick bomb proof door closed behind him.

'I'm going to bring Tim down here from London, Kit just to lend a hand, and I think now we'd better get you up to the Balearics, then you'll be there for when Carlos II arrives. Any ideas how we get Kit there, Commander?'

'We've nothing here at the moment. The Spanish police have their anti-drug helicopters at Malaga, but that would mean involving them. Or we can charter a Jet Ranger, also out of Malaga. The 'Medi Assist Company' use it, so it isn't unusual for it to come down here to pick a passenger. Then route it up the coast, re-fuel at say, Alicante, to minimise the sea crossing. The other and impractical alternative, as there's no direct flight, is to fly back to the UK and then re-route to Mallorca on a scheduled airline'.

'A chartered heli from Malaga would be the best, Sir,' I said, 'providing this bloody wind drops, but mightn't it be out of limits at the moment?'

David butted in to say.

'Hopefully it'll drop a little in the late afternoon, usually does.'

'Right,' the O.M. said. 'Let's get that sorted, say for three o'clock and get Kit. away from here and up there, if the wind drops then that should give them ample day light. I'll have you booked into the 'Victoria' overlooking the harbour in Palma, I'll also get our Consul to meet you, and take you to the Victoria,' he said looking at me.

'Now, gentlemen, let's make some plans and decisions. If, and it is if, Carlos II is carrying Scud missiles or even Scud parts, what are we going to do about it? I don't think a Spanish bulk carrier acting suspiciously has any right to them. If Kit's search proves correct, and I am beginning to think that it will, this ship is going to be sat in the middle of Palma harbour, one of the largest in the Mediterranean, a huge port for tourists and pleasure yachts, there will be over a thousand yachts just berthed there. I doubt the Spaniards would welcome any fracas, we know the crew are armed and the packages may be booby trapped. Also, we should take into consideration, that in the event of them being arrested. I cannot imagine that the would-be recipients of this cargo would just stand by and let the world grab it from under their noses. I have a good idea where this lot is going,' then after a pause, 'Or was,' he added as an afterthought and laughed.

'Do we speak to the Americans? Kit what do you think?' speaking in a more serious tone.

'Let me try to clarify matters first, its all hypothetical Sir, and anyway she really wants apprehending in International waters,' I said and 'Well out of the way of other interests.'

'You're right, you're quite right, but the only vessel we have is the frigate on its way from the south? Commander, could you get them to confirm the soonest that they could be here?'

'Will do, Sir,' the Commander said, leaving the table and going next door to speak to the Lieutenant.

'In the meantime, I'm going to speak to the Ministry in London, also, C-in-C Home Fleet and tell him I'm about to borrow one of his ships.'

I took this as a signal to leave the O.M. alone for a while.

'I'll go back and make ready to leave, Sir.'

'No need to rush,' whispered the Commander, winking and passing me a coffee. I looked across at the O M. who was oblivious of us, and now quietly formulating a plan, desk covered with papers, phones ringing, and the fax chattering.

It had been agreed that if she was carrying the missiles, then there would have to be a mid-sea seizure somewhere past the Balearics, that is if her route was still going to be southeast. The justification for a seizure had still to be decided, but it would still have to be a covert operation.

It was therefore agreed that the frigate would now increase speed to the maximum possible, given the conditions, and would be in Gibraltar for fuel by 02.00 tomorrow. If needed she could then be dispatched into the Med to locate and shadow Carlos II, and to stand by for instructions; that is, if and when Carlos II sailed from Palma Mallorca.

From the anemometer I could see that the wind had dropped to 25 knots, it was time to get going. I asked the Lieutenant to tell the pilot from Malaga I was clear to go and we might as well go half an hour or so early. Within moments he came back to me,

'Sir, he's already on the ground and waiting.'

'On my way 'I said.

The Commander handed me a folder.

'Your contact codes and numbers are all there. Have a good flight. We never did get that night out,' he said earnestly.

'Next time, hopefully,' I said, as the O M. scowled, wondering what that was all about.

'And by the way I've organised a lift for you. The car's outside,' David said with an expressive grin.

'I'll check in the moment I'm at the Victoria,' I said to the O.M.

'Do that Kit by then I should have the current position of Carlos and her E.T.A. with you, that is if her speed remains constant.'

I made an unnecessary casual salute and closed the door behind me. When I passed the Royal Marine sentry at the outer end of the tunnel, I saw the Bay below was no longer streaked with foam, but had the waves still had white tops. Turning I looked for my lift, but I didn't have to look far.

'Hi, I'm Debbie,' came the cry. I looked across at the source of the cheerful hail, a peacock blue MGB convertible, contrasted with the dull blue backdrop of the Straits. Debbie was spread-eagled across the seat posing in her diminutive splendour of white lace, a beautifully bronzed young girl with cropped sun bleached blonde hair, with a permanent laughing smile. 'Hi, you must be Kit, David asked me to drop by. We were supposed to see you the other night,' she said cheerfully.

'We,' I said, looking at Debbie, admiring her

slender form, scarcely concealed by the expensive lace just hanging on to her athletic frame.

'Oh yes, David promised we would dine and go to the Casino, all four of us.'

'Four?'

'Sorry, yes, his er, you know.'

'No, I don't,' I said smiling, but I can guess. 'He does seem very well organised,' I commented.

'He is, he is, her name's Josie, lots of fun. Come on, get in. I've got to give you a lift, you're in a rush. Didn't you know,' she laughed.

I climbed over the door and dropped into the seat. She leaned over and gave me a kiss, leaving a lingering fragrance of Miss Dior behind.

'In shock? Do, you know you've hardly spoken a word?'

'I've hardly had time,' I said laughing. 'My eyes have been too busy,' as I looked across at her tanned legs.

Without wasting a second, she slammed the MG into a non-synchro first, and we growled off with a jerk.

'Rock Hotel for your bits and pieces?' she shouted over the noise of the engine, laughing.

'If we can get there alive,' I said as we shot down the hill and round a corner on the wrong side.

'Relax, they know me,' she screamed.

'Well, they'll hear you, if they can't see you,' I said, mesmerised by her taut breasts trying to escape whilst simultaneously doing a jig.

Within seconds it seemed, we hurtled up to the entrance of the Rock Hotel with a screech of brakes and a cloud of dust, to the horror of the liveried doorman.

'Er, this is Debbie,' I said, and the doorman looked resigned.

'I know the lady well, Sir,' was the weary reply.

'I'll go and get my bits and pieces,' I said.

'Thought you'd have them with you,' she giggled.

I vaulted out of the car and ran up the steps to get my equipment and settle my bill.

On my return the sight of Debbie was just as spectacular. I threw my gear in the back and we scorched off through the streets of Gibraltar toward the airstrip.

I wished now that I had taken the Commander up on his offer.

Fifteen

Across the airstrip, waiting stationary by the old hangars, I could see the white Jet Ranger, rotors drooping, the pilot standing by, his obligatory green Ray Bans reflecting in the afternoon sun.

The road or entrance leading across to the mainland, between La Linea and Spain, as well as access to the runway and airport, where also the barriers. They were up and the lights at green, so no delays, but as a precautionary measure, as we crossed the runway, I double checked there were no aircraft on finals, in case the barriers had been raised by mistake.

As I doubted that Debbie would have stopped anyway, and what I would have done I did not know. We crossed the runway as if at Le Mans, and up a taxi way, coming to yet another screeching halt close to the waiting helicopter.

Climbing out of Debbie's MG, the heat of the tarmac hit me as it came up to meet me. I looked back ruefully at my hot blooded chauffeuse, reached in for my luggage and blew her a kiss.

'I'll be back,' I smiled. She laughed, waving both

hands in the air, breasts jiggling, then let out the clutch and left two black lines on the tarmac.

'Afternoon, Sir, that's some lady!' the pilot said, thrusting forward a hand, and we shook.

'Jerry,' he said, introducing himself.

'Kit,' I said, still watching the MG disappearing into the distance, and then regretfully said, 'Ready to go?'

'OK to put your baggage in the rear compartment?' Jerry responded. 'They tell me you hold a current licence for one of these, Sir?'

'I do, but don't worry, just you crack on, I don't want to lose any of the light.'

'We'll be OK, Sir, but it may be a bit bumpy for the first half hour. It'll get less as we get away from Gib and the Straits though. We'll need to re-fuel as well, probably at Alicante, before we go across to Mallorca.

'OK, whatever you say.'

'Right then, Sir, pilot or co-pilot?' Jerry said, smiling and opening a door, I hesitated for a moment then,

'What the hell you win. Pilot,' I said and climbed into the right-hand side of the green tinted Perspex cabin, and reached back for my shoulder harness and clicked it shut. I looked up for the head set and put it on, at the same time turning on the radio. It crackled as I operated the squelch.

'Jerry,' I called checking the system.

The voice came back,

'Yes, loud and clear.'

'OK for the start?'

'Go ahead,' he said.

I checked that we had no obstructions; the blades were clear, no on lookers in the way, and leaning forward I pressed the starter. You could immediately hear the slow whine as the Benelux starter wound up the Allison turbine, and at 7% I cracked open the throttle. Poof! The turbine burst into life. I watched the sudden rush of heat on the temperature gauge as it approached the danger area of 900 c, only as normal, to fall back to 700 c and settle. As the turbine whine increased the rotors began to turn, the cyclic shook slightly, I eased it back a shade. One minute to wait for warm up and I did my pre-flight checks, while Jerry did the radio bit and called the tower.

We were cleared for an immediate take off, for a left hand turn out toward Marbella, and we had no known traffic here.

I moved into the hover at about six feet and checked the gauges again, now under load.

'OK,' I said to Jerry through the head set, which shut out most of the roar of the turbine.

'Fine. Away you go, it'll be a bit bumpy.'

Turning within the circle of her rotors into wind, she gathered speed forward up to 45 or 50 knots. With the ground rushing away below, I gently lifted the collective and climbed out left hand into the blue, turning toward the Costa Del Sol on heading

035º, leaving the huge grey white fortress and docks of Gibraltar and the Rock behind for now.

The coast of Andalusia lay to our left, Malaga, Alicante and the Balearics all before us. To the right the odd ship riding the white topped waves, battering its way eastwards into the Med. Jerry called up Malaga Airport air traffic control and asked permission to cross overhead, which was granted. It would save us some time and fuel rather than having to go around the back into the hills to avoid the air space if it had been busy.

'Now all we have is miles and miles of topless beaches,' he laughed, as we clattered on with an airspeed of 155 knots.

To save time I did a running re-fuel at Alicante, and then lifted off straight for Mallorca. The overall trip was uneventful save for the near overwhelming desire to head off to sea and look for Carlos II. Soon the blue grey mountains of Mallorca were showing dead ahead, in a shimmering heat haze. I called up Palma approach, they routed us down the coast at two thousand feet, and told us to report over Andratx for a direct approach, we should then move over to the control tower frequency.

Andratx came into view, a narrow inlet with a fishing port, the hills either side lined with the villas of the rich and famous. Minutes later Palma was dead ahead, with the Cathedral standing proud over the red roofs of the town. Looking down to the left at the port, one could not help noticing the enormous amount of shipping coming in and out of the harbour, some vessels riding at anchor in the outer bay waiting for entrance, a maze of masts pointing skyward from the two packed marinas, a white cruise ship followed by the Barcelona ferry, just clearing the light at the end of the mole.

I wondered how much security the docks had, but with so many people milling around surely, I could slip by unnoticed? I was making a mental note of the layout when the relative silence was broken, as air traffic crackled on the radio verifying our position. I confirmed we were on course and within only minutes it seemed, I was letting down onto Palma airport, the buildings a mass of re-construction, and a row of holiday Boeing jets standing in front of them.

On instructions from the tower, I hover taxied, following a yellow SEAT car with flashing lights toward the *Aduana* Diplomatic, found the H circle emblazoned on the tarmac and let down slowly, touched skids, and lowered the collective to the floor. Turning I said.

'Thanks, it does me good to keep my hand in, I don't always get the chance nowadays, maybe I will when I retire?'

'Will you retire?' Jerry said curiously and obviously wondering how I earned a crust.

'Sooner than most people think,' I said laughing.

'Somebody has spotted you,' he said, pointing

over my shoulder. I looked, a gentleman in the doorway opposite was holding up a paper to attract attention.

As we waited for the obligatory two-minute cooling down period, I couldn't help wondering where Carlos II was now, already here, or still making her way? And how was I going to board her tomorrow. I shut the turbine down, the rotors slowed. I jumped down and waved goodbye to Jerry.

I carried my own bags toward the *Aduana* Diplomatic. The gentleman in the pale suit and white straw hat turned out to be our Consul in Mallorca, who introduced himself as Sir George Corn.

'Welcome to Mallorca, my dear Sir,' he said, kindly taking one of my bags from me. As we entered the hall he said that it would be far quicker if he handled any formality; in the event there was none and we were waved through by an uninterested official sitting at the far end of a long thin cigar.

Once outside the building, the heat was oppressive, with the chatter of evening crickets vying for supremacy with the noise of passenger jets.

A white BMW waited for us on the yellow no parking lines, the chauffeur had the engine running, and a *Guardia* stood by the door.

'Gracias.' Sir George said, looking at the officer and passing him a note or two whilst holding open the rear door for me. The welcome coolness of the air conditioning greeted me. Once inside and moving off into the traffic, Sir George was more talkative, too much so for my liking.

'Well, to what do we owe this visit and your arrival in that impressive manner,' he questioned eagerly.

'Oh, nothing much,' I said. 'Just the possibility of a drugs bust, we've been following it for some time.'

'Then why not bring the Spanish into it?'

'Well, the contacts are British, based in England,' I lied.

'But now you are in Spain, and they are very keen to pick up any leads. The expatriates on the Costa del Sol include a lot of villains who are running the stuff,' he persisted, afraid he was being kept out of something. 'We must pass on what we know to them as well.'

I could see that from where this was going, things might become difficult.

'Well, I'll tell you more when I know more, I'm still a bit in the dark myself,' I said. hoping for the moment that would suffice, and rapidly changed the subject by asking about the maze of yachts and masts that were becoming visible to the left in the port of Palma.

The Paseo Maritimo was busy with tourists and traffic as we drove slowly along toward the hotel, under the long shadows of the magnificent twelfth century Cathedral, in the setting sun.

'Will you be staying long? Will you require anything? A car for instance? How can I help? Is it really as secret as London suggested?' he said excitedly.

If we are not careful, not anymore, I thought, I nearly said no, nothing thank you, to his proffered help, not wishing to get further entangled; yet not wishing to appear too rude either, I relented, realising that I was very much on my own, and I could yet need help. So as to leave the door open, and realising that his staff could help my legs in a strange town.

'Yes,' I said, 'I would appreciate a very light weight black jogging suit and some trainers also in black, must be black,' and I started to scribble the details down for him. 'If you could get them delivered to the hotel, I would appreciate it.'

He looked at me, obviously thinking, and a little surprised at my request, then after a moment.

'Fitness freak eh, on Government funds,' he said laughing approvingly.

I nodded, then, noticing that we were approaching the Victoria, surrounded by palm trees, exclaimed 'Ah! the hotel.' It was an impressive building, and, as the O.M. had promised, it overlooked the port.

I somehow managed to avoid further conversation for the time being. He gave me a sheaf of contact numbers and several addresses; I apologised for my secrecy, and with relief bade Sir George farewell for the moment.

As I entered the hotel the soft tones of a piano played gently in the reception area, adding to the ambience of the impressive foyer. I checked in quickly, eager to shower and get out to explore the area of the port.

Sixteen

The O M had made a good choice, from the room I could almost throw a stone into the harbour. This was ideal, I wonder how he knew of this place, I thought. A dark horse the O M. I decided to make a night of it, have a look at the harbour itself, and see how easily entrance could be gained to the commercial quay, especially at night, and also try to gain some local knowledge.

The entrances to the quayside area were not the easiest I had seen, both of them having armed guards. The reason for this being that the commercial harbour backs on to the Marivent Estate, formerly owned by the President of Chile, now a holiday home of the Royal family of Spain. Access without the correct papers would not be easy. I needed an alternative. On inspection the ferry terminal didn't look any easier, guards and Customs officials in all directions, the problem compounded by a high steel fence. No, that was a non-starter. The more I thought of it, access from the seaward side was the obvious choice. I decided to walk down to where the Marina joined the commercial quays; then noticing a chandlery across the road from the ferry terminal, my mind shot back to the hold of Carlos II, and to the danger of trying to move in the wheat cargo, like trying to walk in quicksilver.

The chandlery provided me with the two very special items I needed, 20 metres of dark blue rope carbon but soft, I would need that to secure myself tomorrow, and a Marine Band scanner radio. Half past nine and he was just closing, thank God for Spanish opening hours. I paid for it on the spot, saying that I would call back in the morning, when he had had time to splice two spring clips onto the rope, but the radio I took back to my room at the Victoria. Now how the hell to get to the quay, and which quay? And where would her berth be? Only tomorrow would tell.

Thirst and a little curiosity for the heady Palma night life was getting the better of me, and I am often a believer of fate working for me, I have never been let down even in the most peculiar of circumstances, or does fate help one who helps himself?

Leaving the hotel behind, I walked off into the late evening and towards the fishing quay. A line of wooden hulled boats with nets hung up to dry lay moored to the quay wall. To the left an interesting street with dimly lit bars with hanging lanterns outside, and rustic tables where a few fishermen sat, a bottle and glasses on the table, olive stones trampled under foot.

I chose a table and sat on my own, looking up the street at the ladies of the night. A buxom woman in a rusty black dress and a greasy apron came out eventually and I ordered a glass of red wine and a plate of olives. But as ever my privacy didn't last long, an unshaven but friendly faced fisherman slumped into the chair opposite, belched and smiled.

'Hola,' he grunted, 'Oyga! un cafe es una Cognac,' he drawled at the ample waitress, then looking across at me, 'English?'

I nodded in amusement as he started to sing and hum. Then in reasonable English he said, "olidays, ors yachty?,' waving expansively toward the Marina.

'One, two days business,' I replied, then after a moment I said slowly and thoughtfully, 'Have you a boat, Señor?'

'Si amigo, I have. Every night now I go feesh-ing, and eveery day I drink, sometimes I sleep,' he belched and smiled again.

'Is your boat close by, do you ever take a small charter?'

'You meen like taxi? Si amigo, all the time, when I forget to feesh,' he laughed again.

'Could you take me to the commercial quay at night,' I asked, wondering if it was a wise move con-sidering his condition, apparently habitual. He said he could, but tomorrow would be better; today he celebrated the day of his patron saint, tomorrow he don't drink. Of course, I agreed, but I wondered.

But then again, I didn't think that his craft would be too conspicuous, it might be just the thing I needed. He'd be in the fish market tomorrow if I needed him, he said, and at least it would be another string to my bow.

'I'm Kit,' I proffered my hand.

'Si, si, I Juan.'

First thing next morning I spoke to the O.M. at the communications centre down in Gibraltar. They'd heard Carlos II on the radio several times, her position now was about forty miles off Mallorca, and as we spoke she was in contact with the Port Authority, asking for a pilot to be on board at about 14.00 hours. The frigate had arrived at Gib and was being re-fuelled and victualled as we spoke. He had not fully decided what action to take, but thought it would be prudent to have the frigate in the Med. and on its way toward the Balearics, to lie off shore, as a just in case move.

As yet the Spanish authorities had not been made aware of our suspicions, and for that matter there as yet had been no liaison with the Americans either, which surprised me, but we had let her slip away. It wouldn't look too good for us; then again I had no definite proof of her cargo yet.

'Just sort it Kit one way or the other,' were his last words to me that morning. He sounded a little tired.

Looking down from the balcony onto the quays and streets of the port, busy and noisy with shipping,

I still stood by my original plan to come in from the seaward side of the commercial quay. I'd need a boat, so I set off to find Juan in the fish market at the other end of the harbour, over a mile away in this vast bay teeming with shipping.

The fish market was easy to find, but not so Juan. I wandered round the great echoing building, staring back at a thousand or more blank glazed fishes' eyes, splashing through puddles of tacky salt water, seeing an octopus being battered so as to tenderise it, and having the odd lobster waved at me, I made for a far door, with the sun streaming in through it. It led back onto the quay, and looking over the edge, there I found him singing quietly away to himself, legs swinging from the stern of a small brightly coloured fishing boat, fettling his nets, basking in the morning sun. Quite a picture.

'Hola, Kit,' he greeted me with enthusiasm. 'Was a good night, eh! you want go now?'

I jumped aboard and sat with him, and told him what I had in mind.

'Contraband no?'

'No,' I said firmly.

'Oh!' and he looked disappointed.

Then I suggested that about midnight would be the right time for me to visit the quays on the far side. That was no problem, he said, nothing out of the ordinary, fishing boats were about all night long, and I should meet him here. Shaking a brown calloused hand. I wondered just how reliable he was, but I reflected there were plenty of other craft I could procure if it came to it.

On returning I called at the chandlery and collected the multi coloured poly propylene rope, now fitted with its spring clips. Back at the hotel a parcel was waiting for me from Sir George.

I ordered coffee to be sent up to my room, and sat on the balcony and waited for the arrival of Carlos II. By 13.00 hours I was picking up regular transmissions on the scanner between Carlos II and the pilot launch. She was a little late, her E.T.A. would be about 15.00 hours, and because of her size she would be docking on the far outer quay as I had suspected.

At 14.00 hours I had her in my binoculars, she seemed bigger and a little more care worn, in this bright sunlight. By 18.00 hours she was alongside and made fast, but showing little sign of activity. I informed the O.M. of her arrival, and he requested that I should let them know the moment I left the hotel to go on board. He seemed unusually anxious because he went on to say the moment I returned I must make contact with him in Gib.

A bit obvious, I thought.

Seventeen

Nothing else now remained to be done except check, and double check again, my weapon, then pack the equipment carefully in the ruck-sack. The Sig 9mm and its silencer now lay ready on the bed. I waited patiently, taking a look through the glasses every so often.

At 23.00 hours I changed completely into the black track suit and trainers delivered by Sir George's runner. Underneath it I had the Sig 9mm in a belly holster, and the silencer strapped to my calf. The coil of rope was in a small black rucksack on my shoulder. To avoid notice I walked down to street level via the service steps, turned left, and hailed a taxi further along the street. He dropped me by the fish market, and I headed off round the back towards the fishing quay. Juan was waiting, sober and eager, engine running; maybe I'd misjudged him. I threw down the black ruck-sack and climbed down to the boat. He untied his craft and we motored quietly into the night, the oppressive blackness of the water accentuated by the bright lights of Palma town. Rusty black weed covered buoys appeared as ghosts as if from nowhere, and then faded into the night as we passed.

As we approached the outer harbour the swell of the sea increased. We headed out between the two moles which protected the shipping within, a red light on one and green on the other. Straight away Juan swung the tiller over and we followed the outer side of the concrete wall, behind which Carlos II hid. I could hear the sea gently breaking on the irregular concrete blocks which lined this seaward side to absorb the power of storm waves. Juan slowed the boat, and nodding in the direction of the quay

'You weesh over there,' he said quietly.

'Yes, can you get close enough for me to jump?'

'Si, Señor, but it is very sleepery, those concrete pieces, you can fall in betweens, breaking you,' he said, shaking his head.

I could see our navigation light reflected by great blocks of concrete jutting at all angles as a weather break for the quay, too late to change plan now I thought.

'Can you give me an hour or more,' I asked.

'Si, Señor, I feesh over there. I will watch for you.'

We were now under the shadow of the quay, and it became very dark as the glow of the lights of Palma were hidden. I strapped on the ruck-sack and waited a moment while Juan got as near as he could. I jumped, landing with a slap of trainers on the stone, but the surface was like grease and I fell on my face.

My nails broke as I dug into the weedy concrete for grip, feet scrabbling, mussel shells digging deep and cutting into my shins. My slide stopped inches above the water, and I hung there breathless. Juan had quietly moved off into the distance oblivious of my struggle. Gathering my senses, I waited to see if I had been noticed, was there a customs guard? Was there a guard on Carlos II?

All seemed quiet, but I decided that it was better to get to the end of the quay and go around it rather than go over the top; any person going over the top would stand out on the skyline. It took about ten minutes to complete this, struggling over the huge blocks, and pulling myself up onto the quay.

I lay there for a moment, letting my breathing settle, eyes adjusting to the new light and reflections cast from the town once more. Further down the quay I could see a uniformed man, his face illuminated as he lit a cigarette. After a moment he turned and walked away along the quay. I rose, moving swiftly at a crouch to the cover of a crane on the rail tracks in the middle of the quay.

I could see Carlos II moored further down. She looked huge and daunting, but from here there was no sign of a watch or guard. I was soon at her bow, still no sign of life, but with the bulwarks high above me it appeared impossible to get on board, the only possibility was nearer the stern where a gangway sloped down to the dockside. Beside its foot there was an untidy heap of boxes amidst a pile of metal parts, had the new parts gone on board I wondered?

Laughter, music and clapping was coming from within the accommodation just aft of the gangway, but nobody appeared to be on deck, so, taking a deep breath and checking in all directions, I casually walked up the gangway and stood still in the shadow of what I knew to be the doorway to the galley. Light and cigarette smoke poured out of the cabin scuttles from several hatches, from the passageway inside came music and laughter, the crash of glass and more laughter, speech was bawdy and slurred, the crew were obviously having a party, confirmed instantly by a girl's screaming laughter.

The decks seemed clear and the main hatch covers were shut as before, although I could not see from here whether the small trimming hatches were open. Moving forward but in the shadows, I thought I'd better see how many of the crew were on board. Cautiously raising my head, I peered in through the side of the nearest of the large square glass ports across the front of the accommodation block, relying on the fact that nobody inside the lighted saloon could see anything in the dark outside.

Then I could see the subject of their amusement. Beyond a table scattered with bottles and a couple of dirty plates a crew member sat on a large chair, straddled by a near naked dark woman. She might have been Brazilian, her long black hair covering his, whilst his head was buried deeply in her breasts that bulged from under her armpits, the pulsating shimmering cheeks of her black bottom a startling contrast to his white legs and pants shaking hopelessly under her. Two men watched avidly, clapping their hands to the rhythm of the strident music, another was undressing yet another girl, with enormous breasts just held in a cheap yellow bra, her hand viciously pulling at his crotch, they would all be occupied for some time.

I moved away slowly and stealthily down the deck, bag in hand. The lids of the trimming hatch all seemed to be up in the open position. There was no point in looking elsewhere when I already knew where to start, so I climbed down the steel ladder of the first one, the same one that I had entered before. The hot air came up to meet me, and I paused with my head level with the deck and looked all round, but nothing moved. I moved cat like down the rest of the ladder, my eyes adjusting all the time, at the bottom there was not a light nor a sound, save for the hum of the fans and generators deep in the bowels further aft.

I laid the bag on the floor and took out my torch, magnetometer and rope. Moving quickly now, I went to the edge of the platform and held the magnetometer out over the wheat. I must have moved about three frames further aft, when I got a reading that seemed possible, a metallic object or objects at a level of about three feet below the surface of the wheat was indicated.

Now I needed a shovel or something similar to dig with. Cursing my lack of forethought, I suddenly remembered there had been a bucket beside the top of the gangway. A baler, I thought. I ran back to the ladder, switched off my torch and climbed up. Nobody in sight again. Climbing over the coaming I bent double and ran to the gangway. There it was, smelling as though it was used to dump the refuse from the galley over the side. I seized it and ran back, then hooking it over my arm dropped down the steel ladder yet again.

The torch picked out my ruck-sack lying where I had left it. Straight away I clipped one end of the rope to the rail and swung myself over and down onto the wheat, starting to sink almost immediately. I caught a bight of the rope below my hand, and passing round my back I tied a bowline knot. I was held up by the loop under my armpits about level with the top surface of the wheat, or else I would have sunk right in. Now, with the utmost difficulty I started to bale-out the wheat from beneath me. The infernal grain seemed to pour back into the hole as soon as it seemed to be starting to get deeper. The heat and exertion made me sweat like a pig, the dust stuck onto the sweat and dried my gasping mouth, it was impossible. I couldn't breathe, but the job had to be done. In spite of the Old Man's words ringing in my ears, I was feeling I could go on no longer, when the bucket struck something solid, and simultaneously footsteps clattered on the steel deck above me, more than one. If I stopped digging, the wheat would refill the hole in a minute so I worked as one possessed, clearing what I hoped would be sufficient to see what I had found.

The footsteps had stopped. Dare I turn the torch on to see what was below my feet? During my frenzied digging had the hold been entered? I shone the shielded torch beam between my feet, sweat and salt dripping into my eyes. My head throbbed. To my relief I stood partially on a wooden packing case, as I moved my feet I could read the beginnings of Russian letters stencilled into it. I stooped to brush the wheat clear and could just make out in the dim light of my shaded torch,

'Scud Mk 11 A4'. A result!

Eighteen

The relief was immense, it was confirmed, the torch had been on only seconds, but I would still need to convince others. I took out my small Minox and photographed the box, the flash increasing my already furious heart-beat. I turned the torch off and waited in silence, trying to regulate my breathing and get myself back under control. There were no obvious sounds in the hold, it all seemed quiet now. I hoisted myself out of the wheat and up to the walk way, still there was silence. I quickly stuffed the equipment in the bag, and listened again. Nothing, save for the odd curious bump and knock from the deck above.

Now to find the locator beacon, I thought. If I can check it is still in position, and possibly find a better position on deck. As these thoughts shot through my mind, I moved further down the walk way to where I thought the ventilation fan was. I remembered where I had stuck the beacon behind the metal casing of the fan only a few days ago in Gibraltar. Moving slowly now I could just see the dark mass of the chest high fan motor.

Kneeling, as I felt behind it in the darkness, the shadows moved. A blinding pain shot through my neck and shoulder, something hard crashed down on my skull. Nearly losing consciousness, in desperation I lashed out at the unknown. A knee came up into my chest, grabbing it I drove my teeth through the cloth and deep into the flesh. It or he reeled back, as I flung my other arm upward and grasped his wrist.

He fell backwards, My, full consciousness was returning, blood poured through my lips, flesh and cloth in my mouth, he stank of old liquor. I had his hand now, it held something, training said got to release it.

I smashed it time and time again against the sharp edge of the fan motor. He hit me hard now with his free hand, but he also lost the battle of the weapon, it clattered over the side and into the wheat. He hit me hard again, my left eye losing its sight temporarily, then his arm went around my throat. I drove my hand up and with fingers deep in his eyes, wrenched his head back, now forcing him to loose his grip. His throat gargled, as I rolled and got clear. I came back as he knelt, and drove his head against the pump with a sickening thud. Blood and sweat spattered up to me, and with a groan he sank to the deck.

Breathlessly I dragged him to the edge of the platform, rolling him over and over until he dropped into the hold, the wheat slowly enveloping him with an eerie rustle he sank, like the sound of a snake moving on dried leaves. As if in swirling quicksand he vanished.

I crouched breathing heavily, my head spinning. Recovering, I unclipped my holster, eased out the Sig a proper weapon if needed, and moved slowly toward the ladder and the shaft of pale light, coming down from the deck. I reached the vertical side of the ladder, was there a sound from above? Reassured, I climbed two at a time until my head was level with the deck; all looked quiet, apart from the music still coming from the crews quarters. Taking a deep breath, I climbed over the coaming and onto the deck, moving stealthily to the side and looking over. The height from here to the quay was too much for a jump, I'd have to brazen it out. Five strides and the noise started again. I froze, looking to my left and there, behind the main hatch cover, on top of a pile of tarpaulin, two fleshy bodies writhed, bright yellow knickers thrown to the deck. The moaning started loudly again as her legs parted, as their heads went down, I moved swiftly past to the gangway. Some crew were obviously still at their revels in the saloon, I could hear them singing drunkenly as I walked past on my way to the gangway. I walked slowly down and away to the end of the quay, as if I were one of the crew, the cool sea breeze a merciful relief.

Juan was waiting just out of sight from the main quay in the shadow of the breakwater, and fishing merrily. I flashed the torch; he was watching and up went his hand. I replaced the Sig. in its holster, and tried to tidy my track suit up. Juan arrived and this time he edged the bows closer in. I jumped aboard from the slippery concrete, taking care not to slip this time. He went astern, and into the blackness, then swung the boat round and motored quietly round the end of the breakwater and down the vast harbour, under the night's mist that hung just above the water.

Juan said.

'Everee things is OK?'

'Fine,' I said, getting my thoughts together.

'Then I weel not ask where you have thoses,' he said, waving his hand at my head.

'M'm, don't,' I said, thinking of the man who had gone to his dusty grave. It wasn't the first time I'd killed a man. But the result, it was never ever pleasant. I consoled myself by thinking of his cargo of death, and that it could have been villages of the East desimated, and me lying under the wheat, but it was subjection what where doing?

Juan dropped me on the quay not far from the hotel. I gave him a ten mill in a peseta note. He looked delighted, but then a little unhappy that I had to go straight away.

'Work calls,' I said, 'Perhaps I see you around tomorrow.' I raised an arm, jumped out and walked up to the side entrance of the hotel, jogged up the stairs and into my room, the bag feeling heavy now. Glad to be here, I thought, I was absolutely black, and stinking, cut and bruised. Putting my clothes in a laundry bag, I ran a bath and poured in an antiseptic

Next, taking the phone codes I rang the O.M. He was on the second number I tried, he could not disguise the relief in his voice.

'Good, good, so we're not wasting our time then, Kit you've redeemed yourself in the nick of time as always, how many do you think are down there? Silly question, sorry, how the hell would you know,' he grunted, never at his best in the early hours.

'We're only half way there yet, Sir,' I said, pausing, then 'Now what, Sir? What is the next move?'

'I've got a plan Kit, certainly got a plan all right, but get some sleep now and call me at eight o'clock, Oh! No injuries I trust?' was said as an after thought!

'No, Sir, good night.' The phone went dead. I knew he would have a plan

It would not be easy, it never was.

I looked at my Ulysse, 03.30 hours. I bathed and changed, and with adrenaline still flowing in my veins, sleep was out. I took the lift to the Street, and walked down to the still quite busy promenade. Selecting a table at a quiet bar surrounded by palm trees and plants, with candles flickering in the night air, I ordered half a bottle of champagne. Looking over the Marina, a millionaire's playground.

I raised my glass, to tomorrow.

Nineteen

The morning arrived as it only can in the Mediterranean, the sun streaming down and warming the already bustling streets. I breakfasted well, and again sat on the balcony, once more looking at Carlos II through the glasses. She was buzzing with activity. Several men were leaning over the side smoking, another group stood in a circle gesticulating, clearly arguing about something. Were they nursing hangovers or looking suspiciously directly towards the hotel? Had I made a mistake by being dropped off so near? I doubted it, but as a precaution I would change hotels later in the morning.

Eight o'clock came and I rang Gib. some four hundred miles away, imagining the O M sitting there waiting, drinking his Earl Grey tea with lemon and looking out on to the Straits.

'Morning again Kit, fit?' he answered presumptuously.

'Lot of activity this morning Sir, men everywhere.'

'They're not aware of anything are they?'

'Shouldn't think so, Sir, but they'll be one man light.'

'I see. No evidence though.'

'No, Sir.'

'The plan is this, Kit and as usual it is probably all up to us. I spoke to the Americans yesterday, and they are not too sure you're correct. In fact, they are not impressed, and they don't have a vessel in the area anyway. The carrier Saratoga and her support group are over in the Gulf, and that would be a bit over the top anyway, but they did agree with our thinking not to have a go in Palma, as they visit the port frequently. So, really we wait till she is in International waters, but as I say they reckoned it was a non starter. But of course they don't know of your last night's escapade.

'Will you tell 'em, Sir?'

'Not sure now,' an unusual response for a positive man, I thought.

'Our frigate left here yesterday and will be up with you soon, meanwhile I am working on some way of apprehending Carlos at sea.'

'Sir, may I call you back in half an hour? I've been thinking it out also, and I just want to look at distances, areas, etc.'

'Half an hour Kit, yes that's fine, get back to me.'

I had been mulling this over in my mind for some days now, what I wanted was a clean, non violent, legitimate boarding, and a proper search and confiscation. The thought of Carlos II being chased by a frigate or whatever, to me seemed foolhardy.

They could have too much warning, there could

be a show down, and what back up did they have? None! Plus, the Arab states were too far away, North Africa was only over the horizon so to speak.

But if she were to break down again terminally and be stranded at sea, our frigate could, if close by, legitimately offer assistance. Then it would be fairly easy to overpower the small crew that I'd seen. An explosion in the engine room might be a possibility, but there could be a considerable loss of life, and I didn't suppose I would get back on board so easily next time, and I didn't have the correct timers and explosives anyway.

My alternative plan intrigued me, but to check it out I needed a chart of the Med. The answer was at the chandlery. Ten minutes later and five thousand pesetas lighter, I returned to my room. Once the chart of the western Mediterranean was spread out on the glass occasional table my plan began to take shape.

It was this; Carlos II was to be allowed to sail. We had the frigate on her way from Gib she should be able to shadow Carlos II, and from some considerable distance if needed. We knew that we had a sub en route for Malta, what if that could divert? If we had the time to do it? But it was due to go on display in Grand Harbour in Valletta for the celebrations along with the Britannia. If there was time before that, and the timing was all important, she could head directly for Carlos II. Then, if it were possible, the front torpedo tubes would be loaded with wire hawser, at each end and intermittently connected to large black fishing floats, the Sub would position herself at periscope depth, dead ahead of Carlos II. Then she would fire off the floats and cable, which would rise to the surface in the direct path of Carlos II, crash dive and leave the wire suspended by floats in the direct path of the vessel. The floats would then spread with the velocity used. The net result being that she, Carlos II would then sail over the wires, foul her propellers and come to a standstill.

Our frigate waiting in the wings, but some way off, would then go full steam ahead to be at the scene, and could then offer assistance in the form of a diving party to go down, make an inspection and inform the Captain of damage. In that way we could get a boarding party onto Carlos II, apprehend the crew, and make a thorough inspection. We then could decide what final action to take.

Well, I liked the plan, and the more I looked at the chart and the timings the more I was convinced that this idea was a starter. I dialled up the O M. He listened intently, unusually so, and without interruption. Then after a long pause, he said,

'Kit you may have stumbled upon on a superb plan, if it'll work. I like it, but I'm not going to waste time on the phone. I'm going now to speak to all the relevant authorities, find out if this Sub idea of yours is feasible. I'll get back to you.'

'Sir, I'll get back to you if I may, as I'm going to change hotels, and the name I'm registered in, so I'll call you in an hour and a half. Will that give you time, Sir?'

'Ring me anyway,' he boomed, now full of authority. 'Any problems at your end?'

'Don't think so, Sir, just as a precaution. I'll speak to you at about 10.30.'

I placed the phone down, and looked out at Carlos, now making a good deal of smoke. There were also two pick up trucks and a minibus alongside, work was being done.

Changing hotels took about an hour, the Punta Negra not as strategically placed but though further away, I could still see Carlos lying at the quay. Once installed, I called the O.M. again.

'Kit I'm impressed. Basically, it should work, according to all parties concerned, with a few details changed, and I've decided to implement it as of now. The Sub; *The Orca*, will start towards the Balearics in the next hour, although she is considerably east of Malta at the moment, and the frigate *Demeter* is on its way up to you as we speak, but we don't really want to show a presence. With that in mind, we have to get you on board, as I will require you to take overall control, reporting back to me. *Demeter* has a Wasp helicopter with her, so we can get you off the island, but it needs to be out of the airport, so that we are seen to be all above board, under air traffic and there is nothing suspicious,

I interrupted.

'Sir, use the Old Airport, *Son Bonet*. It's now used by private charter flights and the flying club, it's out on the old Inca road. Just a bit less conspicuous than bringing a Wasp into the main passenger terminal in Navy colours?'

'You're annoying but as ever, Kit you may be right,' he said, in a tired manner.

'If the *Demeter* arrives first and I think it will, I'll have her stand off over the skyline until we know that Carlos is on her way, agree?'

'Sounds perfect to me, Sir. The moment she makes any sign of movement I'll come back to you, but of course, Sir, you will already know that, as you will have picked up her transmissions to the harbour control and the harbour pilot.'

'Yes, Kit' he said, even more wearily.

'I'll keep in touch, Sir.' I put the phone down, smiling to myself and walked round my new abode, more palatial, and overlooking the pool, with an excellent sea view. I was further away now, but I could still see Carlos, a thin wisp of smoke coming from her funnel.

By evening I was getting tired of watching, waiting, and the constant transmissions of other shipping on the scanner, but eventually Carlos II broke the silence. She was requesting a pilot for 10.00 hours the following morning; the harbour control answered in the affirmative. She was on the move again.

I rang the O.M; they also had picked up the call and were aware of the time of departure. They would now have to calculate where *The Orca* and Carlos would converge, so that the whole action would happen under the cover of darkness. It would be pointless during the day, when Carlos might possibly see the fishing floats and the wire. Even worse if she saw a frigate trailing her although at a distance making recognition impossible.

It was decided that I should remain at the hotel until Carlos had left her berth. I would then proceed straight to the old *Son Bonet* Airport and be lifted out to *Demeter,* who would proceed to trail her out of visual range by plot and radar. She would coordinate the rendezvous with the submarine *Orca,* and on my reckoning it would be at least another day or 36 hours before we were in position. But then it had to be an 'all systems go' situation as we would only have one chance, she could be nearing her possible destination, which now didn't look like it would be Malta, not with that cargo. Libya, therefore, was a distinct possibility.

I then spoke to Sir George's secretary at the Consulate, apologizing for not being in touch, and yes, I had got my requirements. I apologized again, but I would now need a car at 09.00 hours in the morning to be on stand by to take myself and my equipment out through the diplomatic Customs at *Son Bonet* Airport.

Twenty

Well before nine the following day Carlos was making more smoke, and getting ready for her departure at 10.00 hours. Going down to the reception area, I paid the bill, had a coffee, and from the veranda watched her lines being winched on board, a couple of tugs and the blue pilot launch standing by.

Time to make a move. Collecting my bags, I made for the door, my driver appearing from nowhere to take them from me, and stow them in the BMW. The driver had already been briefed where to take me. We drove down the miles of sea front on the Paseo Maritimo, past the night-clubs, hotels, and the fish market, traffic already was beginning to build up. I turned to look out across the harbour and saw Carlos now in mid channel and under way.

The Old Airport, a remnant from the past, a time capsule to early air travel, and empty now except for private charter, and the flying club. We passed old hangars with rusting doors, it was all ghostly quiet even by the row of brightly painted light aircraft on the far side of the dilapidated main building. Only one door in the building seemed to be open and the car stopped in front of it. I bade farewell to the driver. Sir George had obviously lost interest in me, but apparently by request the diplomatic office was open and he had made arrangements for my departure. The Customs Officer was cordial and friendly, and took my two diplomatic cases out on to the tarmac, and waited with me, chewing on a small cigar, obviously interested in the arrival of a strange helicopter. Soon I could hear the uneven beat of a helicopter approaching from the southwest, a black spot one moment, discernible the next, like an angry hornet it came in swiftly, a heat haze swirling above the rotors, as two jet exhausts blasted out dark fumes. The rotors stressed upwards in the decent, sun glinting on the Perspex nose, the navy blue Wasp came into the hover over the runway, then approached the offices in a shower of dust and leaves, and gently let down.

'Eempresive,' the officer said.

'Noisy,' I countered, not wishing to get into a broken conversation.

The Wasp kept her engines running, a white helmeted Chief Petty Officer unclipped his harness, jumped out and ran toward me carrying a brown holdall.

'Morning, Sir,' he saluted, placing the holdall on the floor. 'Flying overalls, Sir, it'll go on over your Kit,' he said, opening the bag, taking out a helmet, a khaki one piece flying suit, and a blue bag on a belt.

'Lot of hassle,' I said. 'This lots going to be hot,' thinking of my easy flight up from Gib.

'Navy rules, Sir, and we're out over water.'

I didn't argue, zipping up the suit. He dropped the orange stole of the lifejacket over my head and pulled the belt round my waist. God! It was hot.

'Right, let's get going.'

I said thanks to the Customs Officer, and walked out of the shade and into the full heat of the morning.

The C.P.O. Airman ushered me into the back, stowed the bags, clipped me in, and plugged in the head set.

'Morning, Sir,' the Lieutenant pilot said 'great day, not a cloud in the sky, you can see for miles.'

Before I could answer the C.P.O. climbed in, plugging in his head set, and clipping on his harness. Turning he smiled and gave the thumbs up OK.

'All yours,' and we lifted out and into the blue, the sea immediately visible, to the right Palma's old town with the Castle behind, in the foreground the Cathedral, the port of a thousand yachts, and more importantly Carlos II making out to sea, the white bow waves disturbing the near flat calm as she picked up speed.

The noise was still deafening but the heat of outside had faded in a rush of cool air. The C.P.O. did not seem to have shut the door, but was calmly sitting beside a drop of a thousand feet below him.

The head set crackled into life.

'We are lying just the other side of the Island of Cabrera, they are out to the left of us.' He pointed, and there on the horizon I could see some hazy peaks of mountains jutting out of the sea, off the south-west tip of Mallorca. Small colourful fishing boats were dotted below as we skirted the western shore of Mallorca, too far out to see whether the sunbathers on the beaches were topless or not.

It was an impressive sight as we approached Cabrera Island the biggest of a small group with blue brown mountain peaks reaching up toward us, its picturesque Castle guarding the entrance to the little harbour and lagoon, then our shadow flashing across the blue lagoon, and two little fisherman's houses as we went overhead at fifteen hundred feet, over the highest mountain tip, the rocky cliffs then falling away, and sheer down to the Mediterranean.

The *Demeter* lay there in waiting, like a pirate ship that was lying quietly and inconspicuously in the transparent waters in the lee of the islands and cliffs, some crew were swimming and diving. We swung round to the stern of the frigate in a tight sweep, tail skidding out, eyes watching, nose up to arrest our speed. The Wasp slowed, and made a perfect approach, letting down on to the 'H' at the stern.

The Lieutenant smiling, now starting his cooling run down, raised a thumb, and nodded. I started to unclip my harness, and one of the flight deck crew wearing a yellow cloth helmet, rushed to open my door. I handed him the bags, and bending down to be well under the still turning rotors walked clear. I was greeted by yet another Lieutenant, in white shirt and shorts this time.

'The Captain is on the Bridge sir, shall we go?' he said saluting.

Captain Peregrine Trevelyn, was young, tall, forcefully good looking, and determined. I knew instantly we would get on well. He came straight across the bridge, looking directly at me, eyes never wavering. Fine by me! Two could play at that game. As we introduced ourselves, he shook my hand firmly.

'Good morning, your reputation precedes you. I am honoured to have you aboard,' he said, exuding friendly sarcasm. He led me out to the sunshine of the open bridge wing where we could talk in relative privacy.

'How much do you know?' I asked.

'Only that we are to follow a bulk carrier bound eastwards, you are to brief me, and then we'll liaise with Gib and co-ordinate some plan of action if needed.'

'Is that all?' I asked, surprised.

'Indeed it is,' he said. 'You have all the cards.'

'Right! Send one of your lads for some coffee and I'll tell all,' I said smiling.

Trevelyn looked at me, looked skyward, and winked, saying.

'Sun's over the yard arm, fancy a gin.'

Lord! I thought, just like David Bairstow, we're off again but ...

'Why not' I said.

The Captain led the way below to his cabin.

After about an hour I had briefed him to what I thought was necessary for the moment, but including the plan for the seizure of Carlos II and the involvement with the sub, which was now on its way to our night rendezvous, a position which would be determined by the speed of Carlos, and the onset of darkness. I kept the knowledge of the cargo to myself.

He nodded as I outlined what I wanted him to do.

'There's no problem for us. We can do all you want once the Carlos is stopped, but I don't go a lot on your plan for that. Have you talked this through with the Captain of *Orca*?'

The Captain's intercom bleeped.

'Yes,' he listened and then said, 'Right, on our way,' then looking at me, 'Come on, let's have a look at her. Up to the bridge deck, the vessel is passing astern of us now, just in view.'

On the bridge the Officer of the Watch passed us both binoculars, Barr and Stroud 7x50, and stood back from us. Focusing mine I could plainly recognise her as Carlos II, red and yellow striped funnel, rust and all.

'Yes, that's her,' I confirmed.

The Captain nodded, saying that she looked in quite good order, and commented that she could probably travel at about 15 knots, but with a top of about 18 in good weather.

Within moments he was giving orders to the First Lieutenant; play time was over. The swimmers were called in, and shirts were going back on, we were becoming ship shape, the frigate was rapidly and efficiently made ready. The shrill of a boatswain's call rent the peaceful afternoon, followed by the raucous cry.

'Harbour Stations'.

'Don't you think we've been a bit conspicuous here,' I said.

'Not a bit of it,' he said confidently. 'Cabrera has always been used by the Spanish military for training and its nothing new to have a naval vessel anchored here, it goes back many years, in fact we used it during the blockade we enforced in the Spanish Civil War.

NATO think we're here to smarten the ship up before going to Malta. This place is full history before that, right back to the Napoleonic wars; thousands of French prisoners died of starvation here. Hannibal was supposed to have been born here and the ship's divers,' he nodded toward a team stowing wetsuits and diving bottles in a store on the main deck, 'have even seen amphora's on the bottom.'

I was impressed.

Twenty-One

S hadowing Carlos, in the scale of things was quite uneventful, until late in the afternoon of the second day. We'd been watching her on radar all the time and remained too far back for recognition indeed at times we were over the horizon. Her course had remained steady, not terribly swift, but surprisingly she had still been heading on a course for Malta. It was only now, late on, that she chose to alter course, not a definite move, more of a gradual change over the next two hours. We had relayed the information both to Gib and to the submarine *Orca*. On this heading she would be able to make contact with Carlos from about 20.00 onwards that night, so there was quite a leeway in timing if we needed it. But we estimated that we would be somewhere over the Sicilian Banks, which were shallows and actually closer to North Africa than Sicily.

Captain Trevelyan now pointed out that the course was more commensurate with Carlos heading for Tunisia or Tripoli in Libya, rather than Malta. I had to agree.

Looking at the chart, we now proceeded to work

out an area where it would be practicable for the submarine that was approaching from ahead, and ourselves approaching from behind to converge on her.

The Captain was pencilling various calculations on the chart, when he suddenly stopped. I could tell that he was thinking, then after awhile, he said.

'You know, we may have one hell of a problem here.'

'Why,' I scowled. 'What have we overlooked?'

'You have overlooked the fact that where ever this cargo is going, if it doesn't turn up or is delayed without reason, someone is going to get cross, bloody furious in fact, and if it's heading for where I think it is we could be in for a shock. We may even be in range of a missile system. They won't think anything is too wrong if they see Carlos' echo slowing a little on their radar, that is, if it's close enough to be on their radar, because they'll know she's been having problems anyway.

Carlos itself shouldn't be too alarmed about us offering help, but if anybody else is watching they could see two radar blips. We'll need to be quick, nobody who is interested is going to watch her float around for long, and I don't want to be hanging around, taking her into tow or anything like that. That is, if your proper check out is correct anyway.'

I knew now that I would have to tell Captain Trevelyan of the full plan that I had discussed over the radio with the O M earlier in the day. I would need a boarding party, to be able to get on board under the guise of helping the diving team, which would be alongside, preparing to dive and free the propeller.

Trevelyan took it in his stride, and sent for the First Lieutenant. And there it was on the Watch and Station Bill. A well armed and practised boarding party under the Gunnery Lieutenant, a ship's diving team led by the Torpedo Officer, and an Engineering boarding party trained to combat damage aboard other vessels. Two inflatable dinghies tested and ready to be swung out on a davit.

As night fell we were in constant touch with *Orca* as she made her menacing way to our rendezvous, and of course keeping the O M and team in Gib up to date.

Lieutenant Commander Bill Thompson, the Captain of *Orca* now worried me greatly, as he was at this late stage expressing severe reservations on the practicability of shooting floats and wire into the path of Carlos II.

'It isn't on,' he stated firmly. 'Nothing on earth would make me fire coils of wire out of a torpedo tube. There were enough problems when we used canvas bags to ditch our gash. I can see what you want, though and we've come up with a better scheme. Mooring wires sink and need floats to hold them up. And there's a good chance that a propeller blade will cut through it, because it's rigid. But our head rope is 120 fathoms of seven and a half inch plaited polypropylene and it floats. If it's hit by a prop it gives way and wraps round it.'

'Brilliant!' I said, much relieved. 'But if you can't fire it, how will you lay it in front of Carlos?'

'We'll trail it across, and let it go when he's aiming at the middle of the bight. We'll have to surface for five minutes after dark to get the rope from under the casing, anyway. Then we drop the eye of the rope over the search periscope and dive gently to periscope depth, and there we are towing the hawser, 720 feet of it stretched behind us. Then I'll steer to cross his bow so near that he can't avoid the rope, even if he sees it, when I'm half its length across his track, down periscope and the rope slips off and is left behind.'

Well, rather him than me, I thought, but he seems to know what he's doing.

'Sounds fine,' I told him and hoped

'Now the big problem is,' and I thought, what now; 'will your authority cover me writing off two thousand quid's worth of mooring rope?'

As darkness came we reduced our distance considerably, it was now 23.00 hours and *Orca* stated she could be in position easily by 23.45. So, 23.45 it was. We were catching up rapidly now but altered course to a slight diagonal track, as if they had their radar on, we would now be in range, so it was prudent to appear a casually passing vessel on route to where ever. In any event, at night they would not know that we were a warship, more likely the radar 'blip' of a large fishing vessel.

By this time Bill Thompson was manoeuvring stealthily into position, dead slow at periscope depth, with his radar mast up as well, looking for a definite contact on Carlos II, while lying in wait on her known heading. We ourselves were not much more than five miles behind, and in constant radio contact with *Orca*.

At ten past eleven she reported.

'Echo bearing 317, range 9.5 miles, diesel H.E. on bearing.' Six minutes later he came back with 'Target course 142, speed 15 knots.'

At 23.31 exactly the voice of Bill Thompson crackled over the air saying, that he now had visual contact, with a range of three miles. Three minutes later he came back to us with a request for our estimate of the target's speed. Without being asked, the Petty Officer manning the ultra violet lit plotting table in the darkened Operations Room said.

'Target speed 15.4 knots, Sir.'

'How did he do that?' I whispered to Trevelyan, who stood silently watching the greenish blob that was Carlos, and the intermittent tiny spot that showed Orca's periscope uncharacteristically visible above the water.

'Automatic radar plotting assistance,' he muttered back.

Bill Thompson's voice came calmly over the radio as he talked us through his manoeuvres. The range closed steadily minute by minute, then at 23.40, without a change of voice we heard him say Carlos was altering course to port.

'Group up, full ahead together,' he said urgently, then, 'I'm speeding up to get across his bow. I think he got an echo off my periscope and thinks he's avoiding a fishing boat. I'm going deep when I cast off the hawser.'

At exactly 23.43 he said.

'Down periscope. A Hundred and twenty feet. Flood Q.'

We could imagine the sudden roar and shudder as air compressed by the sea pressure rushed in from the quick diving tank. The submarine would lean forward and thrust downward, quietly hissing as she slipped to the depths like a dark cobra leaving its kill. Then they would hear the thump, thump of Carlos 'propellers passing overhead, some fifty feet above the top of the fin.

The tension now for those of us still waiting in the Operations Room seemed to last forever. Nobody spoke. There was silence save for the hum of the ventilation fans, and nothing moved except the eerie green flashes from the radars.

It was a long two minutes by the clock before it came.

'Ops, this is sonar, target H.E. slowing up,'

followed a moment later by 'Possible explosion, and confused H.E.'

Trevelyan looked up from the plotting table.

'She's slowing down all right, that bang might have been the prop shaft shearing.' He was confirmed right away by the sonar operator saying,

'H.E. ceased.'

Captain Trevelyan picked up a hand microphone and spoke to the Main Signals Office.

'M.S.O., watch for transmissions on VHF and interfere with any except Channel 16 Emergency frequency. And try to jam any medium frequency radio.' Then turning toward me, 'That'll slow up any calls for help,' he winked.

Orca must have returned to periscope depth because Bill Thompson came on the air,

'We can hear a lot of banging in their engine room, but I don't think they're going anywhere. If you are happy, gentlemen, I'll bid you good night; I'm going to see the Queen.'

'Many thanks and good night, say hello to Malta for me,' Captain Trevelyan said.

He turned to look at me, 'Right Kit what now?'

'Give her five minutes, to assess what has happened, and then we'll give her a call.'

I spoke to the First Lieutenant.

'Make sure that the boarding party are ready to go, but keep them out of sight and as we briefed them, all weapons must be out of sight. Are the diving team ready?'

'They are all ready to go, Sir.'

I had seen the Gunnery Officer and his boarding party earlier that afternoon, he looked useful enough, he had experience and it was a help to have a known leader amongst the team, the men knew and trusted him.

After another four minutes we called, saying.

'Unknown vessel' and giving our position a mile and a half astern of them, and quoting their geographical position. We asked that as we had been passing astern, we noticed that they had come to a standstill, did they have a problem? And could we assist, as we ourselves earlier had noticed fishing nets in the area and we had a diving team on board.

We did not approach any closer yet. There was a long pause, then eventually we were asked to identify ourselves and what vessel we were. I looked at Trevelyan, here goes, I thought, this is where we blow it.

The Captain said that we were warship *Demeter*, a training frigate on our way to Malta for the national celebrations. We waited for the reply on tenterhooks, the longest few moments I could remember, we stood there watching the radar screens, Carlos II was the only blip indicated, the sea was calm, we held our breath. I blessed the intuition that was preventing Bill Thompson from bringing *Orca* to the surface while still within radar range.

The reply came back after what seemed an age. Yes, they would welcome some assistance, only for a diver team to assess the damage; they appeared to have fouled their propeller on some object.

We then asked them to move to the less public working VHF channel 67, and carried on monitoring the other channels and radio frequencies, just in case. The Captain ordered *Demeter* to proceed slowly, and turning on our deck lights slowly one by one so as to remove the suspicion we had been ready all the while, two lookouts were placed on the bow and signalling lamps were turned on. The last thing we wanted to do was to foul our own props on the floating hawser. Even covering a short distance of less than a couple of miles it seemed an age to have Carlos in full view, but then they turned her poop lighting on and the deck was ablaze with light and a dozen crew all looking and pointing over the stern. They didn't seem too euphoric to see us. We manoeuvred into a position some hundred yards off on her port side. As Captain Trevelyan said.

'Put Carlos between us and the North African coast, we may then look like a single radar echo that is if someone is monitoring the situation. Likewise, if there is anything coming, they'll get it first.' A smooth move, good thinking.

One thing had stuck in my mind, and that was that the accent of Carlos' alleged Captain or Officer whom we had heard over the radio, was certainly not Spanish.

Carlos' Captain spoke once again over the VHF.

No, they did not want us on board, but just to do a dive on the propeller. We argued that we would need to rig lights on the stern, and maybe rig tackles to a winch. We should definitely have a team aboard for safety reasons, but if they didn't like that we would tow them to Malta. All went quiet, then, after further consultation they agreed.

Trevelyan looked at me.

'Right, Kit you're on, look after my men, and whatever you are doing, just remember we're here.' I wasn't sure which way to take that.

Moving in a quick yet orderly way, we lowered the two inflatable dinghies, one for the divers, and one for the boarding crew. Inspecting the men, there was no sign of any arms, all had their instructions. As we boarded the boats from the pilot ladder I looked up, most of our crew were at the side watching in anticipation.

They would go to Action Stations in a flash at a given signal, but for the moment we were just the friendly British.

We motored quietly across, I gave instructions to the diving team, and dispatched them to the stern. The eight man boarding party, nine with myself, grabbed the bottom of the pilot ladder hanging from the main deck. I nodded to the Gunnery Officer, he winked and in turn we climbed laboriously up to the deck of Carlos, followed by the men, leaving a single boat keeper behind.

The Captain met me at the top. He didn't offer his hand. He wore a holster, the flap undone. I looked across at what crew I could see, my heart stopped, the crew and Captain had changed. I recognised no one, they all looked of Arab extraction, dark sharp features with black dangerous eyes, hate burning within. I could see another man who had a gun in his belt, I hadn't bargained for this but it was too late to turn back now, so taking a deep breath, with one sweep of my arm I introduced the Gunnery Officer and his back up team. The Captain nodded coldly.

A noise of shouting came from the diving boat at the stern. Cries of,

'Get a bloody move on,' 'Drop us a line,' 'Get these lights up,' came up from below.

I looked at Carlos' Captain, and he nodded grudgingly. The Gunnery Officer and his men went to the stern, and joined Carlos' crew looking down at our diving team. There was a lot of shouting in both directions, and heaving lines were being thrown and missing. It was all taking a long time.

I waited for a moment at the back of the crowd, then when all backs were turned, I did not seem to be missed as I walked back, ostensibly to see if out dinghy was still safe at the pilot ladder. I turned right and swiftly darted into the shadows of the accommodation, darted up a flight of steps to the boat deck level and another flight to the bridge. Turning aft I hesitated momentarily outside the radio room, listening, not a sound from within. I opened the door slowly, no radio operator.

Entering quickly, I closed the wooden door behind me. Then, systematically I set about cutting wires and destroying all radio equipment, grabbing whatever paper work and notes I could find. The job done, I left by the internal door leading directly onto the bridge. Still no sound, so I moved carefully toward the chart table and there before me was the course and destination of Carlos II.

A pencilled line on the chart led to Tripoli in Libya.

I let out a deep breath, I now felt somewhat vindicated. In the dim light I started quickly folding up the charts and whatever notes I could find, and stuffing them in my ruck-sack.

Then the sound. Foot-steps? A sudden noise? I looked up, ducking as the door swung open, simultaneously came a blinding flash and deafening roar, my right thigh was sledgehammered from under me, catapulting me to the floor. I rolled fast, fast for cover, anywhere. No cover. Nowhere to go. Reaching now for my Sig, another roar and the smell of cordite, wood splintered, into the space under the chart table. I rolled up against a safe, two more deafening blasts slugs thudded home through the table top and into the floor near me, then click, and a curse. Was it a revolver? How many had he fired? Was it an auto? Was it a jam? No time to think, clasping the Sig. I thought, roll!

roll! I spun out from under the table; he still stood by the doorway, his mouth dropped as he saw me. I fired twice in succession, crash he flew back, he hit the map of the world on the wall behind him and slid slowly down, staining the fractured glass dark crimson.

No pain, but nauseous faintness was sweeping over me as I gripped my thigh. I had been lucky, the femur was not broken, it was still load bearing. The bullet had passed straight through, but I was losing a lot of blood, I could feel my heart pumping in shock, blood everywhere. The sound of footsteps, a lot of footsteps coming up the steel steps, forced me roll back under the table. Breathing heavily, I steadied the Sig. at the doorway, at the last moment recognising the blue trousers and boots I rolled clear with a groan. The Gunnery Officer was standing there with a Lanchester at the ready.

'Christ! You all right, Sir.'

'Fine,' I said, 'just got in the way of a bullet.' I pointed at my leg, 'It's not broken, what's happened to your lot?'

'Not in the plan, sir, but as soon as those shots went off we put them straight under guard. One tried to get a shot off, but Pete, the big Welsh lad, felled him from behind, split his head wide open. I disarmed the other, they're now all face down on the deck, there doesn't appear to be anyone else on board.'

'Give me a hand,' I said, as I grimaced, summoning all my strength and stood up.

'I'll call the doc., sir, Christ! Got to stop that bleeding' and he spoke into his radio.

I hobbled through the radio room and on to the bridge deck looking down at the scene below, seventeen men were spread-eagled on the deck, two of our team standing over them. The blue grey frigate was closer now, just abaft the bridge was mounted a Bren gun. I could see a burly seaman in a flak jacket covering Carlos' poop, he waved five fingers as if playing the piano, and smiled hopefully.

'Right,' I said, propping myself up. 'Open the hatches and start digging, but rope everyone on, they must work in twos for safety, and be careful. Check in those holds for anything that may be buried, I suggest you start on hold number four, you should find packing cases at about three feet down in the wheat about a third of the way from the after bulkhead. Some of the others may be too deep, but as far as I am concerned one is enough. Send the diving team back and ask the Captain to send over engineers to come over and locate the sea cocks and open them.'

'Isn't that a bit premature?' he questioned.

'Open them,' I said. 'Let the bloody sea in, it'll take time to sink her.'

'Aye, aye, Sir,' he replied, coming to attention.

'Also, shut all fuel valves, and don't forget the vents. I don't want any leakage, contain it all in the tanks, then get ready a life boat for Carlos' crew, put in fresh water, food medical supplies, fuel, and any waterproofs you can find. Oh! And a compass and chart.

'What happens if it was the navigator you shot?' he said with a whimsical smile on his face.

I looked at him, hard.

'They'll get lost.'

He immediately set off to pass on my instructions, within moments shafts of light from the open hatches below lit the deck, and the whining noise of a winch running out under gravity drifted up to me as the lifeboat was lowered to the sea.

God! I felt terrible. Waves of pain came and went, but I had to hang on.

The Surgeon Lieutenant arrived, took one look at me and pronounced that a stretcher was needed and promptly gave the order.

'Over my dead body,' I said shaking my head. 'I'm staying till the end.'

'Then it may well be your dead body, but I'll give you a shot,' he said taking out a syringe. 'It's a pain killer, and I'll try to get a couple of pads and a tourniquet on, but I am staying with you.' I nodded, I wanted to be sick.

The Gunnery Officer arrived back.

'First three holds so far have got the wooden crates. Some different sizes though, Sir. We've opened one, hell of a job; inside they have a waterproof steel container. It's very big, they are probably in sections.'

'OK, that's all you need to do' Then I thought. 'No

get photos of everything you can down there. Are you sure the sea cocks are open?'

'They are, sir, it's coming in like blazes down there, but it'll still take time, long enough for photos anyway'

'Get Carlos' crew to the life boat, get rid of them, get all the paper work from the Captain's cabin, and take this lot.' I pointed to the charts and papers and my ruck-sack on the bullet ridden table. 'Let's pack up, let's go home,' I said all of a sudden becoming terribly weary.

The Surgeon Lieutenant helped me for the last time down the bridge steps of Carlos II.

Carlos' crew scowled at me, one spat, others muttered, as they walked by, and one by one climbed down the pilot ladder into their life boat, engine running, white steamy fumes wafting like dry ice over the calm surface of the sea. I clung to the guard rail feeling dizzy and watching as they motored between the two huge vessels dwarfing them, only to return shouting, waving their hands and refusing to go.

I looked up at the machine gunner, and nodded. The biggest smile I've seen in years came across his face, his hand went to the gun and two bursts went into the water, bullets zipping into the water by Carlos' crew. They vanished in a cacophony of shouting, engine noise and wash, they vanished into the night, fists shaking.

Desperate to get it all finished with now, I was

helped down the ladder where I could see that Carlos was beginning to lie heavily in the water, but it would still take some time, lucky there wasn't a lot of current, I thought.

Two men now helped me up to *Demeter's* main deck, the Captain watching all the while. At the top I turned again to look at Carlos, and the Captain looked curiously at my leg.

'What are you trying to prove?' he asked.

'I have to see it through, I have to see it through,' I said faintly, gripping the guard rail with whitened knuckles, as I looked once more desperately at Carlos.

I passed out.

Sometime later I awoke to a gentle shake, opening my eyes slowly, not knowing just where I was, then, as pain came back I saw Captain Trevelyan was standing over me.

'You're OK now, Kit all plugged up, can you move?'

'I don't know, I'll try, maybe I can,' I said in absolute anguish, but curious to know the Captain's reason.

'Come on then, I'll show you something,' the Captain put my arm over his shoulder pulled the sheets back, and half carried me to the door, a door that was jammed open by what looked like a bar stool. He sat me on it.

'Thought you'd like to see this,' he said 'but if old saw bones finds us, I'll end up like you … … shot!'

The sight took away all pain. It was early dawn,

with the misty blues and smoky pink tones over Africa, to the far east the most spectacular sunrise was starting; close by mists crawling, steam like, curling over, inches above the calm sea. Carlos now some eight hundred yards away was down at the stern and sinking fast, a rushing of air and bubbling coming from outlets, white foam swirling round and over her decks, wheat floated away on the surface, the sea close by boiled with fish in the excitement of their breakfast feast. Carlos II slipped slowly away in a rush of furious water, a cauldron of hell, doomed for ever to the murky depths, some water spouts shooting fifty feet high or more skyward.

To see a ship go down, is a sad sight, even Carlos, but it would have been far sadder if her deadly cargo had ever reached its destination, and wrought havoc on the world.

After some time the Captain spoke.

'We've been routed to Malta, we're so close we might as well make a presence at the celebrations, along with the Britannia and our friend *The Orca*, fly the flag and all that.

Then I believe after a few days' convalescing you'll be flying back to London.'

'I'll look forward to Malta, haven't been there for a while, my parents have a house there, but they don't use it too much nowadays, I might even stay there,' I said. Just then the tannoy burst into life.

'Captain required in the M.S.O.'

'It's the big boss on the radio from Gibraltar. I'll tell the Chief Sparks to patch it into your phone at the bed side. Oh! and by the way he rang earlier; I don't think he expected you to send the whole shooting match to the bottom. He sounded a bit shocked'.

'A bit late' I quipped.

Part 3

*London, England and
Farewell*

Twenty-Two

Walking down the long and carpeted hallway to your own leaving party is something I had never quite envisaged. I wondered if it was akin to being able to witness your own funeral, the spirits staring down from above, and the living not knowing how to say good bye, it was quite eerie. I knew already that I was no longer one of them, no longer part of the team, the team that had moulded my life for some fifteen years or more.

I never had liked this part of the building, the rooms at the end reminiscent of a small ballroom with double ornate doors, high embellished ceilings, glass chandeliers, and a Persian carpet, reputed to have been given by the Shah in return for a favour.

I was a little late; surely you could be late to your own farewell party? Stuart and the Old Man stood by the open door, drinks in hand.

'As ever, a law unto yourself, Kit' the Old Man said looking at his watch.

'Good evening,' I said, entering quietly. They returned my greeting, the O M saying he would be back shortly as he knew that Stuart would have things to ask. A waiter arrived and I took a glass of champagne, casting my eyes round the room as I brought the glass to my lips.

Even now I could see smart arse looking at me through the crowd, immaculate as ever, sun tanned, in his designer wear. Was I jealous? No, it was just that he stood out so, amongst the unobtrusiveness of normal MI6 dress. Hell! If the rumour was true, that now the powers that be were going to advertise for personnel; glad I'd made the decision, glad I was leaving. I suppose we were all so bloody English, nearly a family, all of us, no need to impress. Stuart and I had even been at Oxford together, we went back a long way, but now the prodigal was leaving.

Stuart spoke first, turning his back on the gathering.

'Have you sorted out your gun and equipment? Oh! And the Daimler, did you make your mind up?' he said authoritatively yet curious.

'I've taken the service weapons to the armoury, but I'll keep my own on my ticket, for the moment, you never know?'

'Still use the Sig.?'

'Wouldn't part with it, that or the Beretta, as for the Daimler, well accounts offered me a good deal, a sort of leaving present, so I accepted it. I'll be giving them a cheque in the morning.'

'Probably as well,' Stuart said. 'You've spent a fortune of your own money on it anyway, I'm bloody glad it's going, you aren't supposed to modify service vehicles, or spend your own money on them. The O M would have had a fit; you can hear those turbo's wheeze all round the Park.'

A big kiss arrived on my cheek.

'Good bye, good byee, good byeee,' Sue sang, having sprung from nowhere. I'll miss you, God! It'll be tame without you, Kit. Do I have to fawn over that 'boy' Liam now?' she said laughing, and looking in the direction of Liam, who knew he was being talked about. 'I'll see you before you go?' she questioned.

'Bet he wears Hom briefs,' I said.

'What?'

'You couldn't fit a gooseberry in those. I patted her backside and winked, Stuart looked mortified, I didn't care, I laughed and walked over to see the O M rubbing shoulders with old friends, shaking hands and saying hello, and a good bye as I went.

When I finally got there, he was standing in an alcove watching the gathering, looking aloof and huge in his tweeds, straight out of the country as ever. Pensively he smoked his pipe, he wasn't even supposed to smoke, but yet it was given to him by his wife, there must be a moral there somewhere.

'Well, Kit you are one of the youngest and yet you're retiring. I should be retiring not you, bet your father is furious.'

'He doesn't know,' I countered, he's not well.'

'M'm, sooner you than me,' he said. 'Anyway, they will have got you on some form of reserve list, so we've still got you for the next ten years or so.'

'That's all I need to know, Sir,' I laughed.

'Happy with your replacement?' he said.

'That's your decision,' I said coyly, then we talked for a while about the past and the new future of the service, but once again I could feel I was not part of the future, open as it was supposed to be, but the shutters had come down.

Looking round the room over the O M's shoulder I could see Liam, now chatting to my secretary, no ex-secretary. Jealous? Maybe, farewells were never easy.

I shook hands with the Old Man, grasping his hand firmly with both mine.

'Excuse me, Sir, I had better do the rounds.'

'I understand, Kit look after yourself,' he smiled sadly.

I made a point of saying farewell to every one personally, a drink here and smoked salmon there. What am I going to do now? Would I live in Yorkshire? Would I have a holiday? And to be honest I didn't know.

As I neared the end of my rounds, and time was getting quite late, I had manoeuvred myself toward the door, only to see Sue standing there; she held my hand, with tears in those big watery brown eyes.

I kissed her farewell, fully on the mouth, did her tongue flick? I'd never know.

'I'll probably never see you again, and it's taken a resignation for you to do that,' she smiled. Taking a white handkerchief from my breast pocket, I dabbed a tear away from her eye. As I was about to say something that I am sure would have incriminated me, the accounts clerk interrupted in the nick of time.

'The log book and receipt will be at the desk in the morning, Sir.'

'Thank you,' I said, shaking his hand, looking at a reflection in his glasses that told me somewhere over my shoulder Liam, my replacement, was still watching me. His interest was too much, I told myself. Why? I questioned inwardly. I'd go over again and say farewell, then leave, at least all the remaining staff would see I was wishing him all the best in his new post.

I turned around and weaved my way towards him. I thrust my hand out, his coming out to greet me complete with fancy shirt cuffs, and huge gold links.

'Well, it is farewell this time, Liam, how does it feel to have your own department?' and then, 'well, under Stuart.'

'Oh! just work, and more work, bringing your department up to date,' he said pointedly. 'What are you going to do with your time, go to your heritage in Yorkshire, and farm? Or the family house in Malta? You do still have a house there, don't you?' he said, a little sarcastically. I was somewhat taken aback, I hoped my reaction didn't show. I doubted it.

'It is not my house,' I replied, 'It's my father's. He spent a lot of time there until Mintoff came to power, and there were problems with Libya, but I haven't been there for some time. I should go, as the gardener keeps sending bills and maintenance isn't cheap, but I just haven't been able to find the time.'

'Expensive toy,' said smart arse. 'How can you afford it?'

'I can't, I've told you, its family.' I said curtly. It was bugger all to do with him and I wanted to finish this conversation.

'I could have sworn you'd been there recently,' he continued, 'anyway how will you survive in retirement, have you enough money?' to my mind he was now being extremely impertinent.

'I'll have enough to survive,' I said, tiring of the man, so bowing in a Germanic fashion with a click of the heels, I took my leave, to the amusement of one or two friends close by. I moved away and toward the raised entrance and double doors. God! I was glad to get away from his aftershave, it was obnoxious.

Walking now toward the double doors and the balustrade through my friends and acquaintances, all together in one room maybe for the last time, I mused as I climbed the two steps. No need for a speech, I thought, although quietness had now descended on the floor. I turned, raised my class and toasted.

'To you all,' I said, holding the glass aloft for a second then downing it in one, raised an arm, and left.

I did not look back.

Twenty-Three

The following day in London dawned beautifully, clear and crisp, I had been awoken by the flower arrangers attending to the flowers in the mews, many flower boxes, something on which the residents prided themselves.

Showered and feeling fit, I poured scalding water on to freshly ground Maragogype coffee beans. I dialled Camilla in Yorkshire, telling her of the leaving party, and of the many friends that sent her their regards. As ever she was cheerful and bubbly, but more interested in going to feed the horses, quite plainly I was interfering with her morning routine in the country. She'd had little or no interest in what my career was or had been; was this a reason for early retirement I asked myself?

What was I going to do with myself now, she asked.

'The estate is run down and there is a mountain of work to be done to put things back in order, you've a lot of work to do. Oh! But don't forget some tea from Harrods if you're passing, No 16 blend,' anyway she was busy at the moment, she'd see me in the afternoon, the phone went click, I wondered why I'd bothered ringing.

Preparing to leave, I put the Yorkshire telephone number onto the answer phone, turned the house alarms on, and heaved the plated door shut. The lock slammed home, till when, I thought, when will I be back?

I hailed a cab for Curzon Street, another last time? On arrival I paid off the cabby and walked over to the Commissionaire.

'Morning Harold'.

'Morning, Sir, not many people are in today, its Saturday and Colonel Stuart apologises but says could you leave your pass with me.'

'No problem, I'll drop it off when I bring the car out of the pool, I won't be long.'

I took the lift to the main office and dropped off an envelope marked for the attention of the accountant. There seemed to be only one or two staff about, all watching computer screens or playing back tapes from the night monitors. It felt strange now, time for me to go.

I walked out and along the corridor, but this time down the winding stairs. Halfway to the first floor, mounted on the wall was a huge gilded frame, a portrait of Churchill, with the inscription below, 'In his finest Hour'. He seemed to be frowning at me. I frowned back, you didn't like boredom either, I thought. Opening a door on the right, I went down further steps into the basement, and the car pool.

The dark metallic blue Daimler was parked on its own, immaculate. I believe that Charles, Stuart's driver, had worked on it yesterday, a sort of leaving present, it looked superb, I must write to thank him. Climbing into the smell of leather and walnut, I fired up the V12 engine, a little rough on first bursting into life, and then settling to near silence, save for the slight hiss of the twin turbos. I loved it. Smiling inwardly, I blipped the throttle to clear its throat, and moved toward the automatic doors. I would be on screen in reception, a warning bell would ring to warn the Commissionaire of my movement. The doors opened, daylight lit the garage, I swung left into the light traffic, then left again into Curzon Street and the front of the building. Leaving the Daimler on the double yellow lines, I walked toward the Commissionaire's office. Harold came out to meet me; half saluted, then grabbed my out stretched hand and shook it firmly with both hands.

'I'll miss you, Sir, we all will, thought you'd be here for ever, Sir, can't believe you're going, Sir.'

'Here's my pass,' I said, smiling wanly. 'It was time to move on, things were just a little quiet. I'll be coming down from time to time, so if I'm here in the Autumn I'll drop you off a brace of Yorkshire pheasants.'

'That'll be kind, Sir, we always look forward to those, Sir.'

He escorted me back to the Daimler glistening

in the morning sun, he closed the door, and I eased into the light Saturday morning traffic and headed for Edgware Road, Hatfield and the A1. I preferred the driving challenge of the A1, the scenery was better than the M1 too, and the chance of a quick bite of something civilised at the 'George' at Stamford. By my reckoning the trip would take about three and a half hours.

Once on the A1, I had a feeling of freedom. Holiday! Going home to the country. Easing the accelerator down, I could hear the whine of the turbos build up their pressures to an indicated pressure of 14 psi, feeding compressed cooled air to the twelve cylinders of now near six litres capacity. The bonnet raised slightly as the tail sank under power, leather creaked as my body was pressed deeper into the seat, but within seconds it seemed I was backing off. The turbos wheezed now, as the air flow was restricted from them, and the speed fell back to the legal limit, with all the dials winding down to sensibility. Oh for Germany, autobahns and no limit, I thought. But it was not out and out speed that interested me, rather the blistering acceleration that was available to get through traffic with ease, and push on effortlessly.

Within an hour or so, Burghley House and Stamford came up on the right. A quick early bite at the 'George,' a fascinating old coaching Inn on the A1, then on up to Yorkshire, towards Ripon and the turn off into the Dales. Another twenty miles further up, I thought and I would be at the Catterick Garrison, where I had first served all those years ago. The signs now indicated to Ripon and I pulled off to the left, enjoying the sheer power as I flattened the accelerator on the exit from the roundabout. Twenty minutes and I would be home.

The landscape was now giving way to small woodlands in green deep valleys, topped with brown moorland in the distance, lambs played in the fields, cattle grazed contentedly, and the odd cock pheasant scratched for grit at the roadside. The Daimler would loose its shine now, for tractors leaving gateways dropped mud on the roads as they spread muck on the fields.

I glanced at my Ulysse and noted it had taken twenty three minutes from the A1 as I was turning into the black wrought iron gates of home. I stopped the car and looked, taking in the scene before me. A drive full of holes, lined with Italian variegated poplars. Hell! they've grown, I thought, casting my mind back, they'd been planted many years earlier, specially imported from Northern Italy, they gave off a beautiful aroma in the summer evenings, quite unique. I drove slowly now, down the drive, looking at the cold sandstone grit walls of the Long House, its small mullioned windows making it look dark, with chimneys towering skyward. A Peacock rested on the roof of the stable block. It all looked like history itself, but it was plain to see that it was in need of a lot of work, and expense, to put it back to how it was in my childhood, and before, and that was only the house. Lord knows what the land was going to be like. But I felt content, if a little apprehensive of my new life. I pulled round to the front of the house, the gravel crumbling under the wide tyres, then stopping, I turned the key and killed the engine. Absolute peace.

As I climbed out, a door of the house opened and out bounded our Red Setter, followed closely by Camilla and two spaniels. Wide eyed and jodhpur clad, she threw her arms round me; I hugged her close and kissed her forehead. I wondered how long this would last; I wondered if she appreciated how much work had to be done. How would she react to me working at home? However, best foot forward! I slapped her bottom, patted the dogs, and walked into the house. The sight was welcoming, old low oak beams, old furniture, dark settles and dressers, long refectory table and a peat and log fire burning in the inglenook fire place. I remembered now, as a young boy how I could stand in it and look all the way up to the sky. The aroma of peat permeated the entrance hall, a Burmese cat poked its head out of the log box, and not liking the disturbance, it gave its distinctive call. It was just as if we were going back in time, if only we could.

Camilla poured us both a glass of Tio Pepe, and I started hauling my cases inside, as Camilla tried to bring me up to date with everything in about fifteen minutes. That would have been about a year a minute.

I was already exhausted, and glad to go into the gun-room to unpack more personal items. A beautifully cool second floor room oozing history and ambience, trophies from a bygone age hung on the walls. I looked up at some of the sad beautiful creatures, such a shame, I thought. The polished oak gun racks were full of old sporting shot guns and rifles, three generations of them now, but I thought as I unpacked them, my guns were for a different purpose. Checking they were clean, I put the favourite Sig 9mm Parabellum, the Beretta 308 9mm, and the Auto Mag 44 into the safe, the magazines and ammunition plus silencer into a locked drawer.

That night we went out, and talked of the future, the plans for the estate, the shooting, the fishing, joint farming prospects and equestrian ideas. Ways in which we could earn money to support ourselves and the future.

Over the next five or six months I worked tirelessly, from dawn till dusk throwing myself into all aspects of country life. The estate was improving, fences were done, the house was repaired, and we had our first Horse Trial in under a month, things looked quite rosy. I hadn't missed London as much as I thought I would, and I had never heard from Tina since the day I left, just as well. I was happy.

Twenty-Four

Then one morning, just after coffee, the peace and tranquillity was shattered as the phone came to life. It was Stuart from London, he was in a call box and obviously distressed. Speaking quickly and urgently, he gave me a number to ring him back, another phone box, and requested that I also do the same, in twelve minutes time. The phone went dead. For a minute I stood there listening to the dialling tone, then I replaced the receiver slowly, thinking what to do. Then, moving quickly, I called to Camilla, shouting that I would be out for about half an hour. The thing was now, where was there a phone box within twelve minutes from here? And the clock was already ticking.

I piled into the Daimler and powered it down the drive, pleased that I had spent money on having the drive re-surfaced. Once out of the gates I powered it towards the village, a big car to thrust down these narrow lanes, often single car width, no turbo whine today, they roared in aggressive response to my urgent need, the brake pedal becoming spongy as the heat built up on the discs and the fluid tried to boil.

Nearly there, past the old Church and to the village green, I was at the phone box by the pub in ten and a half minutes. Leaping out, I fumbled for change and the piece of crumpled paper with the number on.

As I dialled in the number, I could hear the click and the tick of heat expanded tortured metal cooling on the Daimler. The phone was answered immediately.

'Stuart,' I said, 'What's all this cloak and dagger stuff about, what's the problem?'

'Big,' Stuart said. 'Very big, we have to meet urgently, we have one minute on this phone so I'll do the talking. Certain people down here think you have sold us out.'

'What,' I screamed, horrified.

'Well, as you know, you've taken early retirement, you've reportedly spent a lot of money on your family estate, you bought your car, you spent money on it, now some people think that's pretty big money.'

'But I ...'

'Quiet time is paramount!' he boomed. 'The Carlos II file is missing or at least it is not complete, and certainly your computer does not have all the information that it did.'

'I could have copied,' I shouted quickly 'No need to ...' I didn't finish as I was shouted down again by Stuart.

'The O M is unaware of this at the moment. As I'm Liam's superior, he's initially come to me, but it won't be for long. He is also not happy with other aspects of your work, and I have to tell you he is pushing for your immediate arrest.'

'Arrest!' I screamed.

'Listen hard,' Stuart said. 'I'll give you another number, 428000 same code. Ring me at six prompt, the conversation will last one minute.' The phone went dead.

Walking slowly from the phone box, I was aware now that I was sweating profusely. I leant on the Daimler collecting my thoughts. What the hell was happening? With a sigh, I drove slowly back to the estate. Turning on the air-conditioning, it hissed momentarily before the welcome coolness flooded into the saloon. My mind was searching for possibilities, was it suspicions, or just a mistake, and by whom, and why?

There was little point in trying to work for the rest of the morning. Lunch time came, but I just pushed food around my plate, my mind full of the conversation that I'd had with Stuart.

Camilla was leaning on the Aga, looking at me.

'The tranquillity and pleasantness hasn't lasted long, has it? You're like a Bear with a sore head and arse. If you don't mind, I'll go riding this afternoon and get some wind in my hair, and clear my brain as you keep telling me to do,' she said sarcastically.

'There's nothing in the fridge, so if I don't see you before early evening, we'll go down to the wine bar at

7.30, in the far village. HELLO!' she shouted to get my attention, 'That is if you are interested.'

I smiled a little distractedly.

'Er, yes, that'll be fine,' letting her saunter off to the stables, I needed to be on my own now. In the cool quiet of the gun room, now my office, I mulled the problem over, looking up now for guidance to the picture of Father in its new position. However I paced back and forth, there was no escape from those eyes.

I decided it was prudent to put a line indicator on to the phone, to check if the phone line was tapped, I also set up the tape machine. From now on all calls would be monitored, and I also activated the surveillance cameras round the house, and set them to record. I wanted to ring Sue, my old secretary in London, to see if she knew of anything, but it wasn't worth the risk of suspicion falling on her. I'd wait till I'd spoken to Stuart.

I set out early to make the call to Stuart, I would need more time now, having decided to go to a different village this time, and by a different route, not knowing what I was up against, there was no point in leaving anything to chance. I mustn't be seen to be doing anything unusual, normality was the order of the day. I walked out to the Daimler, gravel crunching under my feet, and drove slowly down the line of poplars. I turned left, and closed the electric gates this time, my mind desperate to know what Stuart would have to say. Yorkshire seemed so distant from London and its problems.

I was at the phone five minutes early, bang on six I punched in his number. As ever, it was answered instantly.

'Stuart.'

'Yes, listen. We need to meet urgently, things haven't changed, your successor blames you for the anomalies, and yes we are missing details. Technically it was I who discovered it, not him, therefore I am going to diarise a meeting with you tomorrow for the world to see in my diary, but in actual fact we'll meet the day after, Thursday, out of London, up near Oxford, it's a lovely old hotel, 'The Manor,' at Weston on the Green. Book there for yourself as a husband and wife, use another name. I'll be there at about seven p.m. don't ask for me by name, and cover your tracks, Kit.' The phone went dead.

I leant back in the phone box, who would try and pull a stunt like this? The problem is that it may very well stick, but what had they to gain I wondered? Everything I did was on record and in good order, but if some of the records had gone, I was the only one who knew.

I arrived at the gates suddenly and in a flurry, my drive home had been as if on auto pilot, I had been so absorbed I could hardly remember the drive. As the gates opened, I could see the house in the background, mown lawns, hedges clipped now, all sheltering in the lee of colourful woodland. I could see why it would all cast suspicions, if only they knew.

I walked into the great hall, poured a scotch and soda, turned and stood staring into the fire. Always a fire in this house I thought, as a log shuffled and sparks disappeared up the deep black throat of the inglenook. Somewhere in the distance a Church clock struck seven, pheasants cackled as they went to roost, water was turned on in the house. Camilla would be filling a bath after riding, oblivious to the events of the day. I turned and walked up the stairs, tired now, glancing at the old oil painting of a stag alone on a hill with steam coming from his nostrils. As a child, I had often wondered where his herd was, he stood there alone. I knew how he felt.

'We've to be there by 7.30,' Camilla shouted, 'The wine bar.'

'Yes,' I said wearily. Your little world awaits, I thought. 'Won't take a minute,' I answered. Damn! I didn't want to go.

When I came down stairs she was already in the car, waiting. We drove in silence.

'I do hope you are not going to be boring,' she said, 'Our friends are there.' Yours, I thought, still, make the best of it; I had another day to wait before I had to meet Stuart.

As we approached the village, I could see the light of the restaurant twinkling. I dropped Camilla off at the door, and parked in an inconspicuous spot, not in the lights, and facing the road to leave.

Camilla was already at the bar, surrounded by her friends and would be acquaintances. I could hear the county accents, and the high pitched laughter, so often associated with the horsy crowd. I smiled to myself, the whole place was full of bridles, tennis rackets, damp handshakes and nipped arse waiters, not to mention the insincere smile of the proprietor. I always became a little cynical in this sort of place, blackboards ceiling to floor, displaying the largest menu that you have ever seen, written in small print with chalk, proclaiming fresh fish of the day. Which day? I thought. Willingly I accepted a glass of bright red wine, which must on its travels very recently have passed through Burgundy. It was virtually impossible to hold an intelligent conversation with anybody, so the answer was to keep shaking hands, filling glasses, smiling, shouting, and restraining ones self from falling down the ample cleavages on offer, the only highlight on the horizon.

After a while I spotted an old friend in the corner, quietly watching events. He was a professional diver, who recently had persuaded me to keep my diving certificate up to date. It was easy to train in the forces, but civvie street had been different. I was about to let it lapse, but his support had been welcome, and I had kept at it. He was a typical diver, strong, broad necked and barrel-chested. His down to earth conversation was a welcome relief. However, after a while, Camilla hollered me over, back into society. She had selected a table with eight others, and as I had been preoccupied, ordered my meal for me, fish and tarragon pie. It was pleasant enough, but try as I would, I could not concentrate, my mind was on Stuart and the problems which lay ahead.

As it became late, it was becoming obvious to others that I was struggling with my thoughts. Camilla looked at me, took the cue, asked for the bill, and we bade our farewells. Once outside into the cool of the night air, I felt more at home, it was a merciful relief. I flicked the remote control and heard the door lock open, but, as the lights momentarily flashed, my eye caught sight of something along the road behind the car, no lights, just a brief reflection. I watched, but said nothing as I held the door open for Camilla, closed it and went around to my door, all the time turning my head to watch the spot where I had seen the reflection. Once inside, she said.

'Bored?' then without giving me time to answer, 'Why do you always hide your car out of the way?'

'Force of habit,' I said being noncommittal.

I turned the key, and whilst watching in the mirror, dabbed the brakes. A red glow lit up the road behind, there was nothing, nothing there at all. It was my imagination; I'd been in the service too long. Turning on the lights, we drew into the main road and made for home. Camilla was full of herself, the tennis club, horses, the people. I smiled at her and held her knee, at least she was happy. Once more I looked in the mirror, still nothing. I relaxed for a while, enjoying the drive along desolate country roads, driving a little quicker all the while. Then whilst going deep into a favourite corner, I heaved on the brakes at the last moment, and almost casually checked the rear view mirror, then I saw it. Blurred, yes, but it was surely the chrome grill of another car, there were no lights, just a dim flash of chrome. I said nothing to Camilla, knowing that she would turn around instantly, whoever it was following would know we were suspicious. I started to accelerate now, to speed up events. The more I increased speed, the more chance of a give away. And sure enough, reflections showed in the mirrors, whoever was tailing us was having to use its brakes, a red glimmer now and again was being reflected back from the hedge row, some distance behind. As we powered on through the country, the turbos' whine becoming a roar, we easily had the legs of whoever it was, but this was not the answer. Who actually was it?

As I howled into a bend and trod hard on the brakes, as luck would have it the exhaust's gases flamed out at the rear with a 'pop'. The sudden illumination showed the chrome flutes of a Daimler grille glistening momentarily. I had a dull recollection that I might have seen this car before. No, there were hundreds of them, but not all following me, this was too much of a coincidence. I powered on harder now, to force him or her into a mistake. Camilla snapped out of her euphoric alcohol daze and shouted her disapproval as we flashed past farms and gateways, while gnarled old trees that had lined these roads for centuries nodded disapprovingly in the slip stream, looking like bowed old men ready to pounce.

Knowing now precisely where I was, I mentally ticked off the distance to the house gates, and as they came up I stamped hard on the brakes once more, the anti-lock brakes kicking back up through the pedal. The lane being barely wide enough for the two, we were suddenly lit with a blaze of light, for the car behind had nowhere to go. Its lights now on, it had nowhere to hide, there was a screech of brakes and shredding rubber as a blue Daimler slithered past in a cloud of burnt rubber and dust. It was nigh impossible to see the occupants because of the head rests and tinted glass, but there were certainly two. As it flashed by, I memorised the number, and then the car was gone. Only the smell of burnt rubber and the echo of tortured mechanisms were left drifting in the cool night air.

'Who the hell was that?' Camilla shrieked, nervous now.

I made light of it, apologising that I didn't realise how close the gates were. Opening the gates, we slowly entered the grounds and there was the scent of the poplars, a pleasant tranquil change.

Twenty-Five

The following day, over breakfast I broke the news to Camilla that I was going down to Oxford the next day. She actually looked worried.

'It's to do with last night isn't it, that car, you were being followed, weren't you? God! Kit, when will these spooks leave us alone,' she said in genuine anguish, 'I can't live your life, Kit, what do you do? You never tell me, and your Father never did,' she said with feeling.

'There is just some sort of clerical error that needs sorting,' I said, stretching the truth. I knew she wasn't convinced, she deserved better, but not now, not till everything was clear. I gave her a kiss, and asked if there was any chance of a coffee in the gun room. She relented with a smile.

'Just this once.'

Sitting at my desk, I played back the security tapes of last night, and whilst watching the screen, picked up the phone and dialled my contact at the local Police station.

'Any favours today?' I asked the Superintendent.

'Cost you,' was the reply, laconic as ever.

I gave him the number and the type of the car. It was pointless, I knew what the answer would be, but I had to check anyway.

Fifteen minutes later, the phone sprang into life and my suspicions were confirmed.

'No known vehicle, not even a number close to it. Kit, I thought you'd retired anyway?'

'I have. That's why I'm ringing you,' I joked thanking him for his help, and replaced the receiver. As I expected, I thought, but who could it be? And why? I was not exactly operational, or in hiding, people had only to ask locally to find out where I lived, it was no secret. Anne arrived with my coffee, smiling pensively. However, not much more I could do now, till the appointed hour with Stuart.

The following day came without further contact from Stuart, or any repercussions from the night before, and in some ways I started to discount the Daimler. Just a kid out for the night, I thought, and chasing a similar car, complacency is dangerous, but what had I to fear? I'd toyed with the idea of changing cars for the drive down to Weston, but preferring my own, comfort won and vanity won. So just after midday I bade farewell to Camilla and set off heading south for the M1 and Oxfordshire, leaving the peace of the Yorkshire countryside behind, and wondering desperately what news Stuart would have for me.

By early evening and having made reasonable time, I was on the A 43 approaching Weston on the

Green. To my left lay an old World War II fighter air-field, old Nissen huts still in evidence, and a large grey barrage balloon anchored to a mobile winch showed that the field was now used for parachute training. I wondered how many of the old pilots were left and if they ever visited their old base?

My wandering thoughts nearly made me miss the sign and the entrance to 'The Manor,' as it came up quickly on the left without any warning. Swinging briskly into the drive and slowing, I was somewhat taken aback by the magnificence of this old medi-eval manor, nearly hidden amongst mature gardens and tall beech trees. On a dark wintry night it would be very sinister indeed, even on this summer's eve-ning lights from within flickered through small lead latticed windows. Rooks circled above tall pointed roofs, and octagonal chimneys scowled back at me. Typical of Stuart, I noted there was no sign of his car. So, being the first here, I put the Daimler incon-spicuously to the rear, out of sight in the old cobbled coaching yard.

Climbing out and taking my overnight bag, I stretched as I looked round and noted the rear en-trance, and a fire escape to the second floor. Locking the car, I walked through the walled garden and round to the imposing front entrance, memorising what I had seen. It was strangely quiet save for the squeak of a small branch scratching a window above in the evening breeze, and the hoarse call of jackdaws somewhere in the eaves. Through a low stone arched doorway I could see reception dwarfed by the imposing entrance hall, walls hung alternately with huge old oils in gilded frames and crossed swords with shields, ones you probably could not even lift. And like home even in summer, a fire smouldering, soot hanging like black wool from an iron spit across the deep fireplace.

A huge black Great Dane lay on a threadbare rug in front of the fire, its unusually pointed ears twitched as its startlingly bright amber eyes watched me intently without moving its head.

I rang the polished brass bell and within moments, an aged sallow faced retainer appeared, wearing an equally aged morning suit, but he was more than helpful, and eventually, I was sure, he would smile. I booked in under the name of John Dawson, saying that my wife would join me later. As he filled the form in for me, I idly took in an arresting detail from the hotel brochure. Mad Maud, it stated, had been burnt at the stake here.

'Who was Mad Maud?' I asked.

'Well, sir, now there's a tale,' came back the old but well practised tone, and he shuffled his feet to get comfortable for the tale. I knew the warning signs, and quickly said.

'Well, just the outline'.

He looked disappointed in me, but continued.

'Mad Maud, sir, was a nun, a nun, sir who was caught out.'

220

'Indeed,' I said with a smile, 'naughty girl' I raised my eyebrows in mock horror.

'Most certainly,' he said, disapprovingly. 'Had some kind of an affair, so they burnt her at the stake, right there,' he said, pointing with a wavering bony and bent arthritic finger towards the little tall thin window, that looked on to the small grass circle in front of the hotel.

'You see, she'd let her Order down, let the faithful, her followers down, sold them out. Even by today's standards,' he said with emphasis, staring hard at me, quite unnervingly, as my mind had wandered off to my own problem.

'Thank you, that's fine, number seven, I'll find my own way,' I said, looking at the gold lettered sign, and heading for the stairs.

'An evening paper, sir?' came the call after me, followed by 'Number seven's haunted sir, Mad Maud, you know.'

'Just the papers in the morning,' I answered, anxious only to leave him and Maud to their own devices.

I climbed the old dark stair way, with still more paintings of unknown figures from the past looking down at me. On the landing a long case grandfather clock chimed six o'clock, the spindles whirring as they released the weights powering the chimes. That done, silence returned save for the slow methodical dull tick.

Somewhere in the distance the branch still

scratched a window. The doors along the corridor were all at different angles, but all of old and solid oak. I found number seven, turned the large old fashioned key and stepped in to find a tasteful room overlooking the front, complete with period furniture and a four poster bed. Time had stood still.

I had a shower, poured a Scotch from the hospitality tray, and changed for the evening.

Looking out of the window again, there was still no car I recognised, but as it was now nearly seven I decided to go down to the bar and wait. Closing the door behind me I walked down the corridor to the top of the stairs. Suddenly there was a creak behind me; I turned swiftly to see Stuart standing there. He looked years older than the last time we had met, he seemed grey and gaunt. He took a long hard look at me, for a moment he did not smile.

'Where the hell have you come from,' I asked, breaking the ice.

'I'm checked in next door to you, number six.'

'Have you come by car?' I queried.

Then, as if now relieved to see me, and as if making some judgement, he slapped me on the shoulder and said.

'Come on, let's have a drink.'

We sat opposite each other in two large wing chairs, the fire now crackling brightly, with sparks rushing up the monstrous dark throat of the fireplace. Soon our drinks arrived, two whiskies. I sat without uttering a word, mesmerised by what Stuart had to say, just turning the cut glass tumbler thoughtfully in my hand and watching the amber liquor glint in the reflection of the flames.

The story that Stuart told me was difficult to comprehend, it seemed totally unbelievable that after all these years my integrity should be doubted, after all I had worked and strived for. Now my efforts seemed to be under some kind of review.

'It's not that I have a suspicion or any kind of doubt in you, Kit' Stuart said. 'Neither does the Old Man, but Kit there are vital documents missing, and they were totally in your care.'

'Or latterly in Liam's,' I interjected.

'That's true,' said Stuart, 'and it is he who is banging the drum, actually calling for your arrest. Or he was,' Stuart said pointedly. 'Nothing will happen now, until I have done my report and there has been an investigation. At least, I imagine that's what will happen.'

'An arrest, an investigation.' I exclaimed again. 'But what about the computer back up files, the information is there, that can't all have vanished?'

'That's true, and that is one thing in your favour, but it would appear that not all of the information is there, some files are missing, or have been deleted, and in any event you really need both sets of information, the documents and the computer files, to get the whole picture. One doesn't work without the other.'

'What beats me, is why would anyone want the whole picture, what is there to be gained?' I said. 'I can remember most of the relevant information anyway; I wouldn't need to take the files away with me.'

Stuart raised a quietening hand.

'That's just it! That is precisely what the Old Man said, nevertheless the files are missing and so somebody, maybe to take the heat off themselves, wants your head to roll.'

'So who? Or what?' I said.

'Also, Kit do you realise what you have just said? You are the only one who knows all the details without the files, that puts you in a very vulnerable position, you must be very careful now.'

We were interrupted by the head waiter, holding forth two menus, large scrolls of antique parchment. I had no stomach for dinner, but Stuart as indefatigable as ever grasped his with vigour.

'Not coming all the way here and not eating,' he said, 'It's excellent here,' and gestured to me to get on with it. 'Hell, I know it's nothing to do with you, so let's eat. We will continue our conversation in the dining room.'

The head waiter led us through into a long tall and timbered medieval banqueting hall, with a wonderful maze of beams, king posts and joists supporting the ceiling. The setting was completed by a minstrels' gallery at the far end, and long candle lit dining tables down the centre of the room. Stuart asked the head waiter to put us at a table in the corner where we could be quite alone.

'Stuart, how do you find these places,' I asked.

'Just a hobby of mine, we all have to eat so let's make it interesting, that's my view,' he said. 'You never know when it may all end, Kit you never know.'

We ordered traditional Yorkshire pudding with rabbit and onion gravy to start, followed by roast sirloin of beef and a bottle of Chateau Margaux. After he had departed with our order we sat in silence for a moment.

'Right, Stuart, let me go through this again. After I leave the service everything is quiet, no problems, yes? Then out of the blue the balloon goes up purely and simply because of one missing file. I know it's serious, but why is 'he making' so much fuss? And why, or how, did 'he' notice that specific file or files were gone? What was 'he' doing looking at those files anyway? What was 'his' interest? Those files have been dead and buried for some time now.'

'You're quite right, Kit it's something that has been bothering me for some time now, and with that in mind I have set up a small internal inquiry as to why, and what, Liam may have been, or is working on. It is fortuitous for you, us, that he has had to go away on holiday, it was booked some time ago, and he is away for approximately two weeks, everything looks quite normal. This internal investigation on Liam; it is not going to be easy for me, it is quite irregular and will take a little bit of covering up, especially regarding somebody working at his level, but Kit, I am prepared to do it.'

'I thank you for that,' I said.

'I am doing nothing but my job,' Stuart said, raising an eye brow. 'As I said I, don't believe for one moment that you are culpable, but I am coming to believe that you may be a scapegoat for something that may prove to be infinitely more sinister than either of us imagine. Remember this; I would be in deep shit if anyone knew that I had told you any of this, or that you are under investigation. Not even the Old Man knows I am here, my diarized meeting with you for yesterday was to be an open discussion in London, nobody knows that it did not take place.'

'Ironical though that you yourself asked for an update on Carlos II just before I left?' I said quizzically.

'Wondered when you would mention that,' he smiled. 'But as you will remember that directive came from the top, the Old Man.'

'Yes, I saw the memo.'

We both sat quietly for a while.

'The Old Man perhaps knows more than he is giving away,' I said.

Stuart looked at me.

'Maybe,' it would not be unusual.

Once again, we were interrupted as the head waiter arrived with a magnificent silver carving trolley, displaying a superb side of beef, and another with the 'Yorkshires,' hot in a silver dish over a spirit lamp. We sat in silence as we were served. Stuart tasted the Margaux, and accepted it, then after the wine waiter had left, looking thoughtfully at me he said.

'What state will the cargo be in?'

'I was just wondering that, it's been bothering me since you rang,' I said. 'I watched her go down, she went down straight enough, and slowly, and it is very shallow there, very shallow, she could even be lying upright. I never did open the containers fully, far too much wheat on top, but the Navy chaps got one open, and said it was the devil of a job to get into it. So, the canisters were water proof, but waterproof to what depth? I don't know, there's a fair chance, you know, that they could be serviceable'.

'Are they retrievable?' Stuart asked.

'Everything is possible,' I said. 'But it would be a hell of a job; you'd need some heavy lifting gear, and a competent diving team.'

'The exact location was in the file?' Stuart said, concerned.

'Approximate,' I said, 'she lies southwest of Lampedusa on the Sicilian Banks. But any decent sized trawler has a fish finding sonar that could locate the wreck.'

'You're sure she was not going to Malta.'

'Fine time to ask me now,' I laughed. 'But no, definitely not, the charts on the bridge indicated that she was more or less heading for Tripoli or

Benghazi. That's what finally prompted me to sink her on the spot, it was after all a covert operation, we didn't have the time to remove the packing cases, and Stuart, don't forget we might have been in range of some form of missile system. No, it was the right thing to do.'

'I like the situation even less, Kit' and after a thoughtful pause, 'even less.'

We completed the meal in relative silence; my heart was not in it, but the Margaux was superb, and lifted me somewhat.

'We have covered a lot of ground,' Stuart finally said. 'But there is a lot more to unravel.'

I knew there was. To start with, I hadn't mentioned the Daimler that had followed me the previous night, another nagging question. But there was no point at this stage in loading him up with more worries.

'How far will you go with the investigation of Liam,' I asked.

'All the way, I think. I'm very uneasy with him, surprisingly we don't know too much about his lineage, which is odd really, and the Old Man does not like that. But that said, he does a good job,' and after another pause, 'I think,' he said, smiling wistfully.

Stuart looked at up as the head waiter trundled toward us with the cheese trolley,

'Cheese, Kit?'

'No, I think not. I'm not really in the mood.'

Stuart shook his head at the waiter.

'Diet, you know.'

'Coffee and liqueurs, gentlemen?' the waiter said.

Stuart looked at me,

'No thanks, I'll refrain, I need my brains for to-morrow,' I said with certain finality.

It was the first time in years that we had ever left a table without liqueurs. Stuart rose like Atlas with the weight of the world on his shoulders. I even wondered if he had told me all he knew.

'I shall be leaving early in the morning,' Stuart said, 'so as to be in the office at the usual time. We'll meet again in a few days when I've sorted this out. It's all so highly irregular, maybe because I can't believe you've left us.'

'In the meantime, I'll see if I can come up with anything for you,' I said.

'Just you be careful, Kit you could well be the lynch pin in this one, as you are the only one who knows everything.'

Stuart went off towards reception; I climbed the huge staircase once more, boards creaking under foot, history staring back at me from the gilded frames. I hesitated at the top, and turned to say good night, but of Stuart there was no sign.

I walked down the twisted corridor with its uneven door frames; a strangely quiet hotel, I thought, as I opened the door to my room, there are so few guests.

For no real reason other than the force of habit, I dragged the chest of drawers across the back of the door. I didn't trust locks in hotels, and I needed a relaxing sleep, which surprisingly I got.

Twenty-Six

The following morning I woke early, with sun streaming through the narrow mullioned windows and the birds singing in the tall beech trees outside. I showered quickly, dressed, and pulled the chest away from the door. There was a click! The door handle had been forced into the down position, and stuck behind the chest, now on moving the chest it had sprung back. Odd, I thought, had somebody tried the door? Or had I jammed it by mistake last night?

Anyway, I was in a rush as I wanted to catch Stuart before he left, so closing the door I went quickly down to the breakfast room. There was no sign of him there, indeed there was no one in evidence, save for the clatter of plates in the distant Kitchens, it was too early for most people.

I decided to pay the bill and return straight to Yorkshire. I resisted the temptation to ask the receptionist whether Stuart had gone, as I remembered he had paid his bill last night. Walking to the front of the Manor I recognised none of the cars, so without further ado I collected my things and made my way via the back stairs to the Daimler. The Daimler started instantly and letting out the clutch I purred down the drive, listening to the crisp ripple of gravel beneath the tyres.

It was now eight o'clock and a bright morning, but I realised that I was a little late for a good run north. On the A 43 the traffic would be busy, damn! I turned left out of the drive and goading the big V12 into action, sped north. The trip was quite uneventful; I stopped off at Wetherby to buy some fishing tackle, and a small present for Camilla from the saddlery. I knew the road well, and even with the problems on my mind, today was no exception. I always enjoyed the last few miles of exhilarating driving before reaching home.

As I swung through the gates, to my amazement I could see people milling about at the end of the drive. I slowed momentarily to take in the scene, looking across to the front of the house, and there, virtually on the lawn, stood a helicopter, a khaki painted Westland Wessex. Standing next to it, and as if to attention, was a man in army uniform. More people stood by a car, a Ford Scorpio with its doors open, and two police officers in uniform stood in the arched doorway of my house. As I drew nearer, I could see that the car also had military plates.

As I came to a standstill in front of them, with a crunch of tyres on the gravel, Camilla burst through the assembly, I could see that she was distraught and in tears. I launched myself out of the car and she fell into my arms, she looked up at me, mascara running down her cheeks.

'Stuart's dead! Stuart's dead!' she screamed, her body shaking with emotion. I looked over her shoulder at the police officers, my mouth dry, my body suddenly sweating.

'How the hell, what is this, he can't be, there's a mistake, he's a fantastic driver, he doesn't make mistakes, I was with him last night,' I gabbled. I could feel Camilla's tears seeping through my shirt, she pulled away, looking at me, her mouth moving but not uttering, she grabbed me again.

'He's been murdered,' she wailed, 'I heard them talking.'

I felt a strong grip on my shoulder. I turned, and realised I was facing a Police Superintendent. This was serious.

'I'm sorry, sir, we have to talk. I'll brief you, and then you'll have to go.'

'Go where?' I said.

'With them,' nodding at the Wessex.

The other officer led Camilla away, saying.

'We'll get someone to stay with her, sir.'

I slumped onto the bonnet of the Daimler; looking out across the fields, thinking of Stuart's last words.

'I'm very sorry, but apparently there's been an

unpleasant incident. He's been murdered at a hotel called 'The Manor' at … '

'I know where it is,' I barked, then taking a deep breath, 'I'm sorry, come inside, I need a coffee.'

'You were with him last night, sir?'

'Yes, I was, but how did you know so quickly?'

'Bit out of my brief really sir, but I gather that the gentleman concerned, as some form of security, had told his secretary that he was seeing you, and that if he didn't ring her at 8 a.m. she was to inform the O M, I think you should call him.

He rang the hotel and that's when the room was checked, and here we are.'

Who the hell had Stuart been afraid of? Surely not me, he had given no indication that he was the least bit dubious about me, rather anxious for my welfare I thought.

Leaning against the Aga, I poured us both a strong black coffee.

'So, please tell me more.'

'It's a bit difficult for me sir, we only know what we were told over the telephone and so the information is a little second hand, but apparently, you had dinner last night with the gentleman?'

'You know that?'

'At the Manor?'

'Yes, yes. But how do you know its murder?'

'A garrotte sir, cheese wire or something, apparently it's not pleasant to look at.'

'Oh my God!' I said. 'What bastard would do that?' In a millisecond my mind responded, one I will find I said to myself.

'They want you down there as soon as possible,' and as if by remote control I heard the Benelux starter crack in on the Wessex and engage the turbines to start to wind up, followed by the slow beat of the blades as they rotated gathering speed. I went upstairs to say goodbye to Camilla, and tell her that I would only be away for a matter of hours. She looked devastated, she lay on the bed shaking and looked up at me in total disbelief.

'How are you implicated?' she sniffed, 'I heard one of them say that you must be the first in line, because you were the last one to see him.'

'Who did?' I snapped.

'The senior one, all pips and braid, he rang London from here,' she sobbed.

'We'll see about that,' I said bending down to kiss her; 'I'll be back tonight.'

I walked down the stairs, I just could not believe my lifelong friend was dead. There had to be a mistake. The sound of the Wessex now reverberated through the house, the stench of burnt avtur drifted in, the police officer stood by the door waiting for me.

'We'll leave someone here, sir, till you er, return,' he said a little hesitantly.

'Thank you, I'd appreciate that. It shouldn't take long,' I said. He looked at me dubiously.

Pulling myself together, I collected my jacket from the Daimler and strode across the lawn to the helicopter, ducking under the rotors as I went. The door was held open for me, I climbed in, grabbed a head set and clipped myself in, calling to the Captain in the pilot's seat.

'OK, let's get going.' Because of the restricted area we climbed vertically out from the site, trees and shrubs swirling, then the countryside panorama becoming visible, a green patch work displayed all around us as we gained height. Ripon and its Cathedral came into view, the nose dipped, we picked up speed and headed south, climbing to about two thousand feet for the trip.

I had little interest in the flight, my mind full of the terrible fate of Stuart, of how long we had known each other, at school, at university, and the missions we had accomplished together in the old days.

Would I have come this far without him? I doubted it, he'd been the conventional operator, the one who played by the rules. I'd been the maverick, the risk taker. I'd protected him though! Twice I'd saved his life and now this.

I resign, I leave the service, and right after that, he's dead. I closed my eyes as they welled with tears, then I reopened them dry-eyed as I thought what I owed him. I knew I would avenge him my resolve would not waver! This now was another ball game. They left me alone with my thoughts.

Time not registered but then the radio crackled into life.

'Here we are, sir, dead ahead,' as the Captain pointed out the old airfield at Weston on the Green, now a parachute training centre, the grey barrage balloon flying high over it. He lowered the collective lever and brought the nose up, simultaneously loosing height and speed, we sank gracefully out of the sky, blades clattering more as the direction of motion changed. As we came closer and moved into the hover I could see three cars parked by the Nissen huts, one a dark green long wheel base Jaguar bristling with aerials, the Old Man.

On the ground, but with the rotors still turning, a dark suited man moved from the side of the O M's Jaguar. He came over to the Wessex and opened my door.

'Morning sir,' I heard through the din, somewhat relieved to hear sir, and know I was not under arrest yet. I unclipped and walked toward the OM. who was now standing by the car.

'Good afternoon, Kit,' he said quietly, extending a hand toward me, not using the familiar 'K.' 'A terrible business!'

I nodded.

'Why have you brought me here, Sir, you don't need me to identify him?'

'No, I don't just one or two things to clear up, and I want you to see the situation, I want it to concentrate your mind.'

'And you actually think I need that?'

He did not answer we both climbed into the rear of the car, the O M closing the glass division between us and the driver.

'It is not a pleasant sight, Kit, but you have to see it, nothing has been touched.'

We travelled the mile to the Manor in silence. There was a police officer at the drive entrance, who saluted as we went past.

'I've closed the hotel,' the O M said distantly.

As we came to a standstill in front of the Manor, our doors were opened by two men in plain clothes, I was not sure whether they were Police or part of the service, but what did it matter. I couldn't help thinking that only hours before I had been having dinner here with Stuart. If he hadn't come here to warn me, maybe this would never have happened?

The O M led the way through the stone-arched doorway into the great reception hall. All the staff were seated round the walls, and everyone stared at me as I walked in. Some I recognised from the night before, and they nodded in recognition, others huddled and whispered their premature judgements.

'This way,' the O M said, motioning in the direction of the stairs. As I climbed, the faded eyes of the portraits seemed to smoulder and follow me in disapproval. The clock still ticked its solemn beat, like the sound of a drum beating its slow cadence as the victims were led to the guillotine. Taking a deep breath, I moved on, the floor creaking as it had last night. There was a police officer at the door to number six, I hesitated for a moment, nodded 'Good afternoon' at him, and walked in.

All my years of training could not have prepared me for what I saw and I had seen plenty.

A shaft of sunlight through the lattice window played on the bed and illuminated the scene. Stuart was half on, half off the bed, his eyes bulged, one terribly so, it appeared not to be in its socket, a swollen purple tongue, bitten, with blood congealed, puffed out of his mouth in an agonising death grin. His right hand was trapped under the wire that had cut deep into his throat, fingers driven under the wire and into his own neck and skin, in a desperate last effort for breath.

'I've not seen the use of a Garrotte since Algiers' I muttered, the O M raised an eyebrow as if some distant memory cell had been jogged. I walked to the window and composed myself, then turned. The Stuart I knew no longer existed, it was now I had to lean on strength and training, this was a job, a battle, and one I had and knew I would win.

The O M and a doctor I knew worked for the Department stood looking at me. The O M closed the door behind him.

'The time of death would be about one p.m.,' the doctor said, 'Not a fight or scuffle, so somebody he knew, I think.'

I looked up at the O M, he was watching me intently, looking for any sign or twitch.

'Maybe they chatted for a while? And then, well as said with not too much of a tussle. The assailant stood behind him and took him by surprise. The garrotte was definitely applied from behind.'

I concurred. His clothes were those he had worn last night, they were not disarranged. I came over to the bed for a closer look.

'Anything missing, do you think?'

'No, it doesn't look like it, all his belongings seem to be here, money, wallet, etc.' said the O M.

'I agree with the Doctor. It was someone he knew' said the O M'

I walked to the bathroom, then remembering, said.

'May I?'

'Go ahead,' the O M said.

Everything seemed normal, with no sign of disturbance. I opened his toilet bag, nothing unusual there. I casually opened and sniffed a bottle of Trumper's aftershave lotion that lay amongst his items, a somewhat discreet lime scent that I knew very well.

A voice came from behind me, the O M's.

'M'm, I smelt that, but it's not the same as what lingers in this room, Kit?'

'No,' I said though somewhat thoughtfully, 'it is not, many people been in here?'

'A few,' he said.

M'm, there was a distinct scent in here. My mind searched its archives for help, trying to remember where I had smelt it before. Turning, and moving toward the bed I could see that he was still wearing his watch, his overnight bag also looked as if it hadn't been turned over. Why, why Stuart, I thought?

Going close to the body now and kneeling down, looked carefully at both sides of its neck.

'It's not a garrotte as such, Sir,' I said, 'It's a commercial fox snare, you can buy them anywhere, they self lock, and you can't get them loose,' I said showing the snare's attachment ring.

'Did he smoke ever?' the O M queried.

'Sometimes a cigar,' I said.

'M'm, well there's a cigar here, a Havana but it hasn't been lit, yet there is ash on the floor. We'll check it out, but I reckon it's from a cigarette. Do you smoke, Kit?'

'Sometimes,' I said.

'Cigarettes?'

'Sometimes.'

'Kit were you in here last night? Did you come in here for a night cap?'

'No. I went straight to bed, Stuart wanted an early start. The last time I saw Stuart he had gone to pay his bill. I didn't see Stuart again.'

'There were two glasses in here. One had the remains of a brandy in it, the other a whisky. You drink whisky, don't you?' he said thoughtfully.

'We both did, but not in here. We had them down-stairs, the waiter will remember.'

'He does.'

'You didn't drink up here in the room?'

'No, well, not in here, I had one in my own room when I arrived, a whisky.'

'Definitely not in here?'

'No, look, if you have the two glasses, do a finger print check,' I said, feeling a little ruffled.

'We did,' said the O M.

'And?'

'One was Stuart's.'

'And?'

'The other was yours.'

My world collapsed, but I showed nothing.

'What type were they, cut glass tumblers?'

'No, just the same as you have on the hospitality tray in you room, plain smooth glass. Cut glass is used from the bar down stairs.'

'You will have checked the room I had?'

'Yes.'

'There are two glasses in each room, neither of the two glasses in your room has been used, and neither have your miniature bottles.'

'May I look?'

'You may do as you please, Kit.' I was pleased to hear that!

My room was just as I had left it. I wish I'd tidied the bed a little. The room was virtually identical to Stuart's, but the drink tray was complete and apparently un-touched. Whisky, brandy, gin, mixers, and a book of matches. The glasses were in a cellophane pack, clearly unopened. Some crafty bastard, I thought.

But deep in my mind a bell rang.

Going quickly back to Stuart's room, where were Stuart's matches? There were none on his drinks tray. He had not lit his cigar, but someone had smoked a cigarette. But whose was the ash, did he, she, or them, have the matches?

I held in my hand the new book of matches from my room. I flipped open the cover; it read:

MEDIEVAL
THE MANOR
WESTON ON
THE GREEN

Each cardboard match had a letter from one of the words embossed on its stem, eight matches in a row, eight letters in a row, four rows in total, quite a clever gimmick. I pocketed the book.

There was a cough and a shuffle at the door. I looked up.

'Ah! There you are,' the O M said, and a ferret like man with glasses and a tatty suit, carrying a black bag, shuffled into the room.

'Kit this is Arthur, he has been going over the room.'

'And a lot more to do, too,' he said glowering at me.

I nodded, recognising him now from the past, he cooed like a bloody pigeon, I thought.

'Did you find any matches in this room?'

'No, Sir.'

'Did you find his note book?'

'No, Sir.'

'Pen?'

'No, Sir.'

'He always had it with him, never without it, and his pen, it doubles as a locator.'

'So, then there is something missing!' I snapped, not intentionally wrong footing the O M.

'We tried the locator this morning,' the O M. said, 'and to no avail,' looking at me hard.

'Did he use the note book over dinner?' the O M questioned.

'Don't think so, but literally he never went any-where without it, hated electronic organisers, always committed things to paper.' Paper! My mind jumped, what about his office, I thought.

'I don't like this room,' the O M said, 'shall we go outside, have you seen enough?'

I looked at the little ferret with the black bag.

'Have you found anything at all out of the ordinary?'

'Not yet, sir.'

Neither would he, I knew.

The O M looked at me and then slowly said.

'What about Stuart's watch? I remember you once told me that you had a pact, as you both wear Ulysse Nardin, you left them to each other. Remember?'

'I do, a silly thing, both bought on a giddy day, too much wine in Bond Street. But no. I shall return it to his family, Sir.'

'Quite.'

With that I slowly bent down, and carefully undid the heavy gold clasp, but to my shock, just as it slid it from his hand something fell to the floor

Putting the watch carefully into my jacket pocket, I knelt at his side and there on the floor, nearly under the bed, was a small match, a match torn from the book of complimentary matches that were offered by the hotel and must have been on his drinks tray. Not a used match, one just torn from the book and for some reason secreted under his watch, a watch he knew I would remove. Looking closely at it I could see the single letter 'L' on the stem which came from the word 'medieval'.

I palmed it quietly. No one saw me and I didn't tell the O M, it might have no significance, but why was it under his watch?

'Seen enough?' the O M said quietly.

'For the moment,' I answered, and walked out into the creaking corridor, and headed for the stairs, the outside, and daylight.

Once outside we walked down into the garden,

into the fresh air, warmth, and the scent of flowers. The silence was only disturbed by the hum of the honey bees. It was altogether a stark contrast to that ghastly scene.

Taking a deep breath.

'What now?' I said.

'Well, if I were the police I would be putting you under arrest,' he said, placing his hand on my shoulder. 'You haven't explained away the glass yet, but you will have your reasons, that I know.'

'No, not really,' I said simply. 'At the moment I really can't explain anything, I just don't know.'

He smiled, not believing me leaning against a sundial in the small sunken garden. After a moment he said.

'We both know that it would be counter productive to apprehend you for this investigation. You still have all my numbers?'

'Yes, indeed.'

'Good! I'll give you three days, Kit three days, and then I want some answers. The Wessex will take you back to Yorkshire. Good luck, and speak to me, and me only. And soon.'

'Thank you, Sir, you can trust me.'

I know.

Walking to the tall armoured glass fronted oak gun cabinet; I slid open the drawers as I had done so many times before, and started to select what I thought might be needed over the next few days. I took the Sig. 9mm and the .380 Beretta, a polychromide holster, the bullet pen, infra-red glasses, laser torch, miniature camera, a radio bug, and other paraphernalia that I had collected over the years.

It was sad that it was Stuart's death that had goaded me back into action, and deep down but now I was getting a buzz, the adrenaline was beginning to flow already, even the tastes of my mouth and changed, it does.

Camilla called up the stairs that dinner was ready. I ignored her for the moment as I started to check what equipment I had, once in the field any defects could be life threatening, spares would be impossible to obtain. There was a cough behind me, I turned to find Camilla standing there offering me a glass of wine.

'You're packing all those horrible things again,' she said, looking at what lay on the table, and eyeing my passport wallet, which she knew held more than one.

'Better to be safe than sorry,' I said, taking the glass from her, and pulling a cloth over the pistols. 'Come on, we'll go downstairs,' and I led her out of the 'inner sanctum,' as she sometimes called it.

Dinner was a quiet affair, mostly in silence interrupted only by Camilla saying that she had rung some friends as I had suggested, and was now going to stay in Cornwall for a few days with the Quarrels.

A good name I thought, remembering the last time I had been in their company. I told her that I had arranged for her to borrow a car for the trip, a good one to please her, and we would leave her own car in full view in the open garage for the world to see. It might lead anyone interested to believe that we were at home; mine would be visible at the village garage, on the forecourt perhaps. I doubted that it would fool anyone, but you never know, every little may help.

The following morning, after checking my equipment once again, I turned on the timed lights and surveillance cameras, opened the garage, and generally made the house look lived in. I loaded the Daimler up with Camilla's mountain of luggage, threw my own couple of bags in, and set off for the village. Camilla looked worried and said nothing.

That was until she saw her loan car with its hood down on the forecourt, a silver Mercedes 350SL. She was delighted and all her worries instantly evaporated, that was one problem less I thought. I loaded the Merc for her, kissed her goodbye saying that I would ring her at the Quarrels, a further kiss and sent her on her way, waving goodbye happily.

Paul, the garage proprietor, came up to me as keen to make a deal as ever.

'I kept out of the way,' he said laughing 'but she was happy, you'll end up buying that.'

'M'm.,' was my sole comment.

'I'll leave the Daimler here for the night if that's what you want, O.K, bit of a risk?'

'Fine, no problem. Who would want to nick an old mans' car like that,' I said, looking back at the Daimler.

'I've lent you a BMW. Any good? It's an M5, the black one.'

I looked at it idly.

'Yes, whatever,' I said, 'As ever I'm grateful.'

He threw me the keys, with a shrug as he did so.

'The tank's full, as you asked, when will you be back?'

'I'm not going anywhere, remember, just put it on the bill.'

'Sorry,' he said, adding, 'mystery man,' shaking his head and smiling even more.

I shrugged noncommittally, picked my bags up from the ground and placed them carefully on the back seat.

'Thanks for the help,' I said, winked, slammed the door and drove off into the morning sun. Now, at last I could think.

I headed south for the A1, enjoying the crisp V8 engine, the power sharp under my foot, the handling so much tauter than my own car. I pondered the meaning of my having being shadowed when I was driving the Daimler.

Twenty-Eight

It was early afternoon by the time I was approaching the outskirts of London, with the Swiss Cottage dead ahead. The traffic as ever was heavy, the atmosphere hot and oppressive, and it took a considerable time to wend my way down through Regent's Park, on to Baker Street, across Oxford Street, and down Audley Street.

I hadn't intended to stay, or even go down to my apartment in Ennismore Mews, yet, inexplicably and as if pulled by some magnet of curiosity, here I was turning into Hyde Park, and heading towards it, soon turning left at Princess Gate and left again into the Mews. The cobbles chattered under the firm suspension of the B.M.W., all looked quiet, save for a red Mini, with the female driver asleep. The rows of colourful flowers in window boxes and hanging baskets stretching down the street and reflecting in the windows gave it a chocolate box appearance; but I still didn't like it. I knew I shouldn't be here, this was insanity and for what? Any mail left here could wait, and the answerphone had a remote calling device. I kicked myself for this stupidity, this lack of stealth coming to my pied-à-terre in the Mews, an obvious place to be put under surveillance by whoever was looking for me, if in fact they were? Whatever cover the B.M.W. had afforded me would now have been blown.

I drew up alongside the door to number 12. I looked at the Mini again, the driver of which was now fully awake and watching me. I was becoming increasingly uneasy, but climbing out of the car I went towards the door, when I heard the Mini's starter engage. From the corner of my eye I watched, then at the last minute I decided not to enter the flat. I still felt uneasy, so taking out the video remote and pointing it through the window, I saw the receiver light go on. Now the surveillance camera would record if anybody went in or out. It was time to go.

The Mini was approaching slowly, shuffling along the cobbles. I spun round quickly jumping back into my car, aware that the driver was watching me. If there was any intention to follow me, I didn't give it a chance. I slotted the B.M.W. into reverse and shot off backwards down the Mews, revs climbing, and out accelerating the Mini. At the end of the street, I locked hard over, stamped on the brakes to bring the nose up and round, and banged it into second and shot off into the evening traffic. I would never be sure, but surely, the Mini had been accelerating after me? I would never know, maybe it was just over reaction? I should never have gone there. My mind steady and back on track, I drove to the Hilton Hotel on Park Lane, and pulled round to the rear of the building, leaving the B.M.W. in the underground car park, asking them to give it a wash, and then park it for me.

I was surprised; London itself still gave me a buzz. I was now within walking distance of Curzon Street, Shepherd's Market, and my old office. I could feel the electricity, the vibes and the memories. I tipped the attendant and walked briskly up to the Hilton reception area. A stunning girl with straight long blonde hair, a wide smile, and smartly dressed stood purposefully behind the desk. She asked if she could help.

'Just a room for a night, or maybe two,' I requested.

'One moment, Sir,' as she rattled away on the computer, 'double or single?'

'Single,' I said sorrowfully, looking into her eyes. She knew precisely what I was thinking, but I knew full well that she would have had that look a hundred or more times already today.

'A single on the sixth OK?'

I watched her silk blouse flutter.

'The sixth are you trying to wear me out?

There was not a smile or a flicker face remained deadpan.

'Perfect, thank you.'

She took an imprint of my Coutts card, margin-ally impressed that watching me meanwhile, then at last when the card worked smiled again, and handed me my keys.

'Number 668, anything you want, just call,'

'The card' was it actually yours? she said coyly with a wink.

No need to answer, of course I left her reluctantly, she would wonder and so would I. But things had to be done. I snapped out of it and made for the row of six ornate lifts.

Stepping out onto the sixth floor, I soon found number 668. A good light and airy room with tapestry curtains, and a marble panelled bathroom, overlooking Hyde Park. Nice if I was staying, I thought.

I stripped the bed, and remade it roughly, threw a crumpled towel on the bed cover, and left an old hanky by the phone. From my bag I took an old pair of trousers which I draped over a chair, poured a drink from the fridge and left the glass on the television. I opened some magazines and scattered them on the bedside table, drew the curtains and turned the lights down low.

In the bathroom I placed a glass across the plug hole in the bath and turned the cold tap a quarter on. The water splashed off it, the noise amplified. Taking a small piece of fishing line, I attached it by an overhand knot to the door bolt. I moved out into the bedroom closing the bathroom door after me, holding the line all the while. As the door clicked shut, I gave the line a sharp tug, the bolt slid home, another tug made sure it was firm, then a constant pull made the line slip its knot and became undone. It was removed without trace, and the bathroom door was locked from the inside. Light shone from underneath the door, and I could hear the sound of running water.

Transferring everything I needed to my other bag I closed the main door, and walked into the corridor. My bag was now heavy and it took an effort to walk nonchalantly to the lift, which I took to the third floor. There I walked to the end of the corridor, and down the fire escape to the ground floor. I clicked the fire door open and walked out into the humid late afternoon, where I was soon engulfed in traffic and heaving humanity.

Within ten minutes I was walking in through the rear entrance of the Park Lane Hotel. I said good afternoon to the concierge on the door, and walked purposefully up the steps to the polished mahogany reception, where a courteous young man dressed in the ubiquitous pin stripe asked if he could help me, and once again I booked a room, but this time using a different name and credit card to match. After signing the register, I thanked him, refused graciously the help of the porter and made my way to the fourth floor, and room 408.

This time I collapsed on the bed. I lay looking at the ceiling for a moment, breathing heavily. To hell with everything in that bag, it was bloody heavy, no way could I have let the porter anywhere near it. The police sirens would have already been wailing their way through the evening traffic by now if I had.

Recovering, I relaxed a little now and turned on the two large polished brass taps to run water into a huge Victorian style bath standing on clawed legs. Steam rushed up at me.

I poured myself a small Scotch, closed the full length curtains in the bedroom, and returning to the bathroom, I relaxed nearly afloat, in neck high steaming water. Revelling in this welcome luxury, I thought out my next move. I would need all my strength and wit to execute my plan in the night ahead. Refreshed by my bath, I set the alarm for midnight, and tried to get some sleep.

Twenty-Nine

Rising before the alarm went off, I dressed in dark clothes, pocketed a miniature torch and the spy cam camera, but in the interests of reducing bulk left the infra red glasses behind. I hoped it was not a mistake, but then I knew my way around the office.

Using the stairs rather than the lift, I came out at the rear of the hotel and set off at a brisk pace towards Shepherds Market and Curzon Street. The streets were relatively quiet, with few cars or pedestrians, just the ever hopeful cabby.

A few ladies of the night plied their trade in the Market, secreted in dimly lit door ways, legs in fishnet tights protruding from pelmet-like miniskirts, breasts thrusting forward, eyeing me hopefully. One offered …

'A good time, sir,' as I passed. I smiled, raised a hand and walked on my conspicuously lonely way, down toward the Grapes public house, turned left and up through the arch, and there was Curzon Street in front of me. To the left rose the massive bulk of the 'Office,' a huge grey and daunting triangle five stories high, spreading back to Berkeley Square

I stood waiting in the shadows of the archway for a while, surveying the scene. I appeared to be on my own, not a soul moved, there wasn't a sound, I was lucky.

Coming out of the shadows, I could see the night Commissionaire standing in the doorway.

As I walked out of the shadows he spotted me, and stood bolt upright looking at me for a moment. He turned around and went back into the office without giving any sign he had seen me. I waited. He came out again within moments, and nodded. I went straight across the road and stood by the entrance, to be greeted by Harold.

'Good evening, sir, thank God you've come, I was half expecting you. Terrible business, poor Mister Stuart, what do you think? No, well, you can't say of course. Er, will you come out of retirement?'

I put my hand on his shoulder.

'I'll do what I can, I want to find out what happened,' I said looking round. 'But I'll need to go inside the building.'

'Oh, dear no, bit difficult of late, sir, new equipment installed,' he said, casting an eye at the camera. 'But you know oddly I er, check it when I saw you coming and there might be a fault sir. And that fault will be registered, they will around here like moths in a bit.'

'I could have been a foe,' I said seriously.

'Sooner a foe that I know, than some smart bastard

of a friend I don't,' he said casting his eyes up to the floors above. 'The code system has been changed, you need an entry card now, and no doubt the main offices are the same. I think they all need cards now, sir, and everybody's got their own, but there is access just to the corridors for the night cleaners, that's a green card.'

I raised my eyebrows.

'Be more than my life's worth, sir, we may still be on a camera somewhere, good luck, and they are listening it's a terrible business,' he said as a green plastic card fell to the floor, and he walked down the street into the night.

I knelt to pick it up, then turning inward toward the entrance and keeping my face to the ground, I donned a pair of clear gossamer surgical gloves, and slotted the card into the door to reception. It opened with a click. Head down and walking with hunched shoulders and a limp I made my way to the stairs. A Hoover whirred away somewhere in the building, a telephone rang in an office. I made my way quickly up the stairs to my old floor; there was still no sign of any night staff, although as I got further into the building I could hear the sound of computers and the metallic clatter of printers operating echoing from behind closed doors. Other beings were only feet away, one slip, an arrest even, and this whole mission was dead and so was my life. If not my life an investigation was impossible to continue if I was incarcerated.

A door opened, and I froze against the wall. A bored voice said.

'Well, do you want a coffee or not?'

I didn't hear the answer but the door closed again as they argued. Swiftly I shot down the corridor to my old office door. Damn! A new card system sprouted from where the old digital lock system used to be. I tried the green card knowing it would be totally useless, and it was.

I took three strides back to the door of my old secretary's office. At least this hadn't changed, I punched in my old number minus ten, and the door gave a clunk. I tried the knob, to my relief it opened, just as the door of whoever was calling for coffee also opened.

As the footsteps passed, I sank into the silence and relative security of Sue's office. I closed and locked the door.

It was surprisingly light inside, the reflection of the street lamps, and the monotonous orange flash of a pelican crossing beacon eerily illuminated the office. Letting my eyes adjust, I moved slowly to the dividing door that led into my old office and slowly tried the handle. Damn! Another entry card was needed to get into that room. Things had been changed with a vengeance.

I had to think, I had to get into my old office, now Liam's office. I looked up at the window. The window! I wonder? Rising slowly, I made my way carefully across the room to the windows. No new locks there. Opening the rusty frame quietly, I looked out and to my left. I was not too keen on the height, four stories high, but there was a ledge, a good ledge some fourteen inches wide going all round the building on each floor. It was covered in pigeon droppings and rubble, yet if I could get on to it I could get round to Liam's office, and if the window frame was as rusty and swollen as it always had been, there was a possibility I could force it open. It had never shut properly, just one good kick and I was sure it would swing out, and I'd be in.

'Faint heart never …' went through my mind as I climbed out into the night air, and stood on to the ledge some eighty feet above Curzon Street. A taxi rattled by below me.

Taking a deep breath, I moved slowly but surely along the ledge, shuffling through pigeon droppings and bits of masonry, with the odd piece of mortar spiralling downward.

After what seemed an age I reached my old office windows. I realized a kick would unbalance me and send me crashing into the street below, but I could see that as always, the window was not properly shut. My fingers forced themselves deep into the gap at the top and clinging on to the top of the frame, I gingerly gave the bottom a kick. With great relief, I had not made too much noise, and it had moved. Yes, the handle had definitely moved upwards. Hanging on tightly now, forcing my fingers painfully further down the swollen metal I gave it another kick. To my horror it swung open unexpectedly, with a sickening creak and my balance went with it. I hung on desperately as the rotting window frame continued to open, all my weight now going on those rusty hinges.

My feet scrabbled desperately for a grip, mortar and chippings falling to the street below, I swung with it as it opened wide, my whole body now suspended over the street. Hanging on grimly, I glanced below, my heart beating like hell. By stretching a leg out, I could just hook my heel over the base of the open frame, the top hinged sheared but jammed. I hauled myself back to the ledge and sprang cat like to the office floor. That was bad, I thought, that was bloody close.

Once inside I didn't move, remaining stationary where I had dropped, heart thumping and trying to get away from its crazy owner, my eyes adjusting to the light once more, and getting my breathing back under control. I took in what I saw, a computer and monitor on the desk, as he'd promised. One wall had a huge map of the world, there was a video and television in the corner, the place was a maze of cables and gadgets, yet surprisingly no alarms or sensors flickered.

I moved across the room to the filing cabinet, and spun in the old code. I couldn't believe it, he hadn't changed it. I thought about that for a moment, what did that mean? Was it a mistake? Did he feel there was no need? Or had he lost interest in the filing cabinet once the Carlos file went missing? Or he'd read it and had no further need to safeguard it.

Opening the cabinet I checked just for the sake of it that the Carlos file had gone. It had. Futilely I did the obvious check to see if it had been wrongly filed close by, but nothing further seemed out of place.

The flashing from the beacon below was getting on my nerves, the wall map seemed to grow and diminish, come out of the wall toward me pulsating with each flash. I looked up at the map and to the Mediterranean. Malta and summer holidays, H'm, no. My mind jumped from Malta to the Sicilian Banks, Carlos II I wonder?

I shone the pin prick of light from the laser torch on the map. As I came close, inches from the fabric, examining the resting place of Carlos on the Sicilian Banks, was that a mark, an area with a ring?

I'd bet my life on it, there was a tiny, tiny, indentation that could only really be noticed under this type of light. I was sure of it. Why would anyone here wish to do that? The exact location was not in the file. Was this just a guess or a lucky stab? And why the interest?

Not really sure what I was looking for, I looked again round the room, for any signs or indication of what he was working on, anything involving me. His desk was tidy, too tidy, then again he was on holiday, but there was a shortage of personal items. Maybe that is just the way he is, I thought, compulsively neat and efficient. There were indentations on the blotter; they seemed to be numbers and scribbles, but nothing I could really make out in this environment.

I went to the mantelpiece, there were no photographs, in fact nothing at all. Looking down and into the fireplace, there were some charred fragments. Sifting through the delicate pieces, my heart stopped. The fragments were completely burnt but amidst the fragile white paper ashes and partly hidden by the debris, lay a tiny piece of harder card, small and folded, almost all burnt, yet some colour remained. It was dark green.

Lifting it clear, I knew what it was, the partial remains of a book of matches. No printing was discernible, but I'd seen one like it before.

I went cold. I now knew where the missing book of matches from, Stuart's room was possibly here in front of me.

Lifting it out gently, I took it to the desk for a better light, and placed it on the blotter to examine it. There was no doubt it had been a book of matches.

Returning to the fire place I searched carefully and minutely, but unfortunately nothing else remained. I stood up turning toward the desk, out of the corner of my eye I noticed to the side of the fire place was a small metal waste paper basket. Stooping, I lifted it into the faint light. It appeared empty, but as I was replacing it something small slid across the bottom, something made a tiny clink as it hit the side.

Moving over to his desk, I gently tipped the contents on to his blotter. Only a spent book match fell out.

His second mistake, a mistake made by force of habit. After lighting whatever paper he wished to destroy, the force of habit had led him to throw the match in the bin, rather than with the burning papers in the old Adam fireplace. The match lay there on his blotter. Slowly my hand went forward – I turned it over. Near the top it had one, and only one scorched letter, embossed in gold, a letter 'T'. From 'T' in The Manor? Perhaps.

Every nerve in my body reacted, every vein stood proud, my heart beat, my breath shortened. Slowly I took an envelope from my inside pocket and opening it I tipped the contents onto the blotter. It fell next to the spent match, another, one of the same, but this one I had taken from under Stuart's watch. It lay there as it had fallen, the letter 'L' in gold looking up at me.

Was this Stuart's last message to me? The letter, the initial 'L' for Liam? I now knew that Liam at some time had been to The Manor, but why not? it was a favourite of Stuarts, he had taken me there to, so why not his new counterpart?

Finding it hard to contain myself as the fury of discovery burned inside, I put the items into the envelope and placed them in my pocket. Carefully

I removed and folded the blotter, this may also reveal something in the future, I thought. Suddenly there was a thump at the door and momentarily I could see the shadow of feet on the other side of it. The door knob rattled insistently. Instantly I ducked down behind the desk, then the noise stopped, the shadow went away, only to continue the rattling next door at the secretary's office, and then again in the distance. I got up with relief; it was only a cleaner polishing the doorknobs.

Still reeling with the horror of what was now unfolding; I climbed stealthily out of the window and once more on to the ledge. I took a last look at my old office, now the office of a possible murderer, but why? I endeavoured to close the window carefully behind me, but had no alternative than to leave the rust-swollen frame ajar. Even as I shuffled along the ledge my mind was working overtime, where was Liam now, on holiday? I doubted it, all the pieces were slowly taking shape.

Once inside Sue's office I sat down at her chair to think. I needed to speak to her urgently, yet I dare not call her at home, the phone would already have been tapped, and I was sure she would also be being watched by the service in case I made any contact, because of the suspicions already against me. Possibly she would also be being watched by Liam, as he, I was now sure, wanted me as a possible scapegoat, a cover, a bloody sacrifice.

No, she had to contact me on a public phone, she had to ring me. What was the first thing Sue did on arrival, I wondered, coffee? She always made herself a cup of Nescafé, as she complained mine used to be too strong for her first thing in the morning. Rising, I went over to her tray and took her coffee jar down, removed the lid, tore off a small piece of scrap paper and wrote a short note, just the hotel number and room number. Thinking that to use any name of mine would be stupidity I signed it 'Hom,' part of the conversation I knew she would remember, one that I had had with her on the night of my leaving party. I dropped the note into the jar and replaced it on her tray.

Time to go, time to get out of here I thought. Standing by the door for a short moment revealed not a sound in the corridor and so slowly I opened her door, all was quiet all was clear. Closing the door behind me, I walked purposefully to the stairs, as I had done many times before, and down to the foyer, glancing at Churchill on the way, this time he did not seem to frown.

Approaching the office, I saw Harold sitting there looking at the monitors, hand on a switch. The door wasn't locked so I walked through into the short corridor and out, he didn't look up, he knew I'd passed.

Thirty

Dawn was breaking as I walked out into Curzon Street. The noise of a refuse truck collecting, compacting and grinding away its garbage, belching fumes from its vertical exhaust pipe, brought me back to reality. I crossed over the street and into Shepherd's Market. The Grapes pub smelt of old ale, yet fresh fish and shellfish were being delivered from Billingsgate to the shop in the square, fresh pink crabs were being placed by appreciative skilled hands on a bed of ice amongst the oyster's mussels and seaweed. Another time, I thought.

Walking back to the Park Lane Hotel I was more than aware that I was a little conspicuous, but it was quiet, the city was just waking up. Once at the hotel and safely in my room, I had a shower and rang room service for an early breakfast of Loch Fyne kippers, ground coffee and toast. I donned a complimentary dressing gown and lay back to think of the past twenty four hours, and the way forward.

A knock on the door and a glance through the security peephole told me breakfast had arrived. But, mindful of the implications of my findings, I took no chances, palming the .380 and standing to the side as I opened the door. The trolley with starched white cloths and silver tureens trundled in with a rattle, pushed by a charming Polynesian girl with an outstanding complexion who gracefully proceeded to lay out breakfast. I checked the corridor, no one in sight. I signed for the meal thankfully and tipped her, suddenly realising I had not eaten for 24 hours, I was starving.

Tired out now I fell asleep for a good hour after breakfast, only to be awoken suddenly by the phone.

'Cheeky,' said a bright voice.

'Pardon?' I said, still dazed by sleep.

'Cheeky, bloody cheeky, Hom indeed,' came the happy voice of Sue. 'But what on earth were you doing here? Isn't it a bit tricky?' she laughed.

Shaking off my sleep and getting my head together, I interrupted quickly.

'I need to speak to you urgently, is there any chance?'

'Sure, just say when and where.'

'Better with a lot of people about,' I said. 'Er, Fortnum's for a coffee in an hour, can you make it?'

'Fine, no problem. Anything you want?'

'You, with a tight lip,' I said, 'But if you know where your boss, Liam is, it would help, and, er, any other information that you have gleaned on him. Don't bring any paper out with you just keep it in your head. See you there, top left table.'

'OK, see you.'

I changed swiftly, and was in two minds whether to check out, or not, but decided not to do so, as taking luggage to the car, and then going back later might have been risky. I opened the room door, the corridor was empty. I carefully placed a 'do not disturb' sign on the door and went down the back stairs, out into the street and into the morning air for the second time in a few hours.

Turning right, I walked as briskly as I could towards Piccadilly and Fortnum and Mason's, through the growing heaving mass of people. The traffic was already heavy enough to be standing stationary, heat and fumes diluting the morning crispness. Through the noise and hum I could hear a newspaper seller touting his wares in the usual strident and unintelligible tone. Nothing registered initially, not until I got really close, then suddenly I picked up the word Hilton. So, I unobtrusively took to the inside line of pedestrians, and stopped casually while a man bought the morning paper. As he moved away I read the scribbled billboard. I could feel the hairs on my neck tingle.

'Bomb Explosion at Park Lane Hilton' it read.

I bought the paper, and stood in the doorway of the Mercedes showroom.

It read:

'Late last night, there was an explosion on the sixth

floor of the Park Lane Hilton, although contained in one room considerable damage was caused. The Police and the Bomb Disposal unit are not releasing further details at the moment, other than that no warning was given. It seemed to be aimed at just a single room. The IRA is not believed to be involved, and a feud between criminals is suspected.'

So states our correspondent.

Christ! These people are serious, I thought, but I was somehow pleased that they had shown their hand. I had thought they would, I knew now what I was dealing with.

I walked out of the doorway and stuffed the paper in a nearby rubbish bin. Taking a deep breath, I made my way across the road through the stationary traffic and into Fortnum's. Across the ground floor entrance hall, their large floor clock was playing a tune. In the café area I spotted Sue, she was already seated at a corner table and looking the perfect secretary. She was reading a morning paper.

'Good morning,' I said, surprising her, my eyes scanning the other occupants while pulling out a chair.

She looked at me with a vague smile, and handed me the paper, the word 'Hilton' prominently displayed.

'It reminds me of a track from 'Mac the knife' I see you are back in town, Kit? Is this anything vaguely to do with you?' she said quizzically.

'Certainly not!'

'I'm desperately sorry about Stuart,' she said, looking down.

'Don't say anything please not just at the moment' I said 'It's difficult.'

'I've ordered your coffee. 'Maragogype,' OK?' she said smiling

I realized, I had missed being looked after.

'You haven't answered me.'

'About the coffee or the Hilton?' I quipped.

I knew she wasn't amused by the expression on her face. My flippant comment wouldn't wash; I had to trust some one. I needed someone one my side. I took the unusual step for me of confiding in her and over the next ten minutes or so I told her of some of the happenings that had brought me back to London. It had to be a brief outline, but it mattered that the O M had given me a little time to rebut the accusations. A time that was quickly running out.

'And the Hilton?' she asked again.

'At the moment,' I said, 'I genuinely don't know for certain, but there's a chance someone is after me, or should I say, would prefer I was not around anymore.'

The coffee arrived and we sat in silence for some time, then looking at her I said

'Well, do you know where Liam is?'

She didn't answer straight away, then in a rush:

'He's supposed to be on holiday, but it's unlikely,

he's not the type. He works all hours, never relaxes, yet he did have this thing about Malta, he kept on asking if you ever went there nowadays. A bit jealous that you had a house there I thought, he often mentioned your family interests, and didn't know how you could afford that big house in Yorkshire. He didn't seem to grasp it had been there for years, he seemed to want to make people think you had been on the 'take' as they say, and that you needed money.'

'Why the fascination with Malta?' I said aloud. 'Did he mention Carlos II much?'

'Well I was going to mention that,' she said thoughtfully. 'Quite a bit actually, and I never told you because I didn't see the point really, but he asked me about it a few times even before you left.'

'What questions? And how the hell did he know about it at all?' I said, thinking about it. 'That was a classified operation and only a few knew of it, and only I had all the pieces of the puzzle. Without a lot of effort he couldn't have found a quarter of the details and why the hell should he want them any way? The operation had been wound up.'

'I didn't say much, as I didn't know much anyway' she said. 'I mean, to talk idly isn't on. It's against all training and rules, but I did say that it was one that you had been in charge of, and maybe he should discuss the matter with you.'

'I wish you had told me,' I said quietly.

'I'm sorry. Did it really matter?' Sue said, looking sorrowful.

'I doubt it,' I said stirring a second cup, and looking out of the café precincts and down on to the store's world famous grocery department, as busy as ever, the smell of cheese and ground coffee wafting up.

'Kit what was the cargo of Carlos? Can you tell me?' Sue said, looking directly at me.

I deliberated for some time. Hell! The file had gone and there was a strong chance it would all come out anyway, but what of Sue's safety, the information could be dangerous. I shouldn't impart classified information, yet she was still part of the service and technically I was not. Indeed I was under suspicion by the service.

'Just armaments possibly,' I said, 'you remember? From Murmansk. A kind of weapon,' I said, not telling all and making light of it.

'Could you still get at them? Could they be salvaged?'

'Not really sure,' I said, curious. But maybe they could, it would depend on a lot of technicalities though, my mind now racing with the possibility of the Scuds being salvaged and ending up in the wrong hands.

After pausing a moment.

'I don't think he's English,' Sue said coyly.

This secret revelation shook me, yet somehow didn't surprise me.

'Why, what gives you that idea?' I said.

'He's too swarthy, now don't get me wrong, it's attractive but he makes great play of using sun beds, tropical holidays and the like. I don't think he does either of them, I think it's in his genes, and I've seen him at the Lebanese restaurants in the City.'

'But his father was in the British Army?' I said questioningly.

'Yes he was, but his mother?' Sue said, raising her eye brows.

'Does he talk of his father?'

'Not much. He's dead, he married very late.'

'His mother?'

'Also dead, or so he says.'

'Convenient!'

'H'm, well, I don't believe him; she was apparently much younger. I think she is still alive, I think she is in the East.'

'Are you sure?'

'No, I'm not, but as you well know one of the reasons for his rapid promotion was the fact that he can speak several Arab languages fluently. We are now getting some communications to our section in Arabic, but that's no problem as you know, our Eastern section can handle that. But because of all this, and wanting to be the perfect secretary, I started having lessons in Arabic. I never told anyone, but I understand more than he thinks.'

'Sue, you're a revelation,' I said quietly.

'Not really. I can only understand a little, but when he's on the phone he has used the word 'Omei' which means 'mother' in the present tense and only on his mobile phone when sometimes it has rung in the office. I'm not saying she rang him, but I do think she's been in the conversation, whoever it was to. I think she is in Libya,' she said looking straight at me now.

The last word arrived like a bomb shell.

'It's purely a guess,' she rushed to say.

'Have you told anyone else?' I asked quickly.

Then I realised by her look that there was a problem I'd been slow to see. Suddenly tears welled up in her eyes, and she took a small lace handkerchief from her bag. I let her compose herself.

'Kit I mentioned it to Stuart, that was when all this started, I told Stuart quite casually one day. I think it shocked him, and later we had a meeting in his office, and then I told him what I've told you. I should have told you sooner?' she sniffed.

'You should have,' I said, and I held her hand as a gesture of encouragement.

'Soon after that I know that Stuart had a meeting with him, and shortly after that, Liam, I believe, disclosed that the Carlos file was missing, then the balloon went up and Stuart caught it in the neck. Liam tried to blame you, thus taking the heat off himself, and that's all really, bit of a mix up,' she said, dabbing her eyes and smudging her mascara a little.

We sat in silence thinking, then after a while I said quietly.

'Ok, so why do you think his contacts are in Libya?'

'It may not be, but I believe his father was there after the war for some considerable time, helping establish the oil industry. I believe that's where he may have married' she sniffed.

I now had the full picture, a picture which I suppose deep down I already knew, one I had already began to suspect, but one that I had been avoiding.

'Susan,' I said somewhat formally, 'Your help has been invaluable.'

'But what have I said?'

'Everything, you've confirmed my worst fears' I said stirring yet another coffee. 'I think that we have been here long enough now, you must get back and I must get on. Sue, tell the O M everything you have told me. Tell him of our conversation and that I'll make contact, now I must go,' I said, getting up and leaving enough money on the table for the bill. 'Look after yourself.'

She stood up sadly and I kissed her for the second time in my life.

Leaving Fortnum's I saw no one I knew, I had no feeling of being followed or of being watched. Oblivious to traffic and people, alone with my thoughts I made my way down Bond Street and then up towards the

Hilton. I'd collect the BMW first, then get my gear from the Park Lane.

I entered the Hilton by the Hyde Park entrance. It was conspicuous, yes, but I had to know more. Security guards were now, after the explosion, checking all baggage brought into the hotel. Having none, I was just searched, and this gave me the opportunity to enquire as to the reason.

'There's been a bit of an explosion on the sixth floor,' the burly guard dressed in blue told me, 'but nothing serious, it is all under control. Haven't you seen it in the paper?

The police are investigating, but we can't be too careful. The bird has flown of course, but it makes the guests happier that security is being tightened,' he said casually; I wondered if it really did.

'Any loss of life?' I asked, he didn't think so but no details were being released. I thanked him and walked away, out of sight of reception, to the stairs behind the lifts and out to the rear of the hotel and their car park.

Handing over my ticket, I collected my keys from the office and made my way down to the second floor of the underground park. There, parked at the far side was the BMW, washed and clean. I waited a moment. The area seemed quiet apart from a small man in overalls, coughing and sweeping the damp floor, but otherwise everything seemed normal. All my senses alert, I moved over to the BMW, dropped to the floor and checked underneath the chassis. Nothing there, I looked up through the chrome grill and that looked all clear too, so with a little trepidation I pressed the remote control and the door button popped up. No heart rending explosion, no blinding flash, no searing flame tearing me apart, no sound, nothing save for the slow methodical sweeping of the attendant. Inwardly relieved, I relaxed.

Sliding onto the leather upholstery, I fired up the ignition and pulled out into the aisle, paying at the office on leaving. I struggled through the traffic and round to the Park Lane Hotel, collected my baggage, and signed out in my false name, using the corresponding Coutts card at reception. My mind always became clearer as I drove, and today was no exception.

I headed out of London and headed aggressively towards Oxford, Weston, and The Manor.

Thirty-One

The drive was as hard and monotonous as over-crowded choked roads can be, but the break as such had been useful. I now knew that there was little point in staying in London and that I had to visit the site of the sinking of Carlos II. How, I was not yet sure, but I had to know the state of the cargo, and at what exact depth she lay. Even now it may be too late, but Carlos and her cargo had to be the vital link in all this.

But would I be guiding whoever it was to the vessel? Is that what they intended? No! They already knew. They just needed me out of their way.

A mile or so from the Manor, I found myself slowing at the red traffic lights of a cross roads junction. On my left were the ornate gates to some stately home, across from the lights and to the right I could see a shabby concrete building which appeared to combine agricultural engineers with selling farmers supplies. A faded orange sign offered Eley cartridges. My heart missed a beat, my mind flashed back to Stuart and his bed of hell.

When the lights changed, I pulled across and onto their forecourt.

Locking the car, I walked into the Farm Shop. The old-fashioned bell attached to the door rang out and an old spaniel opened an eye as he lay on the thread bare carpet.

I looked round, a dusty treasure trove of shooters' country paraphernalia, stuffed foxes, rabbits, antlers, saddles and bridles hung from the walls, three or four mole traps and some faded boxes of mole fusees on a shelf. Hanging menacingly from a nail at the corner of the shelf was a bunch of fox snares.

An elderly man in dust covered tweeds shuffled in from the door at the back of the counter, a curved pipe between his lips.

I pointed at the snares.

'Sell many of those?' I asked.

'Aye' came the ample reply, the pipe firmly clamped in his mouth.

'Recently?' I questioned.

'You're the second city gent wanting to buy some in as many days,' he said knocking dottle on to his already inch deep floor.

'Please tell me more,' I said.

'Police?' came the cautious reply.

'Not if you tell me,' I said pleasantly.

'Wrong time of the year to sell 'em, that's what stuck in my mind,' he mused.

'Smart guy, bit like you, kind 'a straight backed fella, fit, looked like he'd been on holiday though, yeah, not from these parts, odd really.'

I took one of the snares from the nail and passed it to him.

'I'll take this one,' I said.

'Won't catch many with one,' he muttered absently to a stuffed fox. 'Bloody one?' he laughed, then demanded two pounds fifty.

'It'll catch what I'm after,' I said menacingly, paid him and left. Did I need any more proof? Others might, I didn't.

Climbing back into the BMW I accelerated hard out of the yard and down the road to Towcester. I knew where I was going now, not to the Manor, I'd seen enough.

On the mobile I dialled in Blackbird Travel and spoke to the girl, asking her to find me a flight to Malta, today, now, and to ring me back a.s.a.p.

Driving forcefully north, I hoped that the airport she found would be Manchester She seemed to take hours but realistically probably only minutes went by before the phone burst into life.

'Four o'clock, Manchester' came the efficient reply. 'Monarch business class, check in latest at three p.m., can you make it?'

The bonnet visibly rose in the air as the BMW kicked down, revs climbing.

'I'll try, believe me, I'll try.' I roared toward the M1, reciting my credit card number to her as I went; my ticket would be ready to collect at the Monarch desk. The deal done, I felt I was on my way.

The next job was to try ring Malta and tell Pilar our housekeeper that I would be staying at the house for a few days. She'd be surprised as I had not seen her, or the supposed gardener, her husband for some time. I was connected swiftly and it was a good line. After the usual cheerful exchanges from either end, I managed to get it across that I was on my way and would be staying at the house tonight, and oh! could they get a car, a Suzuki 4/4 from the hire company, I'd pick it up at Luqa airport. They'd try their best, and they looked forward to seeing me after all these years.

At 2.30 p.m. the BMW, nearly out of fuel and overheating, the warning indicators flashing, I shot up the ramp at International Departures to the short stay car park at Ringway, Manchester's International Airport. I had no time to search for the long stay multi-car park, the bill would be horrendous but how could it matter now?

I parked the car, grabbed my luggage, and headed off at a pace for the Monarch desk, breathing heavily because of the sheer weight of my luggage. I collected the ticket and headed for the check in.

There was no way I had time to re-route my luggage through a 'diplo' channel. I'd just have to take a risk, if it came up, well, I'd have to use whatever means there was available. I checked in and watched the luggage disappear down the conveyor. Christ! If they knew what was in that bag.

Just as I was going through into departures, flight Monarch 1506 was being called for boarding. At W. H. Smith's I bought the evening paper, and smiled tiredly at an air hostess as I handed her my boarding pass. She waved me through and I walked wearily down the aluminium embarkation tube. 'The throat of hope' I mused; it had been a long day so far.

Once in flight I ordered half a bottle of champagne and a brandy. Mixed together, they add just a little tincture to life. Settling back in the reasonably comfortable seats of this Boeing 757, I opened the evening paper.

'Hilton Bomb Mystery' was still front page news, but had now shrunk a little, into two columns. There had been no sign of a body; the Bomb squad thought it had been some form of grenade, and it would appear to have been of foreign manufacture, possibly Chinese. Some 'take away,' I guessed.

I was surprised at them releasing that piece of information, it would have been far better if the O M, who must have been consulted, had said; 'The body is being identified,' it would at least have given me a little leeway. Still he would have his reasons.

The champagne and brandy arrived, a moment of indulgence. I raised my glass as Stuart and I had done so many times.

'Stuart, thinking of you,' I murmured, raising my glass, 'I know you're with me,' and within half an hour I was asleep.

Part 5

Malta

Thirty-Two

'Ten minutes, sir,' the air hostess said as I awoke. She bent down and gave my safety belt a gentle tug. Somewhere beneath my feet wing flap servos whirred, then a creak as they reached their predetermined angle, the twin Rolls Royce jet engines whistled, now free-spinning, losing their thrust.

Pushing up my table, I drank the last of my now warm flat champagne, the glass was swiftly taken away.

More servomotors whirred as with a vibrating clunk the wheels lowered and locked into place. Slowly the big Boeing banked to port, slivers of moisture misting from the wing tips, showing the last few moments of a magnificent sunset and revealing the small island of Malta below, a twinkling jewel in the Mediterranean.

The last rays of sunset pointed skyward, cross like, the island now bathed in orange resembled a golden orb, shadows from the domed Carmelite Church of Valletta were cast across Grand Harbour. Steadily we came level, Valletta and the island disappeared somewhere below the polished wing, the Boeing now sinking onto finals for Luqa airport.

I glanced out of my window again, to the south and far out to sea. Somewhere over there, somewhere, I thought lies Carlos. I wondered what I'd find? Then a shudder through the aircraft as the wheels touched brought me out of my reverie; Malta, I was here.

I hate waiting for luggage especially when it may be opened, but eventually the large squashy bag arrived on the conveyor. I picked it up nonchalantly, went through passport control, and with slight trepidation walked through 'nothing to declare'. The doors opened automatically, and I walked out into the reception area, inwardly breathing a sigh, so far so good.

In the line of shabby offices and car hire hoardings, I located the office of the Modern Hire Company, the one that I remembered. I rang the bell and after a short time a large dark lady appeared from the back. With arms like hams and arm pits bristling, sporting a short skirt she definitely should not have been wearing with her large drooping thighs, with a screech of over taught tights she approached the counter. After attacking me verbally in unfriendly German, she realised I was possibly English and apologised, becoming a little more amiable. Yes, Pilar had reserved a car for me, a Suzuki 4/4, and it was out in the front and full of petrol. I gave her my card and she took an impression, saying that we would settle up on my return.

Walking out of the building; I suddenly re-alised, I was sweating. God! It was hot. The Suzuki was open with the hood down and I threw the bag onto the seat, making sure that the passenger door was locked. I climbed in and set off down the tortu-ous road towards the village of Hamrun, by-passing the Marsa and the way to Valletta and out toward St Pauls Bay and my family house. The traffic as ever was unbelievable, old British cars painted in ques-tionable colours, buses and trucks a blaze of colour and chrome attacked me from all angles.

As it grew dark, it was obvious that many of the land marks had changed. Struggling to remember the area I rattled through narrow streets, and dusty lanes hoping I could find my way. Malta isn't that big I thought, just busy, bloody busy. But within forty minutes I was going through the white gates of 'Bancali,' a home my father had loved. Lights were on and the pool lit up, its aquamarine colour reflect-ing back onto the white walls of the house. Wearily I climbed out, reached for my bag and made my way round to the front, fumbling for my key. The sounds of the shore came up to me, the scent of the sea, and flowers, the lights of a large passenger ship glowed on the horizon, crickets serenaded my arrival.

As I opened the door a gecko ran up the wall, his peaceful sleep disturbed. The house looked clean, Pilar had obviously spent some time on it; the smell of polish and detergent still lingered. The night heat was oppressive, I peeled my shirt off, then suddenly as if driven by some unseen force I tore all my clothes off, and ran out to the pool and without hesitating dived straight in. The relief was immense, swirling round on to my back, I looked up at the stars. It was beautiful, but this was no holiday; coming out of the pool I was refreshed but tired. I would need all my strength in the coming days and I looked forward to a long sleep, bed now was a welcome relief, I had gone more than twenty four hours without sleep. The bed had been made, everything was clean and orderly, within minutes I had sunk into deep sleep.

The following morning with sun streaming through the windows I arose early, not allowing myself too much time to admire the flowered gardens or the view out over the rocky coastline toward Sicily. I had a vigorous swim in the pool, a small work out, then locked the house up and drove down the narrow road to Ta' Xbiex for breakfast.

A coffee and a croissant at a small local café sufficed, as I was eager to get going. I had to go in search of a vessel to take me to the resting place of Carlos. Paying the bill, I started to walk towards the marina at Msida Creek on the north side of Valletta.

Scores of boats, mostly sailing craft, lay stern to the quay, their crews washing the decks in the early morning sun. Dirty detergent foam floated between the hulls and mooring warps creaked in the light swell. A black and white cat with bald patches played with the skeleton of a small fish.

I needed power, speed and range, but most of all, I had to find a suitable craft with a willing owner on board. It wasn't until I was nearly at the end of the quay and beginning to feel anxious that I came across a likely candidate. The boat lay there, a sleek Sunseeker, rather too smart and clean for my purpose, but the first likely one I had seen. She would be about 55 feet in length, glistening white with a tinted windscreen on the open bridge, a useful craft, and flying the Italian flag.

A big powerful bronzed man was cleaning off diesel marks from the stern.

'Morning,' I called.

Slowly and in his own time he finished what he was doing, straightened up and looked at me.

'Si,' he growled.

My Italian was only fair, so I asked him in English if he ever did any charter work.

His answer was in perfect educated English.

'No,' he said, showing a mass of white teeth, and a flash of gold.

I tried again quickly, before he went back to work.

'Would you for a fee, a substantial fee?' I asked, but to no effect.

Then, just as he was going back to work.

'Do you dive?' I asked loudly.

He stiffened, I had struck a nerve.

'Why do you shout? Come on board,' and he did speak perfect English.

Stopping work, he gave me a hand on board, simultaneously shouting down below to his unseen crew for two iced beers.

'A bit early,' I said, he just shrugged. 'Two for me then.'

What happened next, I was not prepared for. His girlfriend, as I presumed by her age and considerable beauty, appeared at the hatch way, topless and impressive, wearing no more than a handkerchief-chief elsewhere. Smiling, she passed us two beers.

'Tova,' he said casually. 'She is Swedish, she loves diving, as I do, but it is very deep round Malta. There are a lot of artefacts from the war but they are deep, so we may go back to Sicily. I come from Reggio in Calabria on the mainland.'

Then with sharp eyes flashing straight at me

'Ivo,' he said, looking at me questioningly and thrusting out a hand.

'Kit,' I said, pulling the beer can ring back with a hiss; the morning sun was hot, the iced beer was welcome.

'So, you want to dive?'

Over the next hour I outlined what I wanted to do.

'Purely to dive on a wreck I know about, see if it was still there, just a bit of fun, a day out,' I stated.

Sitting in the cockpit on this sunny day made me wish that this was a holiday and not a matter of urgency. 'Tova' lay on the forward deck, soaking up sun, and the looks, and smiles from admiring passers by.

'I'll pay for the fuel,' I said hoping to encourage Ivo to decide in my favour. Then suddenly making up his mind, Ivo said he would not charge for the boat. He was interested in a new diving site, and a new found friend. Someone to talk to about serious things he had said, smiling and glancing at the ever attentive Tova.

We agreed to meet later in the day, in fact this evening for a diving discussion. I would bring charts and more details, also by that time I would have acquired all the equipment I needed.

We provisionally agreed to go first thing tomorrow, before dawn, depending on the weather. He would go and get a meteorological forecast from the marina office but the weather looked settled, in the meantime he would fuel the boat, fill his own air bottles and make preparations.

We shook hands on it. I was pleased on two counts, I had another diver to go with, which is essential for safety, and meant we could employ the 'Buddy' system, and now there was a fast boat to go in. Jumping ashore, I was delighted with the mornings work.

I now needed to arrange my sub aqua equipment, and buy a Magellan hand held receiver for the Global Positioning System. This small instrument would enable me pinpoint my position, vital for accuracy in pinpointing Carlos's last resting place, the co-ordinates of which were in my head. I would get everything at Malt Aqua, the diving shop that operated close by Manoel Island.

Jumping into the Suzuki, I drove round the harbour side and towards the island. Looking across I was interested to see amongst a host of vessels under repair, that there were three large rig support vessels lying at anchor in the lee of the island, their cranes, masts and lifting derricks pointing skyward. In the back ground was the old Georgian looking building I knew had been a military isolation hospital in the distant past, I stopped for a while thinking and watching, only one of the vessels appeared to be showing any signs of activity.

On arrival the diving shop was small and cluttered, just as busy as I had remembered it. The little Frenchman that ran it was holding a fleeting conversation with five people at once, yet he greeted me like an old friend. Then he promptly rushed away to serve someone else, yet a sixth. I chafed at the delay. Eventually I managed to hire four air bottles, the regulators, weights, wet suit, fins, snorkel and mask. I arranged to collect them in the evening.

Then, as I waited for a Magellan G.P.S. to be taken from its box and tested, I couldn't help noticing two heavy bull necked divers walking back with equipment in the direction of Manoel Island and the rig support vessels I'd just seen.

It might mean nothing but I decided to check it out.

I bade the loquacious Frenchman farewell, surreptitiously watching the divers as they moved away, I wonder? I let them get well ahead of me, then clambered back into the Suzuki and drove over the small bridge which connects the island with the rest of the harbour.

Along the quay-side there was a maze of private craft, some rotting, some glistening, and as usual in Mediterranean ports all moored stern to the quay. The casual passer by can see right into most boats and guess what the owners are like. Judging by the washing blowing in the breeze many of them were boat gypsies.

I waited momentarily till one or two more vehicles joined the line cruising along the quay, then pulling out, I drove less conspicuously amongst them down toward the rig vessels.

Opposite the old isolation hospital two of the large rig boats were moored together away from the wall, the third, and the one which looked commissioned for use, was alongside.

Wet suits hung from the stays, drying in the sun, while dark skinned crewmen lounged around smoking. I could hear the high revving motor of an air compressor running somewhere on board, charging up the bottles used today, no doubt. I drove past showing no interest, and from this angle I could not see where they were registered.

When darkness came, I'd be back.

Thirty-Three

Needing to buy a chart that covered Malta, Lampedusa and the Sicilian Banks, I went up into Valletta town, remembering there used to be an Admiralty chart agent there.

I parked the Suzuki in the crowded car park that was actually over the old grain silos hewn out of the rock below. Predictably, the centre of Valletta was heaving with tourists. I bought the morning Times of Malta, at the corner by the ruins of the theatre that had been bombed out in the last war, and walked down to Queen's Square, a plaza full of tables and colourful umbrellas, and Cordino's café.

Looking around I found a table in the shade which gave me a good view of the square, and humanity. A smartly dressed waiter with a red cummerbund appeared, I ordered a coffee and opened the paper. One of the many colourful horse drawn taxis trotted by, bells jingling, scattering the pigeons pecking busily in the roadway, only to return and strut hungrily round the tables. I tried to read, but mentally I was ticking off everything that was needed for tomorrow. I'd go to see Ivo this evening, but more to the point, later and at dusk I'd have a look at those rig vessels moored at Manoel Island, some second sense deep down nagged me.

Then snapping out of my thoughts something caught my attention in the far corner of Cordino's, some English being spoken perhaps? They sat closely, talking. What attracted me I cannot say, but foolishly I thought no more of it.

I returned to my paper, and my thoughts, I must ring the O M, Sue, and Camilla in Cornwall. I'd do it all from the house. Suddenly, across the square and followed by a clatter of pigeon's wings, a chair fell over noisily. I lowered the paper with annoyance, and looked toward the disturbance.

There, for one split second in time I looked into the face of Liam. Standing up swiftly, throwing money on the table top, I staggered through the tables, ducking umbrellas, pushing through a milling crowd of people and children, and with difficulty arriving at where he had last stood. There was no sign of him, nothing, the table empty, he'd gone enveloped in the crowd.

Cursing I ran down Republic Street, but he wasn't there, he could have ducked into so many alleyways, dingy doorways and old bars. People stared at me, pointing, so I stopped running. I stood for a moment looking, listening, senses acute, but there was no sound of running feet, nothing unusual to see, just people everywhere, like ants.

Getting my breath, I walked slowly back up the hill, I'd go via Straight Street, the 'Gut'. My mind now racing, was that Liam? Was I mistaken, if it was him he certainly looked different, so was it him? If so had he recognised me? I was sure of it, it must have been, why the hasty exit? But now there was doubt. Yet my second sense was asking where was that bastard now, what was he doing here? In theory I was right on target, the only reason he could be here was because of Carlos II. This would be his base, the chances of this being his holiday destination were slight.

What then was his investigation, was this a double cross had this been sanctioned by London?

I was keen now, my urge to act had sharpened and I needed to return to the house as soon as I could, I needed to phone the O M.

Turning I walked into and up the infamous 'Gut,' a long narrow steep alleyway reeking of piss, cooking fat and garlic, full of seedy sailor's bars with broken windows, and pimps loitering outside. An ageing smudged scarlet lipped prostitute smiled at me in forlorn hope.

H'm, 'knickerless and winderless,' I thought, looking up at the sad old buildings, I walked on by.

As soon as I arrived back to the Suzuki, I drove quickly back to the house at St Pauls Bay. Pilar had been, the bed was made, the pool was clean and circulating, there were two bottles of Maltese red wine by Marsovin on the table, and a note saying that bread and milk were in the fridge.

I don't know why but somewhat apprehensively I dialled the O M in London on his personal number. Yet within about ten minutes or so I had brought him up to date with my findings, of what I'd found under Stuart's watch, at the office in London, the farmers' supplies shop near Weston, the meeting with Sue, and now my possible sighting of Liam. He listened intently without interruption. Oddly there was no indication of surprise in that perhaps Liam was here. So, did London know? I wondered if I had done the right thing by being so open.

Could there be duplicity? I only had to cast your mind back a few years, thinking of Burgess, McLean and Co. monstrous duplicity in the Hall of spooks.

The words of Captain Trevelyn came back to me, 'from what you have told me Kit someone is going to be very upset if this cargo does not reach its destination'

Was I leading him to Carlos, or leading him to myself?

On my instructions, Sue had had a meeting with him, and told him of her suspicions. He seemed amazingly to take it all in his stride.

'I've always been a little wary of Liam,' he had said dismissively.

When I asked him he had no news on Stuart's

murder. I took that with a pinch of salt. He said guardedly.

'It had been very professional, and there are no clues at the moment'.

He wanted me to find and get to the site of Carlos II as soon as possible, to see if there had been any tampering, and in what state the cargo was. He would also start to find me some form of back up, as he felt I could no longer go it alone, but it would all take time, and he'd only give me three days before I presumed the knives would be out for me.

But surely the O M was beyond reproach there were people above, and many below. I knew that for the moment I had no option, no option at all, but to go it alone.

I would call tomorrow, maybe more carefully

Next, I rang Sue, Could she get on to the main air line passenger listings, do a computer search and find out if a Liam De Valk was listed on any flight from the UK. Check also in Malta, if a credit card has been used, a car hired, a hotel booked, anything that you can think of that will leave a data trace of Liam in the last two weeks. Then as an after thought I added please keep it to yourself you and I.

Somewhere in the hills a dog barked, setting off another dog barking close to the house. This was unusual during the day and I had had to ask Sue to speak up. Replacing the receiver, I opened the bottle of Marsovin and washed a glass and looked out of the window at the sea reflectively.

What now? I was hot and bothered, it was early afternoon, and the sun was at its hottest, so, throwing my clothes over the bed once more, I walked out through the patio doors, and dived into the pool. I remember thinking as I went, that infernal dog was still barking, but now only the one up the hill, unusual.

The cool welcoming water beckoned me, I dived deep and swam powerfully underwater nearly to the end of the pool. When I surfaced, turning to do a lazy back stroke, I looked up towards the arid hill shimmering in the heat. There in the distance the sun glinted on something, something was reflecting its light.

Instantly I knew I didn't like it, but too late. To my horror, with a screaming zap and hiss the water erupted ferociously by my side, and a mercury like silver trail spiralled down to the depths of the pool. I didn't need to hear the sound that would follow to tell me what it was. I'd already gone; dived deep again and was flashing across the bottom of the eight foot deep pool towards the cover and protection of the near side. Surfacing slowly, my head well below the pool-side, breathing heavily I could still hear the report, a rolling echoing around the hills. I waited for a full three minutes, then realised I would have to move, as whoever it was might now already be making their way down toward the house. Being caught in the pool was a bad idea. I had to get to the house and my weapon.

The sudden noise of a car arriving in the drive shook me. I'd move to the shallow end, ready to make a dash for the house. Swimming under water, I swam to the far end. Poised to leap, I gingerly raised my head.

'Hello, Mr Kit' said Pilar, and her gardener husband said, 'Every thing all right, the house is good, yes?'

The relief, I hope did not show. I looked again towards the hill. Nothing moved.

'Beautiful,' I said, turning to swim again, and still keeping in the cover of the pool side. Diving to the bottom of the pool and at the far end I found what I was looking for. After surfacing, I held a copper jacketed slightly damaged soft nosed bullet, holding it between my fingers, it glinted ominously in the sun, on inspection it was a 7.62 bullet, the bands showing marks of about two in ten inch twist of a snipers rifle. That would have been nasty I thought as I swam back to the shallow end and climbed out, although moving quickly into the cover of the house.

It was rude, Pilar and the gardener had unwittingly saved my life by their timely arrival, yet I couldn't thank them, neither did I have the time for a chat. Very apologetically I made an excuse, about jogging and being late for an appointment.

I would see them tomorrow, yes the house was lovely, the garden also, yes thank you, yes, yes, mother was fine. I shook hands with them both, hugged and kissed Pilar on the cheek and ran into the bedroom. Once dressed, I grabbed my Sig, and ran out of the gates as if going for a jog, to the amazement of the two Maltese onlookers.

I had marked the spot pretty well, moving at a crouch and under the cover of a small cliff, I moved to the left and round the back until I came across a goat track I had known as a child. It was quite a distance but it would take me to above and behind my assailant, although it gave me little cover as I followed the track swiftly up the hillside. I stopped half way, and crouched by some scrub to listen, then sadly in the distance heard a starter engage and a car engine roar and accelerate away furiously. I relaxed now I knew I had missed him. Moving less carefully now, within minutes I came upon the flattened scrub of his position behind several boulders. He had been tidy, there was no shell case, no cigarette, just a few broken brambles and turned stones and an area of scuffed earth a little redder and moister than the rest. Looking round, I carefully let the hammer of the Sig down, and sat for a moment on my haunches. I was thinking this was a well chosen spot, this had been done with forethought, it was not chosen by chance, someone had been expecting me.

Disappointed, yet thankful for my life I walked

quickly back to the house. Pilar's husband was watering the garden. I showered, packed the things I would need, and following the routine as many times before, left the room looking occupied. Collecting my thoughts and considering my position, I poured a glass of red wine, and sat looking out to sea from the patio. I knew now it was time to move base. I went out, locking the door behind me and threw my Kit into the front of the Suzuki. Then as I was just about to turn the key I had a premonition.

No dogs barked, all was quiet, the evening tranquil, but the hairs on my neck rose. Slowly and carefully I got out of the Suzuki, and heaved a sigh of relief when I was out. There was no reason, I just didn't like it.

Carefully and slowly I dropped to my knees, simultaneously scanning the hill opposite to the house. Then looking underneath the car, I froze; on the exhaust pipe was a lump, an object. I came nearer and looked closer, sliding my head partly under the body. There, resting on top of the exhaust pipe amidst a jumble of wires was what appeared to be a grenade. I examined it closer and got the gist of how it was installed. It was simple but lethal. I would need tools, a knife, and a pair of pliers. There were tools in the pool pump room, I knew. Moments later I was back with the pliers, and gently slid under the car. It was a grenade, and a Chinese one, I guessed.

It was sitting on a bed of Blu-tack, one short wire

from the eye on the end of the pin attached to the chassis, and one longer wire from the grenade body, also attached to the chassis. I understood how it would work; the car would start, the vibration and heat would dislodge the grenade, it would fall and its own weight as it fell would pull its slim pin out. But still attached by the longer wire, it would dangle there, a ticking death attached to the Suzuki, hanging there pin less and now live. An ear shattering flesh tearing bang and no more Kit. Simple but effective.

Cold now, but steady as a rock, I clipped each wire and delicately lifted off the grenade, carefully holding the pin in position. I slid out from underneath, and stood upright. To make it safe I used the split ring from the key of the Suzuki, to act as a safety retainer for the pin on the grenade. Now safe and neutralized, I put the 'Chinaman' in my bag. It may be useful, I thought, maybe Liam would like this stuffed in his supercilious mouth, I mused.

I went back inside and dialled a taxi, there was no point in using the Suzuki; it was now a marked target. The taxi, as usual the ubiquitous Mercedes, arrived in a cloud of dust and blew its horn in the drive.

I locked the house for the second time, waved to the bemused gardener and left.

Thirty-Four

'The diving shop, on the Ta' Xbiex Coast Road, near Manoel Island' I said.

'Malt Aqua?'

'Yes'. Which got me into a conversation with the driver, whose name was Michael, a small tough looking man, apparently ex-naval. It also transpired he had diving experience from years ago, and he had also skippered a diving boat round the Islands. I made a mental note he might come in handy, it's a small world, I thought.

The diving shop for once was quiet. I took the opportunity to ask about the rig vessels; did they normally carry divers.

The answer was inconclusive.

'Some do and some don't, but the one against the quay,' he said pointing, 'is just being re-commissioned, they have many divers on board, and a lot of lifting equipment,' he said, then after a pause, 'Yes, that many is unusual really, it must be crewed up for topping off a well head somewhere. There are some plenty off the Libyan coast, m'm yes the vessel is Libyan, but was built in Britain, Upper Clyde ship

Builders I think, one of the last, they're getting ready to move pretty soon.'

I thanked him, and he wished me luck with my diving, he did not enquire where, he knew better.

After loading the equipment, we set off in search of a small local hotel, Michael recommended one close to the front in Msida and drove me there. I asked him to wait while I booked in. Grabbing my bag, I ran up the white stone steps of an old colonial style hotel, and after fighting my way past the aspidistra I arrived at the desk. Yes, they had a room, the old concierge informed me, sneezing with the dust as he opened the diary. I wasn't surprised, the atmosphere was not exactly oozing prosperity and I checked in. The room was simply furnished but adequate, with a terrazzo floor and a balcony looking out on Msida Creek. I threw the bag on the bed and opening it, deliberated for a second. Wearing a short sleeved shirt but no jacket meant the Sig was out. I slotted the .380 Beretta into my pocket, not terribly accurate, but very useful at short range.

I changed into dark slacks and a dark shirt, and as instructed I rang the O M. He seemed surprised. But I continued and told him of my move in that I was to do the dive tomorrow. He seemed to relax and in turn saying that he had spoken to the Americans and they had an 'arms embargo' frigate cruising in the Straits of Otranto area. I was surprised that he had actually given them the last known position of

Carlos II and they would also try and make contact. He would now confirm my possible E.T.A. on the site to them. Was I becoming paranoid? But I did wonder if I'd done the right thing.

Yet ironically feeling more in control now, I went down the stairs to the waiting taxi, that predictably was blocking most of the street. Michael was oblivious and uncaring, his door was open, 60s music was playing on his radio and he was talking unconcernedly to an attractive young girl.

'The Marina,' I said, and directed him to where Ivo's Sunseeker was berthed. As we approached we could see it, sleek, large and powerful, glistening in the late sun.

Ivo, with a smile raised a clenched fist as we approached. His diving equipment was efficiently laid out in order on the quay. I was impressed. I unloaded my equipment, taking care to keep it separate. I dismissed the taxi but asked him to come back in an hour.

Once on board I spread the chart open and with Ivo worked out a course passing round the south side of the Island. I still did not mark the exact spot, nor would I until the morning, however drew a largish circle round the position. The sea bed depth shown on the chart in that area was about 80 to 100 metres down. The deck height of the vessel, if she was upright, therefore would be about 20 metres less than that, so we were looking at a 60 to 80 metre dive, which was deep. Nearly too deep, as our bottom time would only be minutes, due to the time needed for decompressing on the ascent. We decided as a precaution to hang two bottles from the guide line at 30 metres, to provide a decompression and air stop as we may well be short of air on the ascent. But hopefully she may be lying in shallower water.

Another problem was that at that depth, the anchor of the Sunseeker would also be at the limit of her anchor chain. We might have to extend it by shackling on mooring lines, and if possible, we needed a boat skipper topsides to monitor the dive, and manoeuvre to recover us.

Although Tova had lots of experience, it could well be too much for her, and anyway she would need a hand, hauling dive gear back on board was never easy. But what about Michael?

My unlikely chance meeting with Michael the taxi-driver could pay dividends, and as if on cue, a horn blew, the aggressive 'barp' of a Mercedes. Ivo and I agreed to leave at 06.00 hours. I bade him farewell, wondering if I should have told him everything. Not yet, there would be time enough for that.

I climbed into the taxi and asked him to take me back to the hotel, then,

'Michael, how would you like to come on a trip tomorrow in the boat we've just come from. Could you handle it?'

'Be delighted to, sir, no problem.'

'It'll be early, before dawn, we've a fair way to go.'

'That's no problem, it'll be a change,' he said beaming.

'Fine, pick me up here,' I said as we arrived at the hotel, 'In the morning, 5.45 OK?'

'No problem.'

'Oh, and can you pick me up here in about another hour?'

'Don't you ever eat?' he said laughing.

'No time today,' I retorted. I jumped out and walked up to my room, and collected my small Zeiss binoculars. I came down and walked along the sea front towards the small bridge onto Manoel Island. Dusk was nearly here, there was no rush. Towards the end of the quay, past the line of yachts, I could just make out the old hospital on the left, and the rig vessels, all three were still there, the one alongside a blaze of light. From the yachts the smell of cooking, garlic and herbs wafted on the night air. No washing blowing in the breeze now, lanterns swung and glowed in the night, glasses chinked, there was laughter as couples sat on board with guests. I slipped by, unnoticed in the warm damp air.

I approached the old hospital building through the waste land away from the quay side. Carefully I picked my way through old chains, ropes, paint tins and other shipping waste, until eventually I came to one of the rear doors of the derelict building. Pushing the nearly rotten door gently, it gave way with a hollow echoing creak. I froze for a moment, melting into the shadows, then moving slowly at a crouch, I entered the dark passageway.

Luckily, with what light came from the glow of the town behind me through the remains of the broken old windows, I could see that stairs leading to the first floor were straight in front of me. Testing the bottom one for rot, I found with relief they were solid stone. I climbed stealthily to the top and made my way round the walls and across to a window. A rat, eyes flashing in the dim light, scuttled away, its paws rasping on old leaves and litter.

Kneeling at the window I focused my glasses on the rig vessel.

After a while, through the open galley door I could make out one of the two divers I had seen leaving the diving shop. He had a drink in one hand and was gesticulating crossly with the other, I could not see at whom. There was an argument going on. Systematically, I checked all the port holes, some were open, others misted and dirty. Some men were changing, some playing cards, it was difficult to be sure, but there was a lot of crew, possibly thirty. In no way could I check it out on board, not while they were all awake anyway. Wet suits still hung from mast stays, more air bottles had been brought on deck.

It was obvious she was being intensively used as a diving vessel, and being readied for more of the same. The after deck had been cleared, and one of the crane winches was in pieces with three or four men working on it, possibly they'd had a breakdown.

For nearly an hour I sat and watched as the crew came and went. Many of them were definitely of Arab blood, but none remotely resembled Liam. Then just as I was ready to leave, a dark car with smoked glass windows drew up.

There were possibly two men inside. One of them, the passenger, went on board, striding earnestly up the boarding ladder. Looking through the glasses, I followed his progress through the ship as best I could, then through a filthy port hole, in the yellow dingy light I could see the diver I recognised. He was evidently still agitated, but he retreated as another distorted figure came into view. Surely this was Liam, the movements were similar to his, but it was difficult to see, the angle from up here was difficult.

The argument ended abruptly, moments later an upper deck door flew open and Liam stood there, clearly surprised the door had flown open so easily. Two other men followed him but my total attention was fixed on the leader. Cautiously the three of them came down the gangplank towards the car. My eyes followed Liam, he wore a flowered shirt, typically flamboyant, but he no longer appeared suave, he was visibly on edge.

At the bottom he slowed and looked up at the building. The bastard, I thought, I could take him out now, but then that would only be half the story.

Restraining myself, I watched as I knelt in shadows. Before getting into the car he stopped, and once again he looked towards the building, it seemed our unseeing eyes met. In the darkness he saw nothing, but he knew, he knew I was there, somewhere.

'You do right to worry,' I thought.

All three climbed into the car, one shouting,

'Well I'm not his bloody keeper.' Had they lost someone? I watched the car turn and move off slowly down the quay as if they themselves were also looking for someone. From this height I could see the car after it had crossed the bridge turn left towards Valletta.

I sat back on the floor for a moment, needing to do two things. I had located Liam but was not yet ready to apprehend him.

'Give him enough rope' was to be the motto. I also had to verify the state of Carlos II. But what was Liam's involvement? To be sure I needed Liam on Stuart's account and for my own satisfaction, but there could be bigger fish involved. I needed the whole story.

This was a very expensive operation so who was funding all this and why? I couldn't go off at half cock.

Making my way silently down the stone steps, I came to the door and listened. There was just the sound of warps groaning, fenders squeaking, in the light harbour swell, muffled wailing Arabic music drifting across in waves from the vessel. Satisfied for the moment, I walked in the shadows back to the hotel, where Michael and his Mercedes were patiently waiting. Opening the door and apologising for taking longer than I had said, I requested.

'Valletta town.'

'Ladies?' he said questioningly.

'No, not necessarily, but do you fancy a drink down 'The Gut'?' I asked. 'Then I can tell you a little about tomorrow.'

'It's a rough place, I don't go there, bad ladies, but OK if you say,' Michael said in a retiring manner, then slowly, 'Why not'.

We approached 'The Gut' from the top, at the Palace Square end, this is where I lost the supposed Liam this morning, I thought, eyes scanning the now empty tables.

He'd vanished too quickly, disappeared behind one of the many sun-bleached doors. Somewhere close by he had a contact, perhaps in an office?

'The Gut' looked even more sinister and seedy by night, with the long and narrow street running straight as an arrow down the hill. Red lights flickered on each side showing the entrances to dark little bars and dark flights of steps separated the buildings instead of side streets. As it disappeared down toward darkness and the sea, the smell of fuel oil and fish of the commercial harbour drifted up.

A man was sprawled on his back in the gutter, his half empty wine bottle clutched desperately in his gnarled hand. The lights of a near by bar reflected green in the bottle. He'd pissed himself.

We passed 'Nelsons Bar,' its sign hanging at an angle, then 'Topless Your Choice,' a choice that we did not make. But half way down, and with so many to choose from with no particular reason, we walked into a small dark bar only lit by two candles on the bar top and one on each table. It was full of smoke, dope, and cheap perfume, olive stones crunched under our feet. Several of the tables had only women seated round them and their dress proclaimed fun and business, they had nothing more than a colourful scarf round their hips, breasts dangled in all directions, and the eyes of every one of them swivelled round to follow us newcomers. The rooms upstairs were busy; a constant stream of glistening girls and florid men pushed by, toilets gushed, girls screamed with laughter, men staggered out.

I ordered two beers at the bar and we sat at an empty table just beyond it. At once two ample girls pushed their way across to join us.

'You want company, yes, you buy Champagne for us, yes?

It would be rude not to, I thought, and we would be conspicuous if we didn't. I looked at Michael, who shrugged, but I felt in a hopeful manner.

'Yes,' I said, 'a bottle.'

She kissed me mechanically and furiously, pressing her breasts into my chest, then turning, she ordered the bottle gleefully. The bar man lost no time in ripping off the foil and casting the wire aside.

'I'm Seefa,' my allotment cried, trying this time to put a now extended nipple into my mouth, thankfully in the nick of time the cheap fizz and four frosted glasses arrived.

I dodged by pouring out a couple of overflowing glasses, but when I looked at the reticent Michael he was buried under the other woman, her dimpled buttocks twitching.

Seefa, to the laughter of the bar proceeded to do her party trick, pour the fizz all over her blue veined pendulous breasts, possibly the best place for it. I ordered a brandy for myself.

Amongst the confusion and laughter, the curtains draped in the corner were suddenly thrown open, and from behind, staggering and hanging on to them, emerged one of the men I had seen in the diving shop. He was a big powerful man, unshaven and clearly drunk, his jeans undone and clinging to his arm was an inordinately young girl, quite naked, breasts still not properly formed, the fact accentuated by the near absence of pubic hair, I'd wager this was the cause of the argument on board, this was the man they'd gone to look for, this man was a danger to them.

Liam would be caught in his own trap, away from his vessel he was vulnerable, this drunken oaf would bring them to me. I could afford to wait.

Across the table, Michael moved and came up for oxygen. Seefa, with surprising dexterity started to undo my belt, if only she knew that the only thing likely to be active down there was a .380 Beretta. I took out fifty Maltese pounds, pressed them in her sweating palm, and asked her just to sit with us for a while, saying that I was in mourning, and just her company would be fine.

'In the morning? Oh good yes that's fine,' she giggled.

Luckily for Michael his girl didn't hear, as he re-moved her scarf, Seefa began showing her obvious disappointment and with a sulky pout stuck her now sugary, sticky breasts yet again in my face.

'Why not now not morning?' she frowned.

Shaking my head, I managed to edge away, moving my seat further back into the seedy darkness.

I sat back to wait but I didn't have to wait long.

Soon, in the doorway the other diver appeared, equally large and powerful. He spotted his pal almost immediately and scowling pushed his way roughly through the heaving bodies. He made his way to the back of the bar, knocking into tables and setting glasses rocking. Did he glance at me momentarily as he went past? Was there recognition in his eyes? Reaching the corner table, he slapped his now torpid pal across the face, the naked young girl, in bewilderment slithered to the floor offering hairless undignified exposure, the older women running to her aid, the noise of conversation lowered as those around followed his progress.

Suddenly Liam appeared in the doorway coolly watching. I glanced behind me at the fracas and then looked back to Liam, his now sun-tanned face eerily lit yellow by the dim street lamp above the door, glowing like a turnip lamp at Halloween his lips drawn back in a sinister smile.

As I rose slowly from my seat, I saw Liam deftly palm a small pistol from his jacket pocket, I moved quickly out of the shadows and into the middle of the crowd round the bar, my hand diving for my Beretta. Then from nowhere an earth shattering crash hit me from behind, my head erupted in a million lights and colours.

Liam's head seemed to grow and expand like an orange balloon, and float, up, up and away, the smile becoming grotesque, wider than the room, then it all disappeared in an orange mist. My legs buckled, I knew I was going down among the tables and into blackness.

Consciousness eventually came, thankfully, although it came slowly and painfully. For a moment I wondered about hell, or was it heaven, twenty or more nipples dangled over me, or were they face's out of focus?

A strident noise of jabbering in a foreign tongue echoed inside my head. Moments later reality came back. Michael lifted me up to a sitting position as one of the girls bathed my head with vinegar and water. My body reacted, involuntarily I jerked away from the helping hands.

'Christ! That hurt.' Diluted blood ran down my shirt and dripped on the floor.

'What the hell was that all about?' Michael asked suspiciously.

'Someone I once knew…I think,' I said painfully, every syllable like a finger nail being drawn.

'Some bloody friend,' he exclaimed, 'That guy in the door way had a gun. Bloody good job you were in the crowd, too many people for him, couldn't get a shot but the guy behind, the big fella, he brought a champagne bottle down on you as you moved, they don't break easy you know.'

'Was it full?'

'No.'

'That's a relief, I hate waste,' I muttered.

Slowly I came to my senses and pulled myself up, Michael steadied me.

'Do we owe anything,' I gasped to Michael.

'No, we're all clear.'

We bade farewell to the bar, I raised my hand as we walked into the now cool night air.

There was a ripple of jeering applause as we went out, just another night for them I thought.

Fortuitously, two uniformed Guardia were walking up the alley. As they passed, we fell in behind, a reasonable cover till we got to the top and back to the car, I thought.

I was not in the mood for another Shanghai. We walked in silence.

As we drove down toward Msida, Michael said.

'Why do you wear a gun?'

'Because of friends like that,' I grimaced. Then I said, 'Michael, a change of plan. Go to the Marina, please, we'll knock Ivo up. If you don't mind, I think we should have a meeting. Things are a little different, and I'll explain to you both.'

'Whatever you say, but if you'd told me a little more earlier, I could have helped you back there.'

'I should have, if only for your own safety, I'm sorry.'

'Hell! Don't worry about me,' Michael said reassuringly. 'I've been in many a scrap, and been shot at, too.' He ripped his shirt open, buttons pinging of and thumped a scar in his shoulder.

I could believe it, he was no slouch.

Thirty-Five

As we drove along the quay the Sunseeker's lights were on, I could see the dark powerful form of Ivo sitting on deck.

Recognising the Mercedes, he stood up as we approached, turning on the cockpit lights.

'Hi, come aboard, you're a bit early, I haven't even been to bed yet,' he grinned, as we walked up the gangway.

I was clutching the guide rope, then as I passed him he exclaimed.

'Mama mia! what the hell has happened to you?' He exclaimed, putting his arm on my shoulder and looking at the back of my head, where my as yet unseen wound must have been a sight.

'So we don't go diving now, uh. Phew what a mess, you were very lucky, no diving eh?'

'We will be diving, that is if you agree, but first I must explain a few things. Any chance of a coffee?'

'You cannot dive with such a head wound, certainly not the depth thinking of.'

'I have no choice, I could be a dead man anyway. I also think it's just skimmed my flesh a bottle

325

of that weight would have crushed my skull. Michael nodded.

Ivo passed me a towel for my head, then over the next ten minutes or so I explained to both Ivo and Michael the dangers we could expect in going on with locating Carlos and the dive.

I didn't tell them about the cargo, but all about the vessel and its interest to Liam, a man who was prepared to shoot in public, and that he would try again.

They sat in complete silence.

Surprisingly, Michael spoke first. He had no family, he was bored to death as a taxi-driver, and the excitement of a bit of hassle outweighed any worries he may have had.

'Hell no, my life hasn't been all roses, I've been close to the edge many times so what was one more time?'

Ivo, was much more circumspect, why all this problem?

'There is more to it I think' he rightly surmised, then out of the blue, 'Listen, I'm from Calabria, my father he has men, I also have men. If this is treasure we're after, I'll have men here by tonight, we'll take this Liam shit straight out,' he said smiling and showing a gold filling.

'No. It's not treasure, there's no money to be made,' I said, trying to allay any suspicion. 'In fact till we find it, I am not sure of anything. I just want to go and look, and this man Liam if it is he and his team will try to stop me.'

Ivo looked at me thoughtfully.

'I don't know why, I don't even know you,' he laughed, 'But I like you, and it's exciting. I'm in, I want to bloody well dive on this thing, anyway, I want to see what is so interesting down there. You reckon he is on one of those rig support ships?'

'Yes, I reckon that they'll use the vessel to try to find Carlos. As soon as their cranes is ready, they'll go. If it were me maybe even before, and work on the way, would make more sense.

Now if Liam thinks I have any intention of going to the site, he might try to get there before us, or he could even use us as to show him where the wreck is, I think that is their game! For all I know he may not have the exact spot, but he can find it.'

'There are a lot of variables, a lot of unknowns,' Ivo said.

'I appreciate that, but what else can we do, I just need to get there,' I said trying to reassure them.

'The trouble is rig support vessels, they're quite fast you know,' then as an afterthought. 'Well, for something that size,' Ivo said and drank his coffee, thinking, then,

'Bit of sleep?' he said questioningly.

After a moment, I said, looking at Ivo and Michael, 'There is a change of plan. We need to go now, before sunrise, this minute,' I said quietly.

'Now!' Ivo said in dismay.

'Now,' I said.

'But I have had no sleep and its tricky leaving this berth at night.'

'Even more so,' I said. 'As you will have no lights on, and won't use the search light. We will leave as quietly as possible.'

Ivo looked at me in amazement.

'He doesn't eat or sleep,' Michael shrugged, shaking his head, looking at Ivo.

'No point in announcing our departure,' I said, 'and the sooner we leave now the better.'

Ivo shrugged his shoulders expressively too.

'How noisy are the engines?' I asked.

'OK at sea, but you'll get a loud resonance from the quayside when I fire up. They're big Detroit diesels,' and as an afterthought, 'turbocharged,' raising his eye brows.

'OK, we'll pull her off the quay, well out of the berth, by pulling on the forward anchor lines, that will drag her out into the harbour before you fire up. Michael, you stand on the bow and look out for any lines or buoys, I don't want to foul the props.'

'Yes, Captain,' Ivo said, smiling and giving a salute. 'Looks like I've lost my ship,' he laughed.

Just then the sleepy tousled Tova walked up from below wrapped up in a towel er' just.

I looked across at Ivo.

'I'd forgotten Tova.'

'How could you ever,' she squirmed. 'What have you got on your head?' She looked aghast at the blood soaked towel.

'they couldn't open the bottle,' I quipped.

Then Ivo raised a hand to get attention.

'I'll take responsibility, she comes too,' Ivo said firmly, as he prepared the boat. With his tone of voice, I didn't argue. Beneath all his demeanour secretly he was a hard bastard.

Within twenty minutes, my head still hurting like hell, we were ready to go. I cast off aft, and Michael pulled hard on the for'ard line. Slowly the big power boat moved out into the harbour, Ivo at the helm, the radar and instruments casting a greenish glow on his face.

Down below, Tova made sandwiches, oblivious to any danger.

Michael turned, raising his hand, he'd done all he could, the windlass would have to do the rest. I nodded to Ivo, he turned the starboard key and the Detroit erupted with a bellow, followed by the port, then both engines settled to a deep slow burble as the engine warning lights one by one went out. The anchor chain now clattered into the locker as Ivo activated the windlass. Michael raised a hand when the weed covered anchor appeared.

Now sure we were clear, we manoeuvred at tick-over speed, every now and again knocking her out of gear, as even at tick-over our speed through the water was creating a wash rocking the other moored boats.

We proceeded down Msida Creek with the huge Detroit's grumbling below, their restrained echo coming back from the walls of the old fortifications. I jumped as a voice burst loudly from the radio.

Ivo's hand shot out instantly, flicking it off.

'Sorry,' he said.

We continued as quietly as we could, three men and a beautiful girl straining their eyes for buoys, mooring lines and other floating hazards. Two fishermen watched from their gondola like *dghaisa* as we went by unlit. High to our right, Valletta town looked down on us, some lights in little ancient slatted windows were now coming on, dawn would soon be here.

Keeping under the shadow of Valletta, we passed the entrance to Lazzaretto Creek and Manoel Island. The lights of the vessels at anchor somehow looked different, but then we were on the opposite side of them to my previous viewpoint. Grabbing the glasses, I signalled to Ivo to knock her out of gear, and we slowly came to a standstill, engines burbling, mist from the exhausts laying low over the water.

As we drifted, I focused down the Creek towards where the rig support vessels were moored.

Then a horrible realisation came to me, the one that had been moored alongside the wall had gone. The one that I had seen Liam onboard, was no longer there, only the two vessels out of commission lay there in the darkness.

I sat back with a sigh and passed the glasses to Ivo.

'The one I had been watching,' I told him, 'is no longer there.'

He shrugged.

'So, it is somewhere,' he said passing me the glasses.

'Could they leave at night?' I asked.

'Much easier for them to leave down here, than where we were,' he said. 'Much more room.'

'If they've left the harbour, they've got a start on us, but it can't be much,' I said, looking at my watch and unfolding the chart.

'Which way would you think they'd go?'

'I would think south-west. That would suit them the best, out towards the island of Pantellaria, it's the shortest way, same way as we are going.'

'Suppose we go around the north side of Malta?' I asked. 'Out through the channel by Camino and Gozo, then head west?' running my finger over the chart.

'Longer for sure, but with a good run we could be there hours before them anyway, I'll make nearly forty knots,' Ivo said.

'By my reckoning we would overtake them as they pass up the other side of Malta,' I said.

'Yes, with luck we can do our dive and be on the

way home before they arrive,' Ivo said a bit more cheerfully.

'What about the extra fuel used?'

'No problem, we can pull into Pantellaria on the return.'

'OK, let's go,' I said, 'We'll give it a go.'

Ivo eased the throttles forward, with a grunt she went into gear and the engines' note deepened as they engaged. Ivo flicked on the navigation, radio and cockpit control panel lights, then we moved stealthily out into the centre of the harbour and headed towards the entrance, under the intermittent beam of the lighthouse on the Fort of St Elmo guarding the harbour entrance.

At the entrance there was a slight swell running and we began to lift easily to it. The sea breeze was a little fresher now, blowing welcome cool air into the cockpit. To the east, dawn was now breaking. Picking up the glasses again I surveyed the scene. To the south, far astern lights flickered in the distance, they could be of a large and tall vessel, but on checking the radar there were several echoes there. Some would be fishing boats returning home, but was one Liam? I wondered.

Once clear of the harbour Ivo eased the throttles forward, water boiled at the stern, props snarled as they started to cavitate, the hull shuddered and dark fumes clouded the water as the Detroit's cleared their throat. The Sunseeker growled forward, seeming to dig deeper into the water before emerging with a roar, the noise a shrieking crescendo of howling turbos, muted only as they peaked, overpowered by the cacophony and beat of sixteen cylinders. She came out of the water in a cloud of spray, and rose to the plane, shaking and showing her teeth like a Killer Whale at play, a huge plume of tortured water blasted from underneath the transom.

As we approached thirty five knots the sound was steadily being left behind, increasing the speed still further she became ultra smooth. Ivo set the course on the auto pilot, checked it with the compass, then proceeded to set up the trim tabs, and check the navigation instruments.

Tova, who for the moment we had nearly forgotten, came up with a tray of sandwiches.

'Three men all to my self,' she giggled, then 'Come, eat, I haven't made these for the fish. Any gentleman for a beer?'

Regretfully we declined, we had a dive coming up, and my head still hurt. Michael though held his hand out

Once we had turned around the corner and passed between Comino and the Gozo ferry pier at Marfa I set up waymarks on the G.P.S. It beeped and indicated that we would be on site in about six hours. With that in mind, I decided to organise three watches of two hours apiece, hopefully that would give us all a much needed four hours sleep, they voted me first, I didn't object.

When I awoke, Ivo had laid out our diving equipment on the cockpit seats, air bottles in the shade. It was a beautiful day with only a slight sea. Looking through the glasses, no land was in sight. The sun was climbing in the sky; even at this speed it was hot. Michael was asleep. Checking the radar, there were no echoes within our twenty mile range, although at this speed the display can not always be relied on.

I wondered idly if the O M had got through to the American frigate, would we have visitors? Or was it all a ruse. Well, nothing showed at the moment.

'All yours, slave driver, two hours to run,' Ivo said, handing over the watch. He looked tired.

'Anything else I should know?'

'No, no problems. Keep an eye on the temperature and pressure gauges though; we're hammering on a bit. Stay on this heading and call me in about two hours. I've set the alarms.'

'Where's Tova?' I asked.

'With me,' he winked.

'You're diving,' I criticised.

'I knoweeee,' he said, gesticulating.

The next two hours seemed forever, then almost simultaneously, as the G.P.S. alarm went, the autopilot alarm went and Ivo came on deck. I slowly closed the throttles, and the Sunseeker sank down in her own wake we let the engines cool themselves on tick-over for a few moments, then Ivo shut one engine down. The sudden quiet and stillness as we settled, was a relief, just the tranquil noise of small waves lapping against the hull. We motored to the last known position of Carlos II. After all this time, I thought, I'm back.

I'd plotted the depth contours of the area that we needed to take into the search and consulting Reed's Mediterranean Navigator had enabled me to also take into account the current that was expected at the time of year that Carlos sank. So, moving west and using the sophisticated fish finding sonar, we started to get a print out of the sea bed. After about three quarters of an hour of circles and diagonals we had a print out of the most likely sudden rise of the bottom. We either had a mass of rock down there, or a wreck. I settled for the latter, time dictated that we should waste no more time. The echo sounder indicated a depth of 220 feet or so, approximately 66 metres, falling off to 330 feet. I was sure this was it.

'That'll do us,' I said eager to get going, 'Lets go and have a look, it's the only real object we've come across, time is pertinent.'

Ivo killed the remaining engine and looked at me. I nodded and the anchor with a splash disappeared into the dark depths, the chain rattling furiously through the stainless steel bullring in the bows. When we were sure the anchor was on the bottom, the chain was still almost straight down, we'd have very little chain on the bottom, if any.

Michael would have to be vigilant when we were down there, a watchful eye on the GPS.

Ivo looked at my sore head and remarked.

'Make sure that's well patched up, don't want any blood about, you know. I haven't seen too many sharks in the Med, but there are some and this is supposed to be the breeding ground of the great white' he assured me. Thank you.

I felt he could have put that better, but I examined my head as best I could in a hand mirror. I would need a square of plaster to prevent the strap of my goggles pulling the wound open again.

Meanwhile Ivo sent the weighted shot line down and threw out the marker buoy on its end to follow. Within moments it was bobbing happily on the surface. We would shortly follow the line down to the sea bed, then clip on a reel of line at the bottom, which would be let out as we went on to explore the area round it, using the compass all the time. Reeling it back in later would then lead us to our marker line and slowly up that to the surface.

This depth is severely dangerous and there is little margin for error, if any. I had to kerb my eagerness and observe time. Problem was we did not have too much time above or below the surface.

I lowered the two spare bottles and regulators over the side to thirty metres down on another line, with a loop round the shot line, so that on our return we could put in what would be a much needed decompression stop on the way back to the surface not to mention spare air!

As I looked round, Ivo was already being helped into his equipment by the ever attentive Tova. Checking my own once more, I started to gear up. Fifteen minutes later we were sitting on the stern of the Sunseeker, going through our hand signals for use below, and double checking each other's equipment in situ.

We checked with Michael that he was happy with the situation, we did not appear to be drifting, and the G.P.S. showed little or no movement. God shone down on use it was flat calm

'So what are we waiting for?'

We both held up a hand with thumb and forefinger touching to form an indicated 'O,' and rolled off backwards into the warm sea. Still buoyant, we once again checked and adjusted our regulators, exhaled air hissing out when above the water, bubbling when below it. Clamping the mouthpiece between my teeth, then another 'O' signal, a look at those on board and I reduced the air in my stab jacket, and sank beneath the surface. All looked good.

Enveloped by quietness save for the bubbles leaving my wet suit, and the swish, and sizz of the noise of the regulator as I breathed, I turned to see Ivo moving towards the line. We nodded and set our watches, then slowly descended into the depths. It was quite bright and clear at this depth, with few fish.

The moment I had that thought, a big ray like a delta bomber flapped past on its way to sunbathe on the surface.

At thirty metres I quickly checked the gauges of the spare bottles dangling there; they were fine, no leaks. We continued with the descent, it was getting much colder now and the pressure could be felt. My weight belt was becoming slack, it had to be continually adjusted as my body flesh compressed. My head hurt, my gloves were now too big, my hands becoming like skeletons with the pressure. We continued down, the water getting quite dark now.

At fifty metres I was getting anxious. I had expected to see something by now. Suddenly Ivo put up a hand, then pointing, he fed out the trace line and we headed off due south. He still pointed, then I realised what it was, what he had seen, the vast dark sinister bow of a ship appeared out of the murk. As we finned closer although it became darker in the shadows the faint name of Carlos II could just be made out. She was lying upright, sad and dark with a list to port of about ten degrees. She looked big down here. She was covered in fish netting and wires, nearly as if she had been camouflaged, many a fishing vessel had snagged their nets on Carlos. The light was not good and only the bows of the ship could be made out, the rest of her disappeared into murky oblivion.

I could sense that Ivo was becoming apprehensive, his breathing was a little more rapid and the bubbles that left his regulator spiralling to the surface came twice as often as mine. In passing I sneaked a look at his contents gauge, he didn't notice. I wanted no panic, we wouldn't have long. I checked my dive computer. Time would be short, we must keep going.

I had agreed to lead the dive as I had been on the vessel before, and I had studied the plans at length, so carefully I finned on watching Ivo all the while, we must stick together.

Fishing nets and wires are a diver's nightmare, entanglement and death lurks for the unwary. As we made our way aft along the hull there was evidence of other dive work.

It was obvious that some of the debris had been cut away, and therefore we were not the only one's that knew of her position. How, who and why? flashed through my mind.

So, following the helpful track of our predecessors I proceeded, Ivo following close behind. Down a narrow but cleared way I finned with caution towards the for'ard hatch, to number one hold. To my shock, it had been blown or cut open, a big deep black hole gaped below me. My heart bumped as I turned on the halogen torch, its beam disappearing into oblivion ahead of me as the water particles attenuated its light. I entered through the hole, as I did a scurry of small fish came out in a bomb burst of silver past my mask. Particles of suspended plankton danced in the beam, a large fish, it's jagged teeth prominent, drifted past, black soulless eyes unmoved. Ivo hung back.

The wheat had long gone, floated away in the pull of the current. The hold was enormous, a jet black claustrophobic cavern, the depth of which might take me past my limit, but I had to go on. The pressure of the mask was now hurting my face, and it was beginning to leak. Down we went, into the unknown blackness.

Suddenly a sharp blast of noise set my heart banging furiously again. My depth alarm was alerting me. I felt Ivo tug a little on the line, I was exceeding my allotted depth, or maybe bottom time.

I was feeling the pressure of both mental strain and sea depth as the darkness enveloped me. Deeper I went, Ivo lagging behind, I could really sense his apprehension now, as he slowed his descent. I was putting him in danger.

Suddenly and abruptly the beam of light fell upon some huge crates, as a shoal of silver sprats flickered round them in the light. As the wheat had floated away or been eaten, presumably over the months, the crates and containers had sank in an orderly pile. They were massive long cases, huge, some smaller and square, one of which had been opened down to its water proof container. I moved closer, suddenly an eel flashed out, body as thick as a mans thigh, its vicious serpent-like head lashing out, with jagged teeth that could rip through a wet suit and into a man's arm in seconds. It writhed, swirled and entwined itself between the containers, finally vanishing deeper in the blackness.

His home, my hell.

I moved closer still toward the open container, then wiped away the sand and slime of the metal in a swirl of dirt, one eye apprehensively watching for the eel. To my intense relief, as I read the details on the case, it confirmed that the cargo was still here, because this was the forward hold which they would have salvaged first, and the rest of the ship was still draped in a maze of wires and debris.

Ivo tugged the line, now more urgently. I turned, you could see the look of terror in his dark eyes, I could see his mask was also leaking he wanted to go, he gave the diver's signal for being worried. I didn't hesitate to acknowledge, he was right. I gave the signal to start the ascent. You could feel the relief, the vibes from Ivo, as we moved slowly from the hold out of darkness into the pale light of the deck, we then cleared the old nets, and followed the line slowly up into the deep blue, monitoring our computers all the while, one slip now and air bubbles would appear in our blood stream, and good bye!

Forty metres from the surface, Ivo tugged my side, a look of sheer panic in his eyes. He drew a hand across his throat, his air was gone, instantly I drew air, then hugged him and passed him my mouth piece so as to give him air from my bottle, all the while I was looking up for the hanging bottles. We were nearly there, I could see them hanging in the blue, Ivo did not wish to pass the air back but forcibly I took my regulator back for a couple of breaths and gave it back to him as we continued our ascent, nearly there, so close now, so close, but take it slowly. Any rush now and we would have problems, it could be fatal. Ivo was not happy, he was tense and once more did not wish to give my regulator back, I coaxed him gently I wanted no panic.

Then to my horror, as we approached the bottles they started to move, jerkily at first but upwards, yes upwards, they were being hauled to the surface. A kick with my fins, another kick and I had hold of them, just as the danger alarms from the diving computer screeched.

That burst of speed meant the ascent was too fast, we could burst a lung or at least surface with the bends as the air dissolved in our blood caused bubbles in our joints. I struggled frantically to reach a new regulator and breathe. Ivo still clung grimly onto mine, while hanging tightly onto me. I managed to get the regulator into my mouth, turn on the bottle valve and breathe. My lungs were a searing hell, bubbles rocketing to the surface, as I held on to the dangling back straps of the hanging bottle. Then, Christ!

We were now being hauled to the surface together with the bottles. Why were they moving again? Drawing my diver's knife I sawed furiously at the line. It gave, I'd cut it, I passed Ivo a regulator from a new bottle, then we fell back and remained suspended there trying to relax, adjusting our stab jackets for buoyancy and now letting our breathing come under control. What had gone wrong?

With air to spare now, I put in a prolonged stop, getting ourselves, and our decompression rate under control. When I was quite sure there was no danger of setting off the diving computer alarm, I re-started the ascent, slowly and steadily.

Ivo was back under control, but what had gone wrong on the surface? Why had Michael started to lift the bottles? Looking upwards I could see the silvery rippling blue of the surface, our environment getting lighter all the way, the traumas of the depths below vanishing. The white hull of the Sunseeker was coming into view.

Ivo and I surfaced simultaneously, in a cloud of air bubbles, and spray. Removing his regulator, Ivo said.

'Hell! You run things a bit close, don't you' as he drew breath.

I never had time to answer. The question was answered for me by a voice I knew well.

'He always did, but this time too close' came the reply.

It was the voice of Liam.

I swivelled round in the water and looked up at the stern and into the mouth of a Browning 9mm. Liam was sitting at the stern of the Sunseeker, pistol in hand.

'So, you decided to come to the surface after all, what a pity,' he said with a sickly smile. 'Now what am I going to do with you? You're such a pain Kit'

A large red rigid inflatable boat was tied along side with two massive black Mercury 300 horse power stacks sitting on the stern. A dark evil-looking and unshaven man perched there, an Uzi machine gun in his lap, he smiled, a dark hole of rotten teeth. Another evil creature lounged on the Sunseeker.

Michael apologised.

'What could I do?' he said, spreading his hands with open palms.

I took off my rubber head gear, and seeing me glance at the RIB. Liam gloated,

'Faster than a rig vessel, pity you didn't do your homework, Kit.'

Looking toward the horizon I thought I could see the vessel on her way.

Ivo burst into life.

'What the fuck is this! That's my boat.'

The Browning levelled at him, and Liam twitched his arm.

'Ivo shut up.' I snapped

'Mind if we come on board?' I queried.

'Sure, won't be for long anyway,' he laughed.

Michael took the bottles from us, and we threw the fins on board. Liam moved to the other end of the cockpit, and moved back round to the stern again as we came on board, keeping us covered all the time. I felt that Ivo was just about to ask about Tova, when I pushed a set of bottles over onto him. Scowling, he took the point.

'Who do you work for Liam?'

'I'm sure you've worked it out. We've been waiting for that cargo for some time, you interfering bastard,' he said.

I glanced at the other piece of dubious humanity lounging on the helmsman's seat. He did not seem to have a gun, and the shit with the Uzi was below the height of the gun whales, only Liam could get a clear shot.

Liam knew what I was thinking.

'Oh, and by the way if you were looking for this toy,' he said taking my .380 out of his pocket, 'Er, sorry it's here,' he smiled.

I let my dismay show, and his smile lasted a little longer.

I started to unzip my wet suit.

'Uh, uh,' Liam grunted waving the Browning. 'Keep it on, it's difficult getting a body back into one,' he smirked. 'I think a bullet first and then being run over by those propellers should do it, don't you.' he said questioningly.

'You're an arsehole,' muttered Ivo.

Liam drew the hammer back with what seemed to be a deafening click. The Browning was levelled at Ivo once more.

'Then why kill Stuart?' I said, quickly taking his mind away from pulling that trigger.

'He interfered, he just could not believe that you might have sold this location to a needy nation. I had it all set until he pushed his nose in, you'd have been in the fucking Tower by now, old boy, as they say in some of your stuffy English clubs.

Mr English Gentleman. You were set up, and now thanks to all these problems you have caused, you have to go,' Liam said, now turning the Browning on me.

'They will hunt you, you will never be free,' I said, trying to gain time and looking out to sea. The rig vessel could be seen plainly now, ploughing her way through the calm sea, her cranes pointing skyward.

'That is where you are wrong, Mr Kit' he said sarcastically. 'I am free; it is you who are not. I will be back in London with an explanation, the Scuds will be in Libya, and you will be fish food.'

'You talk rubbish,' I said. 'The O M knows the situation very well.'

'Then he will be pleased to learn of the million dollars paid into your family account here in Malta, two days ago. A small price to pay for me to remain at the Office, don't you think? and of course there is the letter which will be found at your home in Yorkshire, along with other bank information.

No, no way have I lost my position,' Liam went on to say, 'my years in waiting are gone. No, I'll be back in total charge, and a hero.'

Behind the approaching rig vessel, but further to the south I could now see black smoke billowing out of a fast ship, a powerful grey ship with a knife like bow and the boxlike superstructure of an American frigate, the white foam of her bow wave clearly visible. It was evidently gaining on the rig vessel. Liam followed my gaze.

'We have visitors,' I said smiling.

'I have, you don't,' he said raising the Browning. I don't believe he had noticed the frigate powering her way toward us from further right.

Suddenly there was a ferocious bang from the cabin below, a mass of flame and smoke, as like a rocket a red distress signal flare came out of the saloon companionway, clipped the cockpit coaming in a shower of sparks and lay spinning and flaming on the floor of the cockpit, filling the area with dense orange smoke.

Michael grabbed the boat hook and swung it at Liam. Liam ducked, raised the pistol and fired twice in quick succession. Michael's head appeared to vanish in a crimson expanding mist. With a groan his twitching body disappeared over the side like a boxer knocked clean out of the ring.

I dived hopefully at my holdall that lay on the floor, fingers, scrabbling for the SIG. I felt cold steel, my hand clasped round the grip, drawing it out and pulling back the slide.

Then rolling, rolling, across the floor amidst the thick orange fumes still pouring out of the flare, I swung the SIG round to Liam, who was taken completely by surprise and off balance by my action.

I fired in his direction, he groaned and slumped to his knees, firing into the floor as he went down. I staggered upright, Ivo shouted and I whipped round, quickly side stepping a charge from the dreg who had been sitting mesmerised in the cockpit. As he stumbled past, I shot him double handed in the neck and he fell.

Quickly I looked back at Liam, he was trying to raise his gun, looking malevolently at me and muttering. I saw there were flecks of blood on his lips.

'Stuart,' I said out loud. Liam winced, he knew what I was going to do, he knew what was coming, he started to raise his gun once more, I waited a split second, I wanted him to realise as the Sig bucked fearfully in my hand as the bullet exploded his eye and whipped back his head. It passed through his skull, blood and bits splattered on the once white sun lounger, falling back his legs shook doing the death dance, his gun clattered on the deck, a foot still flicked.

Michael, I was sure had been blown overboard into the RIB, falling onto the guy with the Uzi.

He'd be dead, but what of the guy he'd fallen on, where was he now?

At a crouch and below the Sunseeker's sides, I waited, heart pounding, knowing that I had a guy with an Uzi only feet away, somewhere the other side of the hull, just three-quarters of a inch of fibreglass. I looked across at Ivo who was flat on the deck.

In a deafening blast the Uzi chattered into life, punching holes through the fibreglass just above our heads, empty shell cases clattered onto the side deck.

I answered quickly with two double taps from the Sig at point blank range through the hull. Seconds later I could hear the starters of the big Mercury's whirring, they burst into life, a high pitched crescendo of sound. The bow of the RIB cast a brief shadow over the deck as it reared up in the water, waiting a moment I rose carefully and looked at the scene.

The RIB was hurtling away from us, but within moments it was circling and coming back towards us in an arc. At about fifty yards, he opened again up with the Uzi.

Ivo ducked to the floor again as the bullets fell well short in the water. The next burst was better placed, they blew bits of fibre glass and polished wood off the cockpit top.

Seeing me kneel, Ivo raised his head to watch. Steadily I raised the Sig up to the target and above, maybe a foot above, and well in front, moving with the target all the while.

Again, the Uzi burst into life, bullets ricocheted all around, he'd got the range. Hard luck, I held my composure as bullets flew by, then squeezed the trigger gently and after a pause which seemed an age, he threw his head back with a snap as if to gargle. The bullet had hit and he sank forward, falling onto the throttles, turning the wheel as he went. Engines screaming, and in an ever-tightening flat out circle, the RIB somersaulted, catapulting the driver high into the air as the body fell into the sea, the engines died as the 'dead man's handle' activated.

'How the hell did you do that? One shot, unbelievable,' Ivo said, as he sat down, holding his head in his hands, Unbelievable, what a bloody day.'

There was a sudden deathly silence, and the stench of death, cordite and the metallic smoke from the flare became apparent. A brass shell case rolled noisily across the deck as the boat rolled in the swell.

Michael's body lay face down in the sea, dead, a slick of congealing blood floated on the surface. From below Tova's voice weakly called for Ivo. With all the action going on I had nearly forgotten her, the girl who's with the emergency flare had made it all possible.

Pulling myself together, I stood fully upright, and looked out to sea. The rig vessel was much closer, possibly ten minutes away, but so was the frigate, still belching out black smoke from the tall funnel housing under the mainmast and the huge bow wave at her bows nearly washing the decks.

She was overhauling the rig boat rapidly, in the silence you could now faintly hear the thunder of engines and the drumming beat of her large propellers.

Ivo brought me a Hopleaf beer, Tova, pale and hanging on his arm, braving the topsides for the first time. She was shaking and had been crying. Blinking in the sunlight, she looked at the two dead men.

'I'm sorry,' I said, 'but it was them or us.'

'I know, I heard,' she sniffed, 'I didn't know what to do, I just thought of the flares.'

'A good thought' I said

Ivo and I started to climb out of our wet suits, then from the distance there was a loud deep boom, which shook the atmosphere, a guard rail rattled. A blast of white smoke came from the muzzle of the 10 inch gun on the frigate's fo'c'sle. A second later an explosive plume of black speckled spray erupted in front of the rig vessel. As we watched it visibly slowed down, a second shell whistled in, close to the last, a sickening thud shook the sea, the vessel had her engines firmly astern in an effort to come to a shuddering standstill. They did not want to play today.

We could now see a helicopter rising from the frigate's quarter-deck, the word NAVY plainly visible on its body, twin exhaust fumes blasting over the tail. In a couple of minutes, the Sea-sprite helicopter was straddling the path of the rig vessel.

To amplify its presence, it gave a quick burst from

its twin 7.62 mm M60 machine guns, the sea erupting all down the side of the vessel, 'just saying hello'.

The rig vessel finally shuddered to a stop, with a swirl of water as her engines shut down.

The pilot glanced across at us, raising a hand. He continued to hover there for some time as the Knox class frigate manoeuvred closer, guns trained on the rig vessel's crew who were gathered in a huddle on the after deck.

As we drifted nearer, we could see a fully armed boarding party was now getting ready to board and take command of the rig vessel. Drifting still closer, two ratings started to put fenders over on the side nearest to us and another threw us a line. I ran forward to make it fast, then looking up at the frigate's deck.

There to my utter surprise, I saw the O M looking down, perhaps with the making of a whistful smile.

The two ratings threw a pilot ladder over, and one came down to make us fast along side.

Ahead of us, others were lowering the sea-boat and then began the grisly business of getting the two bodies from the sea, and salvaging the RIB.

A party in decontamination overalls and hoods was waiting to remove Liam's remains from the Sunseeker.

Wearily, I gestured politely to Ivo and Tova.

'Shall we go aboard.' The O M and the Captain met us at the top of the ladder. I shook hands and introduced my friends; desperately sorry I could not introduce Michael.

Ivo and Tova were led politely away to the ward-room by an Ensign.

I said to the O M.

'How the hell did you get here, Sir?'

That pleased him.

'Flew into Catania, Sicily yesterday evening and that thing picked me up,' he said gesticulating and nodding at the Sea-sprite that was just landing on aft. 'Thought you might need a hand, but you seem to have managed very well. Are the missiles still there?' he asked, peeping over the side, as if expecting to see them.

'They are, Sir.'

'That's good,' interrupted the frigate's Captain, 'give our men something to do.'

As we spoke six ratings carrying three body bags came past. I held up my hand stopping the first pair, slowly and deliberately I unzipped the bag just about eighteen inches.

'That's Liam, Sir.' I said nodding

'Best place for him,' he said without the slightest sign of emotion, lighting his pipe and looking out to sea, he had dismissing the situation.

I wondered what was really going on in his mind

'Well Kit, what a come back,' he said, looking quizzically into the bowl of his pipe, as if unsure that it was burning satisfactorily.

'Pardon, Sir?'
'What a come back.' He repeated
'I thought you said that, Sir. I've retired, Sir.'
'Will you not come back into service Kit?'
'I've retired, Sir.'

'I heard you. But would you for me, Kit; as a favour?'

Epilogue

About a year later I went back to Malta, just for a few days, taking a short break. 'Bancali,' the family house, had been sold.

There'd be another 'Bancali' sooner or later, I didn't doubt, but not in Malta. Too many people knew of it; it was no longer private and the island now had sad memories for me. Maybe the Balearics?

On handing the keys over to the new owner of the house I promptly left without looking back. I drove out to Hamrun, and to the Catholic graveyard prominently visible on the hill overlooking the two harbours. Those lying there had a good view. With a small case in my hand I walked amongst the mass of white tombs, some simple, others large family vaults like little white houses where on the 'Day of the Spirits' the families would come and visit their dead with an outdoor feast. The men would lay the tables, one outside for the ladies, and one inside for the men; their dead, their loved ones could often be viewed through glass sided coffins.

I walked on, taking it all in, looking at the photographs and images of ones long gone, behind glass and gilded frames, some screwed onto the little doors. Dead flowers now and again littered the small paths. At the top corner, and in the shade of a small chapel, I found what I was searching for: a small white vault, domed and with a black cross at the top. In a little gilt frame on the door a picture of Michael looked back at me. I hesitated for a moment as at each side I noticed there were fresh flowers in two new vases.

He had no family, no relatives, yet here were fresh flowers. I stooped and opening my case took out an engraved brass vase. I filled it with water from the nearby tap and added my flowers to it. In that quiet place, remembering Michael and that fateful day, I knelt and said a short prayer.

Rising, I wondered about the fresh flowers and who could have brought them. Then I turned back and walked down the path again, through a stone arch with a bell hanging from it. I closed the little squeaking gate after me. Sad at heart, I drove down to the quayside at Msida, thinking only of poor Michael.

It had altered a little; there were more boats and bigger boats and more floating pontoons. Stopping the car, I got out for a stroll for I fancied a breath of fresh air; to remember the time over a year earlier when I had last walked that quay.

The 'yachties' were there as ever, working on their boats, the smell of varnish and polish drifting in the air, an electric sander buzzed. Towards the end of the quay and just about where the Sunseeker had been moored now lay a large 'Squadron' motor cruiser in sparkling white, with a powerful rib hanging from its transom davits. A crewman in whites wiped the stainless steel, he looked as if he would be more at home weightlifting. On the quay another crewman in whites stood in the shade, lighting a cigarette and watching me. I said 'good morning' but he didn't answer.

Turning back to the Squadron I noticed wetsuits hanging from the bow pulpit to dry. The Italian flag flew from the stern. Could it be, I wondered.

I called to the crewman onboard; no answer, just a surly stare. This has happened before, I thought.

To hell with it. I stamped with my foot on the gangplank and the noise echoed round the quay. Surprised and instantly alerted both crewman came simultaneously toward me. I stood my ground, just as a voice from within the saloon shouted, 'Kit. Unbelievable. Its Kit, come on Board.' Once Ivo had spoken to me, the crewman on board managed a quick smile while the other had melted back into the shadows.

Ivo looked well, if a little heavier. Tova had appeared, dressed and kissed me on the cheek. She waved her left hand in front of me, her third finger sported an enormous diamond.

I congratulated them both on their engagement,

would I go to the wedding, the invitation could be sent, what was my address now?

'You've done well' I said, 'a new boat'. He laughed and pointed out that he had little need for the old boat full of holes and the Ministry had been generous and anyway, business had been good.

'Business' I queried

'Well you know' he shrugged flashing a gold tooth.

I looked at the crewman and purposely told him they looked like Mafia men. I had struck a nerve. I intended to, but he laughed saying he did not want to take any risks this time; his father had insisted.

'Anyway' he said, 'what is Mafia? Just family trying to do well, eh. So are your Masons, eh and the Jews. Just groups, families who stick together'. As he spoke, he spread his palms with a shrug and a sinking of his chin onto his chest in explanation.

'A Sicilian mannerism' I laughed, I knew what he meant and I remembered the gesture.

Then out of the blue, and changing the subject he said 'Kit, I have a present for you, a gift' He continued apologising for his nerves on our dive on Carlos II the previous year; the deepest dive he'd ever made. 'But now, I've mastered it, I've been back'. He went on to explain.

The Ship, he informed me was now empty and had been blown apart by the Americans, but they missed something.

'I knew where to look, and I have it for you' he proudly announced as he made his way below, shortly to return carrying a large polished mahogany case, it's gleaming brass corners and lock enhancing the colour.

Then slowly with an air of triumph, he presented it to me with a slight bow and a smile.

Placing the case on the aft table I opened it carefully, with genuine curiosity. There displayed, clean and polished was a large merchant ships brass compass, made and engraved by 'B. Cooke and Son Limited of Hull'

It now rests on a brass binnacle at my house in Yorkshire, a subtle reminder of the Carlos II.

Also by James Hayward-Searle

Featuring Kit Martin MI6

Coming summer 2019

'The Meeting'

www.spythriller.com

Printed in Great Britain
by Amazon